TANGLED WEB

A DEADLY CURIOSITIES NOVEL

GAIL Z. MARTIN

SOL

CONTENTS

Tangled Web   v

Chapter 1   1
Chapter 2   11
Chapter 3   29
Chapter 4   41
Chapter 5   55
Chapter 6   76
Chapter 7   88
Chapter 8   97
Chapter 9   109
Chapter 10   123
Chapter 11   146
Chapter 12   157
Chapter 13   169
Chapter 14   176
Chapter 15   188
Chapter 16   200
Chapter 17   208
Epilogue   225

Afterword   229
About the Author   231
Also by Gail Z. Martin   233

TANGLED WEB

DEADLY CURIOSITIES BOOK 3

By Gail Z. Martin

ISBN: 978-1-939704-71-9
Tangled Web: Copyright © 2018 by Gail Z. Martin.

Cover art by Lou Harper
SOL Publishing is an imprint of DreamSpinner Communications, LLC

For my wonderful husband Larry, my children, Kyrie, Chandler, and Cody, and my new sons, Nick and Zach. Much love and gratitude to you.

CHAPTER ONE

I'D NEVER BEEN A FAN OF HUNTING, AND I LIKED IT EVEN LESS WHEN Teag Logan and I were the prey.

"They're getting closer," I yelled, as the wind swept around us, and the sound of braying dogs grew louder. Hoof beats thundered far too close, and I felt sure we'd be ridden down at any second.

Teag didn't move. "They're not real," he replied, raising his head to the wind. In one hand, he held a staff carved with protective runes and wrapped with spelled rope. In the other, he gripped an iron rod. I could see the tension in the twitch of a muscle in his jaw, and I knew Teag better than to think he'd take a reckless chance. But as the pounding of horse hooves and the wild barking of dogs closed in on us, my heart thudded like our days were numbered.

"They can't do anything if we stay inside the salt ring." Teag knew I knew that. This wasn't our first rodeo...or our first spectral "hunt." But this manifestation sounded big and real; and the circle of salt that enclosed us seemed like flimsy protection, although I knew how powerful it was in the spirit world.

I held my athame—the handle of an old wooden spoon—in one hand, and in the other, I grasped a smooth agate spindle whorl, a powerful protective charm. A shake of the dog collar that wound around my left wrist, and a spectral dog appeared beside me, the ghost of Bo, my old golden retriever. Bo must not have liked the barking hounds, since he lowered his head, bared his teeth, and bristled.

"Here they come," Teag murmured.

On the horizon, the shadows darkened, sweeping toward us in a wave with the gallop of dozens of horses, eager hounds running around and between them. If they kept their course, they were heading right for us.

I almost expected the ground to shudder beneath us, but these shadow horses glided across the grass. Even though I'm not a medium, I could pick up the disquieting energy, which felt like a gathering storm.

A horn blew, rallying the hunters. I thought about the old stories I'd heard of the Norse gods leading an eternal, infernal hunt with red-eyed horses and demon dogs. While I didn't see a glint of hellfire in the eyes of these ghostly horses, I had no desire to get a good look up close. The cloud loomed like black roiling smoke, and sometimes the darkness took the shape of horses and other times of dogs before vanishing into the inky mass.

The hunters bore down on us, and the wind picked up, gusting hard. And when it howled past, it swept away the ring of salt that protected us from those pounding hooves.

"Run!" I yelled. But after a few steps, when I didn't see Teag close beside me, I turned. He's taller than I am, with long legs, and he should have been able to outrun me. Instead, to my horror, I saw Teag standing still, staring mesmerized into the roiling darkness, as the ghostly horses headed straight at him.

"Teag!" I focused my will, leveling my athame at the spectral hunters. A blast of cold white force blazed from the tip, as Bo's ghost sprang into action, planting himself between Teag and the apparitions, barking furiously. The white force shredded the darkness, scattering the black fog. I held on tight to the agate whorl in my left hand, drawing on its protective power, and channeled everything I had into the blast of light. A few seconds later, the sound of the ghostly hunters was gone.

"Teag?" I'd never seen him freeze like that, and as I stepped closer, Teag shook himself like he was waking from a dream.

"Cassidy?" Teag was disoriented, and I put a hand on his arm to prove I was real.

"They're gone," I replied. "Are you okay?"

"Yeah, I think so," he answered. I had the feeling he wasn't telling me everything, but sometimes Teag holds back until he's thought a problem through. I'd just have to bide my time.

Teag looked back toward where we had set the salt ring. "They say that Geoffrey Nicholson's horse threw him right over there," Teag pointed to a spot near an old live oak tree, "and he broke his neck. The horse stepped into a hole and busted its leg, so it was put down, too."

"That was in 1878," I mused. "But from what we saw with the ghosts, Nicholson never stopped hunting."

"All of the men in that fox hunt the day Nicholson was killed died within a year, under unusual circumstances." Teag scanned the horizon as if looking for ghostly hounds and riders. A lock of straight, chocolate brown hair fell into his eyes, and he pushed it away.

"Do you think they still ride with him?" Part of me wondered whether their hunting dogs crossed over with them, and I hoped that the unfortunate fox wasn't doomed to a perpetual reenactment.

"That's what the stories say, but I thought it might be a dramatic flourish—until what we saw. Now, I'd say odds are pretty good." Teag walked carefully around the old live oak tree, and I scoured a nearby section of ground. We both looked for trampled grass, hoof prints, anything that would suggest a physical—rather than ghostly—reason for the sightings.

"There's been enough rain that anything out here should have left marks," I replied. Plenty of humidity, too—enough to frizz my strawberry-blonde hair, and pink up my very pale Scots-Irish skin. "So I'm betting on ghosts. But the real question is, are they repeaters, or sentient? And what's juiced them up enough that people aren't just seeing them, they're being chased?"

I'm Cassidy Kincaide, owner of Trifles and Folly, an antique and curio shop in historic, haunted Charleston, SC. The shop has been in my family for three-hundred-and-fifty years, and in all that time, we've learned to keep a secret or two. One of those secrets is my magic—I'm a psychometric, able to read the history and magic by touching an object. Teag, my assistant store manager, best friend, and sometimes bodyguard is a Weaver, with the ability to weave spells into cloth, or data into information, making him a hell of a hacker. Did I mention that my business partner, Sorren, is a nearly six-hundred-year-old vampire and that the shop itself is cover for an alliance of mortals and immortals who get haunted and cursed objects out of the wrong hands and protect Charleston—and the world—from supernatural threats? When we succeed, no one notices. When we fail, the destruction gets chalked up to natural disaster.

"Did Kell and the SPOOK crew get a look at the ghostly fox hunt yet?" Teag asked. Kell Winston is the head of SPOOK—the Southern Paranormal Observation and Outreach Klub—a reputable paranormal investigation group. Kell's an ally, and he's also my significant other.

"He's been out a couple of times to try to get readings," I replied. "Picked up plenty of EMF and some audio of dogs barking in the distance—a lot of them, not the neighbor's terrier. But they didn't see anything themselves."

"Tell that to the groundskeeper," Teag replied. Kell's group had been called in by owners of the historic plantation because a "ghostly fox hunt" had started terrorizing workers and tourists. Kell called us since he's in on our secret.

"Let's check out the house while it's open," I suggested. "And then we can hang around once it's dark and see what we see."

TEAG and I headed to the grand entrance of the Nicholson mansion. Back in the mid-1800s, Geoffrey Nicholson had been a prominent cotton trader and farmer, an influential man in Charleston politics, and an avid fox hunter. We paid our entrance fee and walked into the historic home, stopping to notice the decorations in the front hall.

"No one's going to miss that he liked hunting," Teag remarked.

Paintings on the walls showed red-jacketed riders on horseback surrounded by dozens of foxhounds. Everything from candlesticks to vases had a "hunt" motif, either in the shape of dogs, horses, and riding tack, or with those images painted or inscribed.

"Mr. Nicholson lived for the hunt," a docent said, coming up on us from another room. "We have an extensive collection of his hunting equipment, clothing—even some taxidermy trophies of foxes he shot." She introduced herself as "Patti" and offered to show us around.

I barely repressed a shiver. In my experience, stuffed dead things were trouble. "We'd love to see them," I managed, hoping my smile looked sincere. Teag and I exchanged a glance. If the museum had that many items Nicholson had owned and used; then the odds were good something anchored his spirit. With luck, we could figure out what was keeping his ghost here and find a way to set his spirit—and those of his ghostly hunters—free.

"Did you come because of the exhibit?" Patti asked as she began her tour. We were close enough to closing time that Teag and I appeared to be the only visitors at the moment.

"Exhibit?" Teag asked as I studied a porcelain statue of a fox on a shelf. A sideboard revealed a set of china with pictures of hunters and foxes. Two oil paintings appeared to be portraits of favorite horses and hunting hounds.

"There's an exhibit on The Sporting Life at the Museum of the Lowcountry," she replied, "and another one at the Historical Archive. Just in time for hunting season."

I made a mental note to check those out, and see if any items carried supernatural residue. "We'll look into them," I replied.

Our chatty docent kept up a running patter as we moved from room to room. I quickly decided that Geoffrey Nicholson's wife must have either shared his fixation with hunting and foxes or had the patience of a saint. As we made our way through the house, I called to my power, trying to sense whether any of the objects on display had magic, or carried a hint of haunt. For now, I kept my hands behind my back, unwilling to touch anything before I knew what we were getting into. Old memories, curses, and attached spirits can pack a real wallop for me when they trigger my abilities, so I try to control the conditions to keep all hell from breaking loose.

Now and again, my gift "pinged" on an object, picking up a touch of something supernatural. Each time, I asked the docent about the item's provenance, knowing Teag would help me remember the details. A Limoges porcelain figurine of a fox had been a present from Nicholson's mother; I chalked the emotional resonance up to it being a gift from a loved one. The brass hunting horn that tripped my power was a favorite of Nicholson, another present.

Finding small wells of memory bound to items with special significance wasn't unusual in historic homes. Most of the time the energy wasn't enough to anchor a ghost, not even a repeater—the echo of a spirit reenacting an emotional moment over and over, but without sentience.

Sometimes, an object anchored a ghost enough to keep the soul tethered to this world. In other cases, dark magic or extreme tragedy could curse an item, creating nasty problems. That's the kind of antique I searched for amid the horse statues and fox bric-a-brac, trying not to arouse the docent's suspicions as I lingered to move a little closer to a curio cabinet or hover a hand above a decoration on display. I didn't need to touch to sense power, and if I could get a reading without making physical contact, I might be spared having a strong resonance knock me on my ass.

Teag had smelling salts in his pocket, as well as orange juice and a protein bar in the car. He's had to pick me up off the floor after a potent reading more than once.

If Patti thought we were odd, politeness forbade mentioning her concerns. Teag shot me a look to see if I'd found anything; I gave a slight shake of my head. Still, something felt "off" about the Nicholson mansion, like the energy simmered around us, not quite a full boil, but hardly tranquil. Something was amping up the haunting, and I wondered whether the "simmer" that I felt was a cause or an effect.

"Have you had any new additions to your collection recently?" I asked with my best nothing-to-worry-about smile. At the docent's look,

I gave a little shrug. "Professional curiosity. We run Trifles and Folly downtown—antiques and collectibles."

Patti frowned. "I don't think so. Nothing I've noticed—and they usually point out new items because repeat visitors like to see the collection evolve."

I went at the problem from a different direction. "I understand needing to change things up, keep them fresh. This is our first visit. Have they recently rearranged any of the displays?"

Patti gave that some thought. "The preservation team brought out more hunting memorabilia from storage to play off the big museum exhibits and tie into the excitement," she said.

"How long was that before people started to report seeing the ghostly hunters?" Teag asked.

Patti gave us a deer-in-the-headlights look as if she wasn't sure whether she should confirm or deny the ghost reports.

"It's okay," I said. "The board of directors invited a team of ghost hunters out to document the sightings, and the investigators called us in to look for problem objects."

"Ghost hunters? You're ghost hunters?" Patti's surprised expression turned to relief. "Oh, thank heavens. I'm glad someone is finally doing something."

Teag and I both turned to her. "Can you tell us what you've seen?" I asked.

Patti looked around, making sure no one else was around. "I haven't seen the hunters, but I've heard them," she said, dropping her voice. "Hoof beats, like a stampede, only there aren't any horses on the property—any *real* horses. And dogs howling. We don't have dogs here, either. The plantation has over a hundred acres, so it's not like we're hearing something happening next door." She looked from one of us to the other. "So what is it? Are ghosts real?"

"Ghosts are real," Teag said gently. "But not everything weird turns out to be a ghost. That's what the SPOOK team was trying to figure out."

"Sometimes, if an item was very important to a person when they were alive, it can anchor them to this world after they leave," I said, gauging from her expression how much of paranormal stuff she bought into. Some people dismissed anything supernatural out of hand, either from fear or because it clashed with other beliefs and made them uncomfortable. Patti seemed genuinely frightened and willing to look at anything that might solve the problem. "Do you know if any of the objects on display were particularly important to Mr. Nicholson?"

"I can show you a couple of pieces that I know were his favorites, and if you want, I'll ask around, in case one of the other docents knows more."

"That would be fantastic," I said, and Teag gave her an encouraging nod.

Patti led us upstairs, and while I kept my senses open as we walked, nothing we passed gave me more than a slight nudge as far as power went. But when we followed Patti into a well-appointed gentleman's bedroom, the resonance felt so strong I had to take a step back as if something had given me a shove.

"What is it, Cassidy?" Teag asked, moving closer. I shook my head, letting him know I was all right.

"Show us the pieces," I said to Patti. "I think there might be something here that's important."

It didn't look like Patti sensed anything out of the ordinary, though I could tell from Teag's fidgeting that while he might not have my psychometry, his magic picked up something that made him jittery.

"Mr. Nicholson was especially proud of his hunting trophies," Patti replied, indicating a shelf of sporting awards with figures of horses and guns. "In the armoire," she said, opening the door to the large wardrobe, "we have the jacket he was wearing on the last, unlucky hunt, as well as his collection of favorite walking sticks." I saw a jumble of long staves, including a long staff that looked much older and might have been carved with runes, but the traditional red hunting jacket with black trim caught my attention immediately.

"You said he had that on when he died?" Teag pressed.

"So the story goes," Patti replied.

"Are there any other items he might have had with him when he was thrown from the horse?" I asked, making a slow circuit of the room. The energy I sensed off the trophies felt positive, but the vibes from the wardrobe creeped me out. I suspected we hadn't found everything.

"His watch," Patti said, pointing to a pocket watch under a glass dome. When I looked closer, I saw that the engraved cover was open, and the glass over the watch face had shattered.

"What about that long staff in the closet?"

Patti pointed to the old wooden walking stick that was probably only a few inches shorter than my own five-foot-six height. "This?" she asked. "It's a family heirloom. The Nicholsons are very proud of their Scottish and Scandinavian ancestors, and this piece supposedly belonged to an ancestor."

"Were the jacket and watch pieces brought up from storage because of the hunting exhibit?" I asked. Patti nodded. I made the rounds of the room twice more, but nothing else stood out to me as having any particular resonance. I had no desire to touch either the jacket or the watch, and since Nicholson's death wasn't a mystery to be solved, fortunately, I didn't need to.

"Thank you," I said, as Patti led us downstairs. "I think we've learned what we needed to make a recommendation."

She looked nervous. "You won't tell the board members that I mentioned the ghosts, will you? They only want us to talk about them at Halloween."

I smiled. "Don't worry. Your secret is safe with us."

"Do you think that if they put the watch and jacket back in storage, the ghosts wouldn't be as scary?" she asked.

I didn't want to lie to her. "That won't make the ghosts go away completely. But if those are items that his spirit is particularly attached to, taking them off display might make the haunting less...rambunctious," I said. "At least, that's the recommendation we're going to make."

"What would it take to make the ghosts leave for good?" Patti was more interested than I would have expected, and then I thought about docents needing to go out to their cars at dusk with few people around and decided I couldn't blame her for being frightened.

"If those pieces are really the anchor, then destroying them would probably be the only way to set the ghosts free," Teag replied. "Which is probably not something the board or the family would be willing to do. But it might help to put them in a lead box, not just take them down to storage."

"And even destroying them might not send the ghosts packing," I cautioned, in case Patti decided to take matters into her own hands. "There could be something else that bound the spirits here, and it could take a priest—or someone else with special skills—to get the ghosts to leave." We often worked with a local priest to dispel troublesome spirits—but we also had a Voudon mambo, a medium, and a necromancer on speed dial, just in case. I didn't think Patti needed to know that.

"Thank you," she said, as she walked us to the door.

I looked around. "Will you be all right? You aren't alone here, are you?"

Patti smiled and shook her head. "There are some people in the offices. We all try to go to our cars together. No one wants to be the last one here."

Teag and I walked out to his car, giving a last look in the direction of where we had sensed the ghostly hunt.

"Okay, spill," I said as we got in and buckled up. "You froze back there when we heard the horses. What happened?"

He stayed quiet as we pulled out of the parking lot and drove down the long lane. Century-old live oak trees lined each side of the driveway, and their twisted branches formed a tunnel that dripped with Spanish moss.

"I had a dream," he said finally, as we pulled out onto the main road. "It was about a fox hunt, and at first it all looked like what you see in those paintings. But then the moon came out, and they were all zombies. With red eyes."

Teag chanced a look in my direction. "I don't usually have dreams like that, Cassidy. But I've dreamed it three times this month. I don't know what it means, but it's got to be important, and frankly, it scares the hell out of me."

CHAPTER TWO

"So you brought an audience this time, Teag? I didn't know our lessons were so entertaining." Mrs. Teller gave me a big smile and hugged me tight. I got a hug from Niella, her daughter, as well. Mrs. Teller led us into a room she had repurposed as her studio and motioned for Teag and me to have a seat. Niella came in a few minutes later with a tray that held a pitcher of sweet tea and four glasses, and she put it on a side table.

"So are you here to see what this boy's been up to, or are you thinking to learn some weaving yourself, huh?" Mrs. Teller fixed me with a gaze that seemed to see right down to my bones. She was in her late sixties, with short hair sprinkled with gray, mahogany skin that showed no signs of aging, and piercing black eyes. Niella took after her, in her looks, her lilting accent, and her talents.

"I think I've got enough with my touch magic," I replied. "I'm leaving the Weaving to you."

Mrs. Teller and Niella are some of the best sweetgrass basket makers in Charleston. They have a regular spot down at the Charleston City Market, and their baskets fetch high prices—for good reason. Not only are they true artists with a difficult craft, but Mrs. Teller's Weaver magic gives a "little something extra" to all of her creations. Oh, and she's also a damn fine Hoodoo worker, a Root woman of high regard.

Mrs. Teller laughed, a rich, throaty sound. "Let me know if you change your mind."

I glanced up at Niella and thought she looked more tired than usual. "Have things been busier than usual?" I left it up to interpretation whether "things" meant the market or the Hoodoo.

"Well now, that's a tale in itself," Mrs. Teller said. Out of habit, she picked up an unfinished sweetgrass braid, and her fingers flew while she talked. Teag took down a half-woven basket of his own from a shelf and returned to sit next to me. Where Mrs. Teller's muscle memory was born from more than a half-century of practice, enabling her to bend and twist the sharp dried grass without slicing up her fingers, Teag moved with careful caution. He'd learned the hard way, and I'd seen him come into the shop with fingers covered in bandages more than once.

"Fill us in," I begged. Sharing information was essential for those of us in the supernatural community in Charleston, and Mrs. Teller ran in some circles that Teag and I usually weren't part of.

"Trouble's brewing," Mrs. Teller said, and Niella settled into a chair beside her, picking up her own half-done basket to work while we talked. "People can feel it coming, like a storm over the ocean." The sweet, earthy smell of the seagrass filled the air.

"What kind of trouble?" I asked. Teag's focus was on his basket, and I knew he juggled both the complexity of working the stubborn grass, as well as the magic he channeled through the weaving. He might be listening, but he had too much going on to talk.

"Don't know yet, that's the truth of it," she replied. Her Lowcountry accent rounded her vowels and softened her consonants, and added a musical quality that I found mesmerizing. "But it's big. I feel that in my bones, and my bones don't lie."

I tried to track how she wove the sweetgrass, but her fingers practically blurred with the speed of experience. Even without handling the baskets, I knew they projected a calm, protective resonance that probably attracted buyers as much as the beauty of her craftwork. The baskets of hers that I owned were some of my favorite decorations because they always made me feel better being around them.

"Just a feeling, or have you seen something?" I pressed.

"What I've seen is people making a beeline to my door, asking me for gris-gris bags and goofer dust," she said. "Folks be saying that they can't sleep, or that they hear noises but nothing's there, or they catch a glimpse of shadows out of the corner of their eye." She shook her head. "Uh, uh," she tutted. "That's not good. Not good at all. So I fix them up best I can, show them how to put down the dust or put a dime in their shoe or fix their mojo bag and send them on their way, and the next day, I got twice as many people waiting for me, because they all told their friends."

While the boom was good for business, I knew that whatever had people unnerved sounded like the kind of problem that landed in my lap, sooner or later. Sorren is part of the Alliance, a secret organization of mortals and immortals that take care of supernatural threats. He founded Trifles and Folly with my ancestor nearly three-hundred-and-fifty years ago, and our store is one of dozens Sorren has all over the world. The stores serve as outposts to get dangerous magical or haunted items out of circulation and shut down things that go bump in the night.

"What kind of bad dreams?" I asked, although I couldn't resist a glance in Teag's direction, but he never looked up from his work. "Is there a common thread?"

Mrs. Teller shrugged. "There're all nightmares, for sure. Most people won't speak of their dreams because they think saying it out loud gives the dreams power. Maybe so, maybe not. But the ones who would say told me they were being chased, in the dark, but they couldn't see what was behind them. Except for red eyes."

Teag didn't say anything, but he swallowed hard, and his fingers paused for a few seconds.

I swallowed hard, too. "Yikes," I managed. "Any idea what might cause that?"

"Lots of things could," Mrs. Teller replied. "If it were one or two people coming in, I'd say they got someone real mad at them. But so many at my doorstep?" She shook her head. "Uh, uh, uh. There's something bigger going on, and you and Sorren need to be getting to the bottom of it."

For the rest of the evening, I sat back and watched Teag's lesson. Mrs. Teller managed to combine teaching him about magic along with the techniques of weaving complicated patterns with the sweetgrass. I didn't always follow how it worked, but then again, my magic is different from theirs.

After a particularly frustrating effort, Teag sighed and looked up, angry at himself for not being able to complete the exercise. "I can store magic in knots, and I can weave a general intention—like 'tranquility'—into a piece of cloth, or protective spells. But I'm not doing very well at countering a spell someone else has woven into something. And to be honest, I'm not sure I want to learn how to weave a compulsion into a piece of cloth."

I shivered. Teag was probably remembering a run-in we'd had with something evil that had gotten locked into a rug by a master Weaver. That gave me nightmares of my own.

"Just because you know how to do something doesn't mean you do it all the time. Maybe you know something, and you never use it," Mrs. Teller replied. "But the things you can do with your magic, they're like tools. You never know when you'll need it. You think 'compulsion' and imagine something bad, like hurting someone. What if you wove that into a rope and used it to tie up a creature and keep him from fighting or yelling?"

Mrs. Teller coiled the braid of sweetgrass she wove. "The magic itself, it's not good or bad. Like I've told you before, it's what we do with the magic that matters." She looked up at him over the top of her reading glasses. "Now, try that binding spell again."

By the time the lesson ended, I felt worn out, and I wasn't the one expending magic. Watching the effort Teag put into trying to accomplish his lessons made me tired. Although being around so many of Mrs. Teller's baskets gave me a Zen-like calm like I'd had a stiff drink.

"You're getting better at control," Mrs. Teller said to Teag as we got ready to leave. "And your gift is strong. I been doing this for a long, long time, and no one I ever taught has been as strong as you are." Before Teag could thank her, she fixed him with a look. "That's a warning, not a compliment. Power like that attracts attention—usually the wrong kind. Like a big, shiny beacon. You need to learn to defend yourself, boy. You don't have a choice about it."

Teag was quiet on the way back to my house. I'd known him long enough to recognize the way he bit his lip meant he was turning Mrs. Teller's words over in his mind.

"She's right," he said after a while. We parked at the curb, but neither of us made a move to get out of the car. "I need to figure out how to do more defensive magic. How to shield, so I'm not easy to find." The worry was clear on his face. "I know how to fight. But if Anthony got hurt because someone was coming for me...I couldn't live with myself."

Teag and Anthony had been a couple for several years now, and I kept wondering when I might find a wedding invitation in my mail. Anthony knows about what we really do at the store and about the Alliance, and he has some latent clairvoyance, but he has no magical defenses of his own, and that makes him vulnerable.

"I don't think the fox hunters from the Nicholson mansion are going to come after you," I said, with as much of a smile as I could muster. "And you're doing everything you can to learn more about your magic. You've already come so far—"

"Not far enough," Teag said with a grim set to his jaw. "Maybe I've been lucky that no one's noticed me so far. That luck won't hold. And until I know how to shield my magic, so it isn't so visible, then I'm a threat to everyone around me—you, Anthony, even Sorren."

"Pretty sure Sorren can take care of himself," I joked, although I knew that even with his vampire abilities, Sorren wasn't invincible.

"I know," Teag said, and slumped. Where he had looked ready to charge into battle a moment earlier, now he looked tired and over-whelmed. "It's scary to think about. And with the dreams, I haven't slept well."

"Did you tell Anthony?"

He shook his head. "Not everything. Nothing he can do about it. So

I said I'd had nightmares, but didn't get into the details. We don't know there's anything to them, yet. But…I wish I could sleep."

I reached over and squeezed his arm. "We'll figure it out," I said. "And in the meantime, maybe Rowan or Lucinda could help with a charm to make your power a little less visible." Rowan's a powerful witch, and Lucinda is our friendly neighborhood Voudon mambo. They're both strong in their abilities and lucky for us, they're good friends.

"That's a good idea," Teag said, and I knew it bothered him to admit how much Mrs. Teller's comments had troubled him. "I'll call them tomorrow."

I moved to get out of the car. My house is warded with strong magical protections by Lucinda, Rowan, and several of our other allies. Once I'm past the gate, the bad guys have to be pretty damn powerful to do any harm. The house Teag and Anthony share is also warded, though the protections there are newer, and being strengthened over time. Teag laid a hand on my shoulder.

"Thanks for going to the lesson with me," he said. "I didn't want to go by myself tonight, not after what happened at the mansion."

I gave him a supportive smile. "I understand. You'd do the same for me. Now go home and get some sleep. We'll call Rowan and Lucinda in the morning." I knew Teag would watch to see that I got inside the wall that surrounded my little backyard garden, and I turned to wave before I pulled the door shut after me.

THE NEXT MORNING at the shop was a blur. We were swamped with customers, and while that's a great problem to have, it made doing our real job—busting bad spooks—hard to do. But a nice day brings people out, and a stretch of beautiful weather meant plenty of tourists. I couldn't complain about ringing up sales, but I itched to contact Rowan and Lucinda and get something to ease Teag's worries.

By mid-afternoon, the shoppers had moved on down King Street, and we could finally take a break. "Go on," Maggie said. "I'll be fine here for the afternoon. I can tell the two of you have places to be. And besides, Mrs. Morrissey called."

Maggie is a godsend. She's a retired teacher who got bored with too much free time and works for us part-time. She's a bundle of energy, and since she has a penchant for changing the color and style of her hair on a whim, we never know what new look she'll be rocking. Maggie knows the real scoop about us, and while she dresses like Woodstock, she has a mind for business straight out of Wall Street. When the chips are down, she's exactly the person you want handling the details.

"Thanks," I said, licking the last of the pizza sauce off my lips from the takeout we'd gotten for lunch. "When did Mrs. Morrissey call?"

"Right when that busload of Canadian tourists turned up and bought up all the tea sets," she replied. "I heard it go to voicemail. I think it's important; didn't sound like she wanted to chat."

I pulled out my phone and walked into the back room, a little kitchen behind the shop where we had a table and coffee maker. Usually I didn't need the privacy of my office to talk to Mrs. Morrissey, but Maggie's comment worried me.

"Cassidy? Thank you for calling back so quickly. I know how busy you are." Mrs. Benjamin Morrissey remained the epitome of social grace, no matter how dire the situation. She'd been a friend of my Uncle Evann, the relative—and fellow psychometric—who willed me Trifles and Folly. I suspected she knew more about what we did than she let on, but she definitely knew about my ability to read objects.

"Never too busy for you." I meant it. I considered Mrs. Morrissey a friend, although I guessed her age to be in her mid-seventies, a good half-century older than Teag and I. "What can I do for you?"

Trifles and Folly, as an antique store, has plenty of reasons to collaborate with the Historical Archive, run by Mrs. Morrissey. Sometimes we work together on charity fundraisers or special exhibits. But from the tone in my caller's voice, I suspected she wasn't going to hit me up for a donation.

"We've had a theft," she said. "And it's one of the pieces you told me was 'special.' Could you come by when you have a chance? Bring

Teag—we have a new textile exhibit, '*Under Wraps*' that he might appreciate."

"We'll be there in an hour," I said, glancing at the clock. That would let us cover all but the tail end of the afternoon rush at the store, so I wouldn't feel too guilty about leaving Maggie to lock up. And we'd still get to the Archive before they closed.

"Thank you. I'll be waiting."

I slipped my phone back into my pocket just as Teag wandered into the break room. "Problem?" he asked.

"Sort of," I replied, frowning as I tried to figure out what Mrs. Morrissey thought we could do about her theft. "Something's been stolen, and apparently I had told Mrs. Morrissey that it had juice."

Teag looked puzzled. "If it was malicious, she wouldn't have had it on display. So why would someone take a piece with good mojo?"

I shrugged. "Don't know. And I'm not sure what she's thinking we can do. Any evidence we might find probably wouldn't be something the police would accept. But she did say there was a new exhibit you'd like, so do you want to ride shotgun?"

Fortunately, we were only reasonably busy instead of slammed for the next hour. Even so, we'd sold enough tea sets and trinkets that we'd close out the month with a tidy profit. Sorren not only pays Teag and me well for running the shop, but we earn an additional stipend for the risks of our "extracurricular" Alliance activities. So the shop would stay open even if we didn't break even. But since Trifles and Folly has been in my family for so long, it's a point of pride for it to turn a profit.

The time continued to fly, and before I knew it, Maggie was shooing us out the door, promising to close up. We walked, despite my crack about "riding shotgun" because it was a nice night and trying to get parking near the Archive was a real pain. Charleston raises "strolling" to an art form, and on a pleasant evening, tourists and locals rub shoulders on the sidewalks. Walking tours, shoppers, and foodies check out our world-class restaurants and keep the streets busy until all hours. Even in residential areas, tourists stroll through the historic district long after the carriage tours are done for the evening.

So it seemed odd that fewer people than usual were out. "Where is everybody?" I asked, glancing skyward to see if I'd missed out on a warning about rain.

"I don't know, but something's up," Teag replied, and while he tried not to rubberneck, I could see his gaze flitting from person to person as we walked. "People seem a little tense."

That also seemed strange. Charleston's lifeblood is tourism, and we've aced hospitality. It's not just good business; it's Southern manners bred bone-deep. Not that everyone is happy all the time, but even when we aren't, Charlestonians make a damn fine effort to be friendly and welcoming. It's the kind of city where people say "excuse me" if they bump someone on the sidewalk, "thank you" if someone holds a door, and might even make eye contact and smile at a total stranger.

Today, good humor was in short supply. Passers-by kept their eyes averted, and they walked like they were all late for work. No smiles, no greetings, and when a few people bumped shoulders, I actually heard a snappish exchange. What the hell was going on?

"Did something happen? Have you seen the news?" I murmured to Teag.

He looked bewildered. "Nothing popped up on my phone. Maybe Mrs. Morrissey will know."

I could almost feel the tension radiating from the other pedestrians, and it was getting to me. I felt keyed up, and that wouldn't help if I needed to rely on my touch magic once we got to the Archive. Impressions flow best when I'm relaxed, and although I've used my gift under very dangerous and demanding circumstances, I'd prefer not to feel out of sorts. Especially when I had no reason for my mood to suddenly tank.

The Historical Archive occupies a restored old mansion in the ritzy area known as "South of Broad." Mrs. Morrissey is one of the quiet movers and shakers in Charleston, especially in the non-profit world. Her husband died quite a while ago, leaving her bank account well-endowed. She leveraged the most valuable currency in Charleston—connections—and emerged as a doyenne. Fortunately, she likes Teag and me a lot.

I didn't see any visitors milling around when Teag and I entered, but since it was nearing the late dinner hour, that didn't surprise me. We went right back to Mrs. Morrissey's office, and her administrative assistant waved us on.

Mrs. Morrissey perched behind her expensive antique desk with the rigidly perfect posture instilled from boarding school. Her St. John knit suit skimmed her slender frame, and the understated pearls in her necklace and earrings were real. She looked up and gave us a tired smile. "Cassidy. Teag. I'm so glad you're here."

I had almost skipped bringing her a latte—our usual "bribe" for information, but she looked so weary I was glad I'd gone ahead and gotten one despite the hour.

"Bless you," she murmured as she accepted the hot drink like an offering. "It's been quite a day."

"What's going on?" I settled into one of the chairs in front of the desk.

"You know what it's like around here when we're getting ready for a new installation," she sighed, raising a bird-like hand to smooth her perfect, silver bobbed hair. "Utter insanity. People coming and going, boxes in and out—hard to keep track of everyone."

"You thought something had been stolen?" Teag pressed.

Mrs. Morrissey nodded. "The exhibit is on field sports—hunting and fishing. Fox, deer, quail, duck—all the usual things people in these parts like to hunt. We're focusing on the sporting aspects, and the Museum of the Lowcountry is putting their emphasis on the 'Rural Gentry'—the families that have been noted for their hunts, horse breeding, field dogs, that sort of thing. That way we don't duplicate."

I gave her an encouraging nod and decided that we needed to give Alistair a call at the museum tomorrow and drop by to see.

"One case shows how sporting apparel has changed down through the years—what the well-dressed gentleman wears for a day in the field," she went on. "Many of the outfits were on loan from the families. And the Nicholson family lent us one of Geoffrey Nicholson's duck-hunting jacket. With the jacket was a brooch that they've lent us before—do you know the one? It's very Celtic."

The mention of "Geoffrey Nicholson" sent a chill down my spine, given the events of the night before. But now that I thought about the brooch, I remembered one in particular that she'd shown me from the Archive's collection, a pretty silver clasp, very old.

"The man's cloak pin? The family said it dated to the Vikings."

Mrs. Morrissey nodded. "That's the one."

I frowned, trying to remember details. "I didn't do a reading on it, but from what I could see, they might be right," I replied. "It held a lot of power, partly from its age, but I didn't pick up anything dangerous."

"That's what I recall," she replied. Mrs. Morrissey stood. "Come with me. I'll show you where it happened."

Museum exhibits are a toss-up for me. As I've gotten more control over my psychometry, I'm better able to protect myself from objects with a lot of resonance. I've also learned which exhibits to avoid, like those commemorating disasters or tragedies, because of the nature of the stored impressions. If I've got no choice about being in the midst of a lot of emotionally fraught objects, at least I can rally my defenses to keep me from being knocked on my ass. Although that still happens, more often than I'd like.

In the past, the Archive hosted some exhibits that accidentally included pieces with strong dark magic. Some of those spawned nightmares that are likely to be on permanent repeat in my brain for the rest of my life. But most of the historic objects, fortunately, have little to no resonance, and some have a very positive, calming vibe. Thank heavens, or I'd never be able to visit again.

"We also have a nice exhibit on quilts," Mrs. Morrissey said as we passed one of the smaller display rooms. "I thought Teag might like to have a look around."

"We'll check it out on the way down," he promised, and with the way his eyes lit up, I knew he'd make sure we did.

A mannequin in a traditional fox hunting outfit astride a life-size "horse" welcomed visitors to the gallery. Enclosed in glass cases throughout the large room, I saw a selection of rifles and shotguns, duck calls, hunting horns, traps, and even a tree stand. Taxidermy trophies illustrated the prowess of long-ago hunters, although the glassy-eyed stuffed creatures made me equally sad and uncomfortable.

Along one wall, winners' cups vied with framed photos to celebrate notable hunting and racing events. That's when I noticed the jockey uniforms and realized that the exhibit spanned more than hunting, taking in riding and racing as well. Charlestonians like their dogs, their horses, and their fishing boats. Amid the cases with saddles and riding tack, I glimpsed some fishing tackle, old-fashioned rods, and some wooden canoes. Mrs. Morrissey knows how to put on a great exhibit.

"This is where it happened," she said, leading us to a long glass case. Inside were faceless display dummies wearing hunting outfits that dated from the 1700s through the early 1900s, showing the shifts in both style and materials. "The brooch was pinned on the red jacket in the middle," Mrs. Morrissey said. "And when we came in this morning, it was gone. I don't know what I'm going to tell the Nicholson family."

"You've reported it to the police?" Teag asked.

"Of course. And to the insurance company. But since Cassidy had picked up on some of its…resonance…I was hoping maybe she'd notice something the investigators didn't," Mrs. Morrissey added.

She sounded hopeful, and I didn't want to disappoint her, but my magic wasn't like a supernatural security camera that could back up and see footage of the crime. On TV, ghosts speak in complete sentences, visions provide clear images, and fortune tellers give detailed warnings. In real life, ghosts often can't speak or are just "stone tape" recordings—a few seconds of strong emotion trapped in an infinite loop. Visions are usually jumbled and muddy, and even fortune tellers with real clairvoyance rarely get a complete picture. Part of having a psychic gift is learning how to fill in the blanks without blindly rushing to conclusions. But for Mrs. Morrissey, I'd give it a try.

I moved closer to the case and held a hand out so that my palm hovered as close to the glass as possible without touching. Faint images bound up in the collective memory of the objects inside buzzed like background noise in my mind, and I concentrated, trying to tune the signal to pick out new impressions. I bet on the fact that whoever stole the brooch had touched the case, and any residue left behind from that contact mattered more to me than the blurry memories of long-ago hunts.

When I found it, the impression confused me. I must have frowned or tilted my head because Teag stepped closer.

"What did you find?"

More often than not, the resonance I pick up communicates in feelings or pictures, and sometimes I struggle to put it into words.

"The thief has magic," I murmured, parsing out information from the tangle of sensations. "Female...I think. And the intent seems all wrong. Not greed." I surprised myself as I listened to my own words. "Anger. Desperation. And...loyalty. Or love. I can't tell, but it's fierce and frightened." I opened my eyes and pulled my hand back. "I sure hope the cops got fingerprints because what I could pick up isn't going to help find your thief."

"Well, it was worth a try," Mrs. Morrissey replied. "Thank you for making the effort. I know that sometimes our displays have given you a rather disconcerting impressions."

I'd picked up glimpses of long-dead serial killers, hanging judges, and scary-as-hell Nephilim from prior exhibits, which went way beyond "disconcerting," but Mrs. Morrissey didn't need to know that.

A call over the intercom sent Mrs. Morrissey hurrying downstairs, but as she left, she thanked us again and insisted we take time to walk through the quilt display, even though we were already past closing time.

The "Under Wraps: Quilts and Community" exhibit exuded a happy, peaceful vibe, and I relaxed as if I'd snuggled into a warm blanket. Quilts of all sizes, patterns, and colors hung in glass cases, but they were close enough that I could get a look at the tiny, intricate stitching.

"They're beautiful," I said. I've always been in awe of the time and attention to detail it takes to create a quilt, as well as the exquisiteness of the colorful designs.

"And powerful," Teag added. I looked over at him, startled. He grinned. "Can't you feel it?"

Now that he mentioned it, when I paid attention with my touch magic, that tranquil vibe definitely was due to more than the calm music playing over the speakers. "Does Weaver magic work for quilts?" I asked.

He nodded. "It's really about all aspects of making or working with fabric. Magic can be part of making the thread or yarn, weaving the cloth, or stitch work." He pointed to a white-on-white quilt where the very small stitches created a pattern. "That kind of detail requires a lot of will and intent. Whether the quilter knows it or not, focus like that marks the cloth. If the person doesn't have magic, then it's more like the kind of thing you pick up—the dominant emotions the crafter felt when he or she made the quilt. But for someone with Weaver magic, it's basically like tracing sigils and runes with thread."

I thought about that for a moment, remembering the quilts my mother had on all our beds when I was growing up, and how they always made me feel happy and safe. "I'm impressed," I said, and I didn't only mean by the beautiful handiwork. We made a slow circuit of the room, admiring the original designs and craftsmanship, and when Teag headed for the door, I paused for a moment to soak up a little more of the serenity radiated by the quilts.

Which made me think of something. "Did anything strike you as odd on the walk over?" I asked as we headed down the stairs. By this time, almost all of the Archive staff had gone. We waved goodbye to Mrs. Morrissey, and let ourselves out, making sure the door locked behind us.

"You mean how everyone was in a lousy mood?" Teag answered my question. "Yeah, I noticed. If looks could kill…" He frowned. "Why? You think it's important?"

I wasn't quite sure how to wrap words around the gut feeling that wouldn't leave me alone. "Yeah. Maybe. Strange that it was *everyone*, don't you think? Did you start to feel out of sorts?"

Teag considered for a moment. "No…did you?"

I shook my head. "And I didn't notice anything wrong once we got to the Archive. So maybe it's a fluke."

The look in Teag's eyes suggested he didn't agree. He glanced at the agate and silver necklace I wear most of the time, and the silver and onyx bracelets. They're not just pretty, the metal and gemstones protect against evil. Teag wears an *agimat* charm and a hamsa on cords around his neck. "Maybe we were protected against whatever's causing the mood shifts."

"Could be. Assuming there's something supernatural afoot, more than a collectively lousy day."

I could tell that Teag kept turning the idea over in his mind as we headed back to the shop, where both our cars were parked.

"What would someone—or some*thing*—get out of making people cranky?" he mused. "Where's the benefit for spending that kind of power?"

"Maybe it's a side-effect of something else, not the main goal," I suggested.

"So why didn't people at the Archive seem to be affected?"

I thought about it. "If our amulets protected us, then maybe the benign heirlooms at the Archive create some kind of protective field," I speculated. "The way the quilt exhibit made us feel peaceful. White light. Or static that drowns out the bad mojo."

"Speaking of mojo," Teag said, "do you think what Mrs. Teller said might be related? About people being afraid, having bad dreams, and wanting gris-gris bags?"

"Could be," I admitted. "But what would bad dreams have to do with people being in unusually foul moods while they're awake? How about the ghosts at the Nicholson mansion being stronger than usual—how's that connected? Or the missing brooch from the Archive?"

Teag opened his mouth to answer when we heard a low growl from the alley we passed. We exchanged a glance and reached for the weapons we never left home without. I pulled my spoon-athame from my purse, and let the dog collar jangle down around my wrist. Bo's ghost shimmered and fell into step beside me, giving me a big doggy grin.

"Maybe it's a stray dog," I posed, although both of us knew better. Teag loosened two of the knotted cords tied to the belt loops of his jeans. The knots stored magic, helping him charge up his power quickly. He reached into the backpack he always carries and withdrew a thin metal coil. The silver whip played havoc with ghosts and supernatural creatures, although I hated to think what a cop would make of it if we got stopped.

The street seemed unusually deserted. No one in sight for blocks— a rarity for Charleston so early in the evening. That meant trouble.

The growl came again, closer this time. I felt my hackles rise. The air around us grew cold. A dog howled, and then another and another. A whole damn pack of dogs, in the middle of a city with strict leash laws. Something was definitely wrong.

"Run or fight?" Teag asked in a low voice.

"How about a little of both?" I wasn't about to turn my back on whatever headed for us from the alley. I'd much rather stand my ground and face a threat head-on than be run down by wild dogs. If something supernatural did lurk down that dark street, we couldn't walk away and leave the next jogger to pay the price.

I glanced around once more, but the streets were empty and the houses around us dark. "All right. Let's see what's going on."

We approached the entrance to the alley warily, weapons ready. The wooden spoon in my hand once belonged to my grandmother, and it held a lifetime of strong positive memories imprinted in its grain. Bo padded along beside me, and while most people think of Golden Retrievers as happy-go-lucky, they're also fiercely protective of their people, and ninety pounds of solid muscle with sharp teeth is nothing to sneeze at.

Shit. Three pairs of red eyes stared back at us from the shadows, and when the darkness stirred behind them, I could make out another three sets farther back.

I didn't want to go into the alley after the ghostly dogs, but the idea of battling them in the middle of the street didn't appeal to me, either. I felt in my pocket for salt and found a small bag, but hardly enough for a pack of hellhounds, or whatever they were. My mind raced, trying to think of what kind of demon-dog creatures might be loose in the city.

The lead dog raised his head and howled, and then I knew. Not *grims* or hellhounds or the "black dog" of legend. These were hunting dogs. And we were the prey.

The pack moved forward, but we had an advantage if we could keep them bottled up in the alley. They couldn't chase us, and they couldn't surround us. We might win this fight without too much effort.

Then I heard more howls from the alley on the other side of the street. This was about to go wrong in a big way.

Teag and I stood back to back, knowing that running would be the wrong move for dogs trained to chase their quarry. Didn't matter whether they were banshee beagles or ghostly greyhounds, they could probably outrun us, and a trained hunting pack could harry and herd its target. Screw that.

"Go for it," I murmured to Teag.

The dogs sprang forward, growling and snapping. They looked solid enough to do damage, with black bodies and hellish, red eyes. Lips drawn back into snarls and heads lowered made their body language completely clear. I didn't know whether those teeth were solid or spectral, but I learned a long time ago that something doesn't have to be "real" to be dangerous.

I raised my athame and sent a blast of bright white energy streaming in a brilliant cone of power at the dogs attacking from the left. One of the dogs tried to duck to the side, and Bo leaped toward it, snapping his teeth. The blast from my athame forced the demon-dogs to retreat. I motioned for Bo to stay beside me because I didn't want to accidentally hurt him while I was aiming for the hunting hounds from hell.

Teag's silver whip snapped, and the black dog it hit vanished. I didn't have any silver, but I did have salt, and when the ghost hounds surged forward again, I hurled a handful of Morton's best right into their midst. Their shapes wobbled and faded, like the image from a weak TV signal, and I doubled my effort, throwing more salt. Then while they looked staticky, I blasted them with the white light power.

The dogs vanished, with a howl that made my skin crawl. Bo wagged his tail, bumped against my leg, and blinked out.

I turned and saw Teag warily reeling in his silver whip; the spectral hounds were nowhere in sight. Without needing to discuss it, we both moved to lay down the rest of my salt in lines at the mouth of the two alleys. It might be gone by morning, but for now, it would deter the ghosts from coming back right away.

"What the hell?" Teag said, as we finally began the walk back to the shop. Instead of the leisurely stroll we'd had on our way here, we kept a brisk pace, shy of a jog. The streets were still too empty for my comfort, although if demon dogs were prowling around, maybe that was for the best.

We made it all the way back before a low growl sounded behind us. Where the dogs from the alley had been indistinct, hard to figure the breed, the huge shadow-cur that burst from the darkness stood as tall as an Irish wolfhound, and probably weighed as much as a full-grown man. Hunting dogs came in all sizes, including extra-large.

The ghostly dog growled again, a low, dangerous rumble. I seized on a plan.

"The warding," I said. "Get to the doorway!"

I ran, with Teag sprinting beside me. We hurled ourselves into the alcove where the door to Trifles and Folly is nestled a few feet deeper than the shop windows. The huge black dog lunged, stretching out to its full length, and bared its sharp teeth, going for the throat.

Teag and I backed deep into the alcove, weapons ready if it came to another fight.

Before the ghost dog came within a foot of the store's windows, light flared almost too bright to look at, and a curtain of shimmering power sprang up between us and the specter. The hound was already airborne, with no way to change its trajectory. It hit the light barrier and vanished in a spray of sparks, like the world's biggest fly in a magic bug zapper.

"I guess Lucinda's wardings are still good," I said, a little breathlessly.

"Yeah, I guess so," Teag replied, sounding as weirded-out as I felt.

We nosed out of the alcove warily, then edged beyond the warding and hurried to our cars with the promise to figure things out in the morning. But as I drove home and the shakes hit me, I had the awful feeling that the storm Mrs. Teller predicted was about to break loose.

CHAPTER THREE

Magnolia Cemetery would be a perfect final resting place, if it weren't for all the damn zombies.

"Where did they come from?" Teag muttered as we looked out across the moonlit grounds at the staggering, shuffling undead lurching beneath the ancient live oak hung heavy with Spanish moss.

"Offhand, I'd say their graves," Chuck Pettis remarked with a sidelong look and a grin. No one would mistake Chuck for anything except ex-military, with his sturdy build, thick neck, bald head, and no-nonsense attitude. He's an Army vet, mid-fifties, retired. His Black Ops unit de-fanged alien and dark magic threats. Now he teams up with us on occasion to fight the good fight against supernatural bad guys, or as he thinks of them, "ectoplasmic terrorists."

Teag rolled his eyes. "I meant, what made them rise?"

Before Chuck could suggest an answer we all might regret, I jumped into the conversation. "Maybe it's tied into the other weirdness. You said it yourself: we don't get coincidences in our business."

I could hear Chuck ticking from here. Don't get me wrong: Chuck is a valuable ally, and he's done us some real solids. He has more than a few tricks—and explosives—up his sleeves for dealing with the preternaturally perturbed. But he's also a little battle scarred—with good reason—and he believes that if his massive collection of clocks ever wind down and stop, he'll die. So Chuck's jackets are all lined with working wristwatches—just the clock part—and you can hear them when he's standing close. If the watches make him feel better, I'm fine with that.

"Since I don't think St. Peter's blown his horn to call the dead to heaven, then I figure some son of a bitch is playing around with magic," Chuck replied. "And that's usually trouble."

We had a heap of trouble shuffling across the lawn. If they'd been smart enough to avoid the headstones, they probably would have been on us by now. But all across the cemetery, I could see zombies stuck behind granite markers like those toys that keep on walking when they hit the wall.

This would have been like shooting fish in a barrel if we were going to go all *Walking Dead* on their asses. But that would leave a major tourist attraction littered with the rotting corpses of historically-significant dead people, and the fallout from that wouldn't be pretty.

"Archibald is on his way," Sorren said, coming up behind us so quietly I didn't hear him. Of course I didn't—vampires excel at stealth.

"Can he make them go back into their graves?" I asked, nervously watching one of the zombies bang into a headstone, back up a step, and run into it again, over and over. "Because making them all fall down isn't a whole lot better than shooting them, and there are too many for us to rebury by the time the groundskeepers get here in the morning."

"He's a necromancer," Sorren replied with a shrug. "I leave the details up to him on this sort of thing."

Sorren is slender, with high cheekbones and gray eyes the color of the sea before a storm. With his trendy haircut and ripped jeans, he looks like a graduate student, but he's centuries older. I took comfort from the fact that he wasn't freaking out about having dozens of shamblers roaming the cemetery. Then again, we'd seen a lot worse.

"Why did some of them rise, and not others?" I asked, then hoped I hadn't tempted fate. There are thousands of burials at Magnolia Cemetery, dating to before the Civil War. A few dozen zombies we might be able to put down without too much of a fuss, but a cast of thousands would be terrifying.

"I think the right question is—why have *any* of them risen?"

I turned to see a tall, broad-shouldered man striding across the lawn toward us. With his British accent and his mutton-chop sideburns, Archibald Donnelly looks like he should be wearing a pith helmet. Since he's the immortal overseer of a time-traveling private club for adventurers-gone-missing, maybe his fashion sense really is left over from the days of the British Empire. All that matters to me is that he does some damn fine magic.

"It's going to be all over the news if corpses with their heads blown off are strewn around the cemetery," Sorren pointed out.

"Can't have that," Donnelly agreed. He put his hands on his hips and surveyed the scene as if he were overseeing a work site. "Do we know who they are?"

I shook my head. "We've been focused on containing them. Didn't want to get too close, and we figured we could find the graves they dug open after we put them back down."

Chuck and Teag had moved to counter some of the zombies that ambled toward where we stood. Teag had a long wooden staff, and when he prodded a shambler in the chest, the creature stumbled backward, then headed randomly in another direction. Chuck had a rifle with a night scope and used it to poke a zombie in the shoulder to send him back the way he came.

"All right, let's send them packing," Donnelly said. "I'd gotten to the best part of the book I was reading, and I'm keen to pick up where I left off." The idea of sending dozens of undead walkers to their graves didn't seem to perturb him, as if it were a common occurrence. Then again, maybe for him it was.

Donnelly raised his hands in blessing, drew in a deep breath, and spoke words of power. I don't know what he said; I tried to listen, but the words seemed too slippery to hear. All across the cemetery, the zombies stilled, raising their heads like dogs listening for a whistle.

Two of the creatures stood about twenty feet from us, and I watched them stop their shuffling and then begin to tremble. I backed

31

up a step, fearing that we'd be caught in a spray of rotting guts if Donnelly accidentally overshot his goal and blew them up. After a few seconds, the zombies began to shuffle again.

Donnelly stared at them, astonished. "That shouldn't be possible," he murmured. He raised his hands again, shifted his stance, and spoke words of power that sounded different, with a stern tone not to be disobeyed.

Once again, the zombies stopped, but this time they turned, orienting on the source of the command.

"I don't like this," I said, and the look on Sorren's face told me he agreed. I had a long knife and my athame, with Bo's ghost at my side. Sorren was old school; he had a sword in each hand. Chuck had a rifle, a handgun, and enough ammo that his pockets bulged. I knew that in addition to his staff, Teag had a short sword, and dagger, and probably that silver whip as well. But usually, all we needed was Donnelly's necromancy, and the zombies would give themselves a dirt nap.

If the creatures were hearing a dog whistle, it sounded "charge" instead of "retreat," Every shambler in the cemetery started toward us, giving a new meaning to "dead run."

"Shit," Donnelly growled, staring at his hands as if they had betrayed him. "I didn't expect that to happen."

"What now?" I asked.

Donnelly raised a bushy white eyebrow. "Now, we fight."

Before I could ponder how a bunch of shuffling corpses managed to defy an immortal necromancer, the game was on.

Chuck climbed a nearby mausoleum, taking up a sniper position on the roof. Teag and I stood guard beneath him, to make sure none of the shamblers tried to climb. Donnelly pulled out an honest-to-God cavalry saber and waded into battle, and he and Sorren slashed their way through the zombies, who lacked the brains or instructions to try to get away.

The crack of Chuck's rifle rang out across the garden landscape, a steady staccato beat as Chuck aimed and fired, over and over again. Teag and I had our hands full down below. Half a dozen zombies at a time closed in on us, but I couldn't tell whether they meant to attack or just started walking this direction and didn't think to stop.

I raised my athame and loosed a cone of cold white force, catching the nearest shuffler in the chest and throwing him back into a granite obelisk. I must have overdone it, because his rotted corpse split open on impact like an overripe watermelon, splattering the area with formaldehyde-scented gore.

Teag spun his staff, slamming into the skull of a zombie that came in range, and then looked on, appalled, as the head tore loose and flew through the air like a two-base hit at Wrigley Field. Two of the zombies came at me, and Bo sprang at the closer one, knocking it flat with his full weight. He grabbed the corpse's shirt front with his teeth and shook the body back and forth. It came apart, arms, legs, and head falling away, like a rag doll with its stitching cut.

I didn't have time to throw up, though my stomach rebelled at the smell. My blast of cold force missed the next zombie who lurched to one side as he tripped at the fateful instant, so I buried my knife hilt deep in his chest as he straightened, then pulled the blade back out and lopped off his head before he could get his balance.

Chuck must have packed enough ammo to stop a small army because he kept shooting. With all our combined efforts, after several long minutes, few of the zombies remained on their feet. Thank God Magnolia Cemetery lies outside of town in an area that's surrounded by industrial sites, or we'd have brought every SWAT team in the Lowcountry down on us by now. Even so, I knew our luck wouldn't last forever, that someone must have heard and called the cops. I hoped we were long gone before anyone arrived and started asking questions.

Finally, no more shots rang out. Donnelly and Sorren moved across one side of the huge cemetery, looking for stragglers, while Teag and I worked our way past row after row of headstones, peering carefully around war memorial statues and fancy Victorian angels in case any of the shamblers had gotten themselves stuck somewhere.

Along the way, we spotted the graves where the zombies had dug themselves out; hard to miss with the spray of fresh dirt and an open hole. I snapped photos of the headstone by each open grave with my phone camera, thinking maybe we could make sense of the whole thing later.

"I don't get it," Teag said, scanning the next row of gravestones. "Some of the zombies are soldiers, most aren't, some are really old, but some of those headstones look fairly new. Who woke them? Why those corpses in particular? And what were they supposed to do?"

I shook my head, busy taking pictures before we had to dodge the cops. When the ground gave way beneath my foot, I nearly fell into a half-dug grave, just as its occupant burst from the dirt, late for the party.

"Holy shit!" I yelled, scrambling back and trying not to lose my phone. I really didn't want to leave evidence at the scene of a crime, since someone would eventually be blamed for desecrating graves and abusing corpses.

The zombie reached for me, and I kicked hard. My boot connected with the creature's chin, snapping the bone and sending the skull flying into the gravestone with a wet thud. The body flopped on, not quite ready to give up, until Teag sank a knife through its back.

"Watch your step," he warned, giving me a hand up. I'd been splattered with gobbets of dead flesh, and the graveyard smelled like a high school biology lab on dissection day. In the distance, sirens wailed, heading our way.

"That's our cue to vamoose," Teag said, and we sprinted back toward where the others waited. Chuck had climbed down from his perch, and I wondered what the cops would make of long-dead corpses sprawled throughout the cemetery with fresh bullet holes in their heads. I wondered...but I didn't want to stick around to find out.

"Take the back way out," Donnelly instructed. "I'll lag behind and see what I can do to slow down the police to give you a head start." He always seemed unflappable, but after the way his magic failed to stop the zombies, Donnelly looked perplexed and bewildered.

"Come on," Sorren said, leading the way to where we'd parked the cars. "We can sort this out later. Right now, we could all use a hot shower and a stiff drink."

Teag came to my house to get cleaned up, because while Anthony knows the truth about what we do, he's still a lawyer and having Teag show up looking like he'd been grave robbing when the aftermath was going to be all over the news would be a really bad idea. We tried to leave Anthony as much plausible deniability as we could, and sometimes that meant our own version of "don't ask, don't tell."

Nights like this are why I keep plastic sheeting in the back of my RAV4, so we don't get blood—or worse—on the upholstery. We rode with the windows down, even though the night air was chilly, because we couldn't stand the stench. I kept to the speed limit exactly, since we couldn't afford to be pulled over, not looking and smelling like this.

When we finally reached my house, I'd never been so glad for the distraction spell Lucinda had placed on the parking spot right next to the door to my piazza. It makes other people completely forget about the empty space, leaving it open for me. A godsend, since I didn't want to traipse down the street looking like an extra from *Night of the Living Dead*.

My house is a white clapboard "single house," a uniquely Charleston style that situates the side of the house facing the street, with a door that leads onto the front porch. The porch and the real front door face a walled yard or garden. Back in the old days, that allowed people the privacy to take off their coats or lift the hem of their floor-length dresses without scandalizing the neighbors. Now, with Lucinda's wardings, the sidewalk door is the first line of defense, and no one but trusted friends could enter without being invited across the threshold. Of course, Teag, Sorren, Chuck, and Donnelly were among those on the short list with permission to come inside.

Once we neared the main door, I heard Baxter, my little Maltese, yipping up a storm. He's a six-pound bundle of attitude. Heart of a warrior, body of a guinea pig. I knew Maggie had come over to keep him company, and as Teag and I came in covered in zombie-spatter, she scooped Baxter up and retreated to the far end of the foyer.

"Merciful heavens, what the hell did you get into tonight?" Maggie's eyes watered, and Baxter gave one last yip and buried his nose against her arm.

"Greasy grimy gopher guts," I replied, toeing off my boots and leaving them on the porch. I debated stripping down right there to avoid tracking awful slimy stuff through the house. Maggie must have read my mind because she came back with Bax in one hand and two old bedsheets in the other.

"Pretend you're in middle school gym class," she ordered. "Wrap up and strip down without showing anything. I'll put on some water for tea. When I leave, I can bundle those clothes into a big garbage bag and take them to my cousin's place out in the country—he's got a burn barrel."

I didn't intend to argue because I know from experience that some things just don't wash clean. I hoped a good shot with the garden hose would save my boots.

Teag and I complied, then shimmied inside wrapped in my mom's old sheets from the 1970s. The big floral prints looked ridiculous, but they let us retain a shred of dignity, and I directed Teag to the downstairs guest bath while I scooted upstairs for a shower. Maggie's been on hand enough times for the aftermath of bloody battles to know where Teag's spare clothing is kept.

I scrubbed with soap until my skin turned pink, and promised myself I'd bleach the bathtub for good measure tomorrow. Even after I knew I'd gotten all the gunk off of me, the smell was still in my nose, and several squirts of my strongest body spray wasn't quite enough to overpower the stink.

Still, I felt a lot better when I came downstairs to find Maggie and Teag already at my kitchen table, with Bax dancing around their feet, shamelessly begging for treats. I scooped him into my arms, and he recoiled, making me wonder whether it was the perfume or the formaldehyde that offended his nose.

"Is it okay if I stay here tonight?" Teag asked. "Anthony was going to be late working on a case, and if he's gotten to sleep, I don't want to wake him. Besides, I'm too jazzed right now to rest."

"Anytime," I said, and meant it. Teag is my best friend and brother-from-another-mother, and Anthony is a close second. Maggie's the smart-mouthed aunt I never had. It's crazy, but it works.

"Thanks," Teag said and texted Anthony that he'd be staying

over. Now that we'd settled that, Maggie got down the good bourbon and three shot glasses. After the night we'd had, I figured we'd earned it.

"What I don't get is, why were the zombies only in Magnolia Cemetery, when all of Huguenin Avenue is one long necropolis?" Teag asked.

Maggie raised her eyebrows at "zombies," but didn't ask.

I sipped my bourbon and considered the question. The street where Magnolia Cemetery is located is home to about a dozen other smaller cemeteries. Bethany Cemetery, down a side street, is still pretty big and has the graves of many of the area's early German settlers. There's a Jewish graveyard and several small AME Zion lots, some of which are very old. Yet as we made our escape, we didn't see any shamblers in those sections.

"That's a good question. I wonder if there were problems elsewhere."

I didn't wonder for long because my phone buzzed. "Father Anne," I mouthed to Teag and Maggie. "Hi there," I greeted my caller and glanced at the time. Midnight. That meant this wasn't a social call, even in our circles. "What's up? And can I put you on speaker? Teag and Maggie are here. We've had an interesting night."

I put the phone down on the table so everyone could hear. "Hey Cassidy, I wanted to give you a heads up," Father Anne said. "Lucinda and Rowan and I have been riding more back roads than a bootlegger, putting down zombies at little rural cemeteries."

We all looked at each other. "Say again?" I replied.

"Zombies," Father Anne repeated. She's a highly unorthodox Episcopalian priest who's also a member of a secret society of ass-kicking warriors against the Darkness. And a great poker player. "Popping up like zits all over the place, in these little bitty old churchyards in the middle of nowhere."

"Are you guys still out there?"

"Just heading back."

"I've got a couple of frozen pizzas and plenty of bourbon. If you want to do a slumber party, why not come over here and get cleaned up, then we can compare notes? We barely got back from Magnolia Cemetery, and it's gonna be all over tomorrow's headlines."

I heard some mumbled comments as they conferred. "Sure thing. But we're all kinda nasty right now, on account of the brain bits," Father Anne warned me. "I think I can rustle up clean sweats for all of us from the bag in my trunk."

"If you can't, I can," I promised and decided to swing by a dollar store tomorrow to pick up more disposable t-shirts and drawstring pants for exactly this kind of occasion. "See you when you get here."

Maggie begged off on the practical consideration that someone needed to be awake to open the store tomorrow. She headed for the spare bedroom after Teag and I showered her with our everlasting gratitude.

I heated up the oven, got the pizzas ready, and grabbed a two-liter of soda from the fridge. Teag knows his way around my kitchen, so he dug out some chips and a jar of salsa. Then I dragged the big white-board out of my office and into the living room, along with one of the gazillion paper maps of Charleston I keep for things like this. If none of us were going to get to sleep for a while, we might as well get something done.

Once everyone had devoured the pizza, we all gathered in the living room. It felt like being back in middle school, except this crowd knew better than to look in the mirror and summon Bloody Mary.

Father Anne's colorful St. Expeditus tattoo showed in all its glory with her tank top. He's a patron saint of monster hunters and the founder of a secret society of hunter-priests. With her pompadour haircut, Doc Marten boots, and penchant for black leather jackets, Father Anne isn't your average parish priest.

Lucinda, our local mambo, looked as unruffled by the night's events as usual. She's tall and statuesque with dark hair and dark eyes, and tonight she had her hair done in braids and wound into a tight coil around her head, which accentuated her chiseled profile. When she's not hunting evil, she's a professor at the University specializing in folklore and mythology. I wondered if she'd taken the next day off from class.

Rowan had her long blond hair in a messy top knot. She rocks a Hitchcock blond elegance no matter what she's wearing, even in jeans and a t-shirt. Although Rowan might look like a fashionista, she's a hella-powerful witch that we're lucky to have her on our side.

"You're telling us that Archibald Donnelly couldn't lay the dead to rest?" Rowan marveled. "Now there's a first."

Lucinda shrugged. "Maybe not such a surprise. The Loas wouldn't answer when I made offerings. It's not like the Baron to ignore a plea to help souls in trouble." I knew she meant Baron Samedi, the Ghede Loa who helped the dead pass over, and probably Papa Legba too, the keeper of the crossroads.

Father Anne looked troubled. "We figured out pretty fast that the bodies weren't possessed when exorcism didn't work. I actually felt sorry for them. They all acted like they'd been woken out of a sound sleep and had no idea why they were wandering around."

"The ones in Magnolia Cemetery were the same—until something Donnelly did seemed to piss them off, and then they came after us," Teag added, nibbling on the last piece of pizza.

"Maybe they weren't supposed to rise," Lucinda mused. "Maybe that was an accident, a side effect of someone else doing something somewhere they weren't supposed to be doing."

"Helluva side effect," Rowan said with an incredulous snort. "It would take a lot of power for someone like Donnelly to raise a zombie —not that he would. But I don't think even he could raise half a ceme-tery—and not just in one, but in cemeteries all over."

I frowned. "But it's not every cemetery, is it? Teag and I didn't see any other zombies in the cemeteries on Huguenin Avenue, only Magnolia."

Father Anne nodded. After the shower, her usually spiked hair lay smooth and flat, giving her a less edgy look. "You're right. We passed other rural graveyards with no zombies at all. And in the places we found some, it wasn't all the graves."

"So why some and not others?" Teag asked.

"Did you note the names of the people who were brought back?" I asked, taping up the map to one side of the whiteboard.

"No time," Father Anne replied. "But I can go back under the guise of 'saying a blessing' over the next couple of days and make a list. It'll be easy to tell from the freshly filled in graves."

"I got some of the headstones on my phone, but not all. Maybe Sorren can do some recon and find the rest. He's the least likely to get arrested," I said.

"Let's start with the locations." Teag finished his pizza and took a drink of his bourbon and cola. "Then we'll start listing the names." For the next half hour, I marked the cemeteries on the map that Father Anne and the others had visited, then Teag read off the names and dates from the photos on my phone, while I made a list on the whiteboard.

When it was done, I sat back on my heels and looked at the work. "Does anything stand out to you?"

"It's got to be significant that only Magnolia had zombies, out of all the other cemeteries right next to each other," Lucinda said. "What's Magnolia got that the others don't?"

We brainstormed for several minutes. War dead, famous ghosts, celebrities, notable historical figures, politicians, and shady figures—nothing seemed to fit.

"Landowners," Teag said. We all went still. "What you said, Cassidy, about it being related to the other weirdness? What if the people who heard this magical 'call' were all landowners—people who liked to hunt?"

CHAPTER FOUR

WE FELL ASLEEP IN THE WEE HOURS OF THE MORNING AND DIDN'T GET
up until almost noon. After a quick breakfast from the odds and ends in
my kitchen, I sent everyone home, except for Teag. Maggie was long
gone, making sure the store opened on time.

"I'd better get home and change, then I'll meet you at the store,"
Teag said. "I need to call Anthony. He's probably worried. Even if he
doesn't want all the details, he knows enough to figure that me being
out all night means trouble."

"Yeah, and I should give Kell a heads up about the zombies, in case
his crew runs into them elsewhere," I said. "I'll see you at the store in a
bit. Gonna need some extra coffee to recover before I can face
the world!"

When I got to the store, Maggie had her hands full with a room
filled with shoppers. Teag showed up about fifteen minutes later. We
both slid behind the counter and got right to work. We didn't have a
chance to talk, but I got a strange vibe from Maggie, and I noticed she
was tense. That's not the norm for her; in fact, it's pretty hard to rile
Maggie. Rainy days and crabby people don't get her down. Now, she
looked ready to chew nails.

"Are you the owner?" A woman with frizzy bottle-blond hair

muscled up to the counter. Besides her hair and the scowl on her face, the hand-woven shawl around her shoulders caught my attention because the bright shade of pink heightened the flush in her cheeks. "I want to talk to the owner!"

"I'm the owner," I replied, with my best customer service smile.

"Why aren't there any opals?" she demanded.

I blinked. "I beg your pardon?"

"Opals. Why don't you have any?" She sounded like we'd run out of cake at a party.

We don't stock opals because they're dicey when it comes to supernatural mojo. Some people believe they're bad luck, and others think just the opposite. I've run into more than my share of the pearlescent gemstones that carried the emotional resonance of their last owner whose belief in bad luck brought about the very thing they feared. But I couldn't really tell her that.

"Our stock changes almost daily," I said in my most soothing voice. "And since everything we carry is one of a kind, there's no way to predict what we'll have from one day to the next."

"Everyone told me you carried the best estate jewelry in Charleston," the woman argued. "But I can see they were wrong if you don't even have any opals!"

My smile strained around the edges. "We have some lovely rubies and garnets, and a very nice sapphire set—"

She leaned in and fixed me with a nasty glare. "Did I say I wanted any of those? I came here looking for opals, and you don't have any!"

I took a deep breath. "I'm very sorry that you're disappointed, but all of our stock is in the cases. We do get new pieces in frequently, but I'm not expecting any opals."

"I'm going to make sure everyone knows what a terrible selection you offer." The irate customer looked like she might bite. "I'm never coming back here!" With that, she stomped out, slamming the door hard enough that I feared the glass would break.

The other shoppers had frozen, studiously looking away but hanging on every word. When the woman left, they slowly went back to browsing. I looked at Maggie, who seemed torn between punching someone and having a good cry.

"Are you all right?" I asked.

All the fight went out of Maggie, and she sagged to a seat on the tall chair behind the counter. "I will be. Thanks for drawing her off. She was quite a handful."

I stared at the door, trying to figure out what had just happened. Something niggled in the back of my mind, a detail I hadn't quite caught, or that my mind didn't process. "Well, she's gone," I said. "Good riddance. I hope she calms down before she busts a gasket."

Maggie had already begun to recover. She slipped off the chair and headed for the break room. "I need some sweet tea. You could use some, too." I didn't argue. Between the sugar and the caffeine, a good glass of sweet tea was the next best thing to a stiff drink.

My phone buzzed, and I looked at the caller ID. Alistair McKinnon, from the Museum of the Lowcountry. "Alistair?" I answered. I barely had time to get the word out before he started in.

"Cassidy, I need you and Teag to come over as soon as you can, please. I know the museum is haunted. But most of the time, the ghosts don't do much. Now, it's like they're supercharged. And there's been a theft of something you'd be interested in. When can you come over?"

Teag stared at me across the shop like he knew something was up, and I gave a nod in acknowledgment. "I can come over right after we close up if that's all right," I said. "But I know Teag has plans—"

"Get me home by seven, and I'll be fine," Teag said, making it clear he intended to come along.

"Wonderful. Thank you." Alistair didn't usually freak out, so I figured something big must have been going on.

Despite our late arrival, Maggie shooed us out the door and promised to lock up. I decided she was definitely getting a bonus—or maybe combat pay. Getting an early start seemed like a good idea since I didn't want to ruin Teag's night with Anthony. Teag and I drove separately so he could head out from the museum. That meant I could meet Kell for dinner as well, so I couldn't complain.

Alistair met us in the lobby. "Thank you for coming so quickly," he said. Alistair looks born to the role of Museum Director, down to the tweed jacket with the leather elbow patches. He's held his age well, with a trim build and a full head of gray hair, so he could be anywhere from mid-sixties to a decade older. He and Mrs. Morrissey teamed up on plenty of fundraisers, charity events, and soirees to attract well-heeled donors and patrons—and Trifles and Folly is often involved.

"Come this way." Alistair ushered us upstairs toward the main exhibit floors. Huge banners in red, black, and gold proclaimed "*Rural Gentry,*" the name of the new installation about Charleston's foremost hunting families. Smaller banners read "*Common Threads*" and tried to lure visitors into a room full of needlework, lacemaking, and similar crafts. I knew Teag would want to swing by that on our way out.

"You've been to the Archive's exhibit?" Alistair asked as he walked. I figured he and Mrs. Morrissey had probably already spoken; they once admitted to talking shop nearly every day.

"It's very nice," I replied. "But they've had a couple of problems," I added, dropping my voice so it wouldn't carry.

"I heard," he replied. "And for some reason, everyone is out of sorts these days. That makes everything twice as difficult," he fretted. "It seems there's no pleasing people. Sometimes it doesn't pay to get out of bed in the morning."

Teag and I exchanged a glance. Usually, Alistair was practically the definition of "unflappable."

"Did something happen?" Teag asked.

Alistair sighed. "No one particular thing. Just that people seem to have a shorter fuse than usual. Maybe it's got something to do with the phase of the moon or the alignment of the stars, but they're extra crabby lately."

I felt certain that he'd had a more potent adjective in mind, but Alistair is quite the gentleman. "There seems to be a lot of that going around," I said carefully, remembering the woman in the shop, and the edgy pedestrians. In fact, now that I thought about it, for a city that has a reputation as welcoming and hospitable to a fault, Charlestonians lately were downright pissy. Odd—and perhaps not entirely a matter of chance. I'd have to give Rowan a call when I left the museum, though I had no idea what kind of spell could make an entire city grouchy, or how to break it.

"Tell us about the new exhibits," I said to lighten the mood. Alistair brightened immediately. He's passionate about the museum, and he's in his full glory showing off a new installation.

"You know that the Charleston plantation class love their sports, almost as much as they do their charity balls," he added with a chuckle. "There's quite a legacy in many families, and that makes for interesting stories. So we decided to highlight the most notable triumphs in hunting, fishing, boating, horse racing, even field trials for hunting dogs. Those successes have been celebrated individually of course, but never brought together to show a bigger picture."

Smart, I thought. The Archive focused on the fashion and decorative angle, while the museum celebrated the big-name families, and plenty of potential donors got their egos stroked, right in time for the next fundraiser.

"And Common Threads?" Teag couldn't contain his interest.

"Oh, you'll like it. Very different from the last display with all the rugs and textile art," Alistair replied with a shudder. One of the pieces from the previous display had led us to a serial killer, although the public was none the wiser. I sincerely hoped nothing about the new exhibit turned out to be nearly that "interesting."

"How so?" I wanted to keep the conversation going. Just being in a museum raises my stress level. So many of the objects carry a sad or even violent resonance; I have to be very careful not to be overwhelmed. I've learned the hard way to steer clear of problematic exhibits, but sometimes the whammy comes from an object as innocent as a serving dish or a piece of jewelry.

The new exhibit hadn't opened to the public yet, but everything appeared to be in place, and none of the museum staff were in sight. Glass cases filled with photographs, silver trophies, and glistening Winners' Cups were arranged throughout the room, interspersed with display kiosks with pictures, personal items, and other memorabilia. To my relief, the taxidermied animals appeared to have been sent to the

Archive's storage. I'm always certain that they're watching me. Sometimes, that's even true.

We moved through the displays, and I noted the names that appeared over and over again. Charleston's inner circle has remained much the same for centuries. The true Old Guard is a network of family ties and old business connections. Now and then a line dies off, or a side branch comes to prominence, but it's not a club that can be bought into, and it's about blood as much as money.

"Looks like the Nicholson family has made a good showing over the years," I noted.

Alistair nodded. "Oh yes. Of course, they're not the only ones, but they've been prominent since the early days with all the field sports."

I made a note of the other family names that came up, jotting them down so I could compare them to the list of newly dug-open graves and see if any of them had come back for another run for the roses.

"Tell us about what's missing—and what's up with the ghosts," I said.

Alistair's smile faded. "Museums—and theaters—are always haunted. It goes with the territory, I guess. Some of the spirits are part of the 'permanent collection,' while others come and go with particularly poignant exhibits. But most of the time, they're on fairly good behavior. Oh, there are strange cold spots, lights that flicker, odd shadows, and some disembodied voices, but the only times it's escalated have been when I've called you in," he added with a pointed glance.

Right. Poltergeists, serial killer ghosts, and the restless spirits from natural disasters tended to cause problems. We'd helped Alistair and moved the spooks on their way. I'm not a medium, and neither is Teag. We bring in our friend Alicia Peters for that. She's got some serious mojo. But sometimes ghosts became attached to an object and followed it around from place to place, lost and confused. They didn't mean to disrupt anything, and some of them didn't realize they were dead. We could usually send them into the light with some salt and sage, and if not, Father Anne made house calls.

"Four of my staff saw shadowy forms among the glass cases, but when they turn on the lights, no one's there," Alistair admitted. "They swear they aren't seeing reflections. And I believe them." He looked down and fingered the keys on his carabiner nervously. "Because I saw Josiah Nicholson, standing in front of his fox hunting trophy, looking like his photo, except that I could see right through him."

"Did he do or say anything?" Teag pressed, his voice quiet.

Alistair shook his head. "He didn't say anything that I could hear, although his mouth moved. I had the oddest feeling, like he was trying to warn me about something. But I have no idea what that might be."

Ghostly hunters, demon dogs in downtown Charleston, zombies, and restless spirits. And it wasn't even Halloween. "Do you know anything about how Josiah died? Maybe he's a repeater. Those aren't really sentient; they're more like a film clip imprinted on an object or place that plays on an infinite loop. Kell calls them 'stone tape recordings,'" I said.

"Josiah Nicholson died with his boots on—in his saddle," Alistair replied. "A stray shot in a large hunting party. No one knew who fired the bullet, or at least, nobody was ever charged. They ruled it an accident, and since no one appeared to benefit, folks didn't fuss about it." He stared out over the display floor.

"How common is that? Fatal accidents in these sports?" Teag asked.

Alistair looked up. "Quite common. Tragic, of course, but that doesn't stop people from doing what they love, even if it kills them." He walked among the cases, glancing at the trophies and memorabilia.

"Getting thrown from a horse or drowning in a boating accident are two of the most common causes of death." He pointed to photographs beside trophies as he spoke, indicating those who had met untimely ends. "Of course, being rolled on by a horse that steps into a hole happens more than you'd think, and catching a stray shot like Josiah isn't unheard of. Untreated tick bites, getting attacked by the wild animal they meant to shoot, stepping on a copperhead, those are all pretty much par for the course."

As he moved around the room, Alistair continued to point to the people whose memorabilia were displayed, and I started to wonder if they had all died from their sport. "And then there are the oddities,"

Alistair continued. "Getting appendicitis or having a heart attack when you're miles from nowhere before cell phones and helicopters. Drinking bad water, or cooking up the wrong sort of mushrooms."

"That really happened?" I asked. "The mushrooms?"

Alistair nodded, indicating a smiling man in the middle of a picture of cheery hunters. "Their camp cook decided to get creative, and 'harvested' some wild mushrooms. Two of the party died, two others went into kidney failure, and the others were sick as dogs. I understand the cook shot himself."

"Yikes," I replied.

"Indeed."

"Seems like a lot of trouble for a shiny cup you can't even use for a fancy vase," Teag noted.

Alistair shrugged. "I'm not sure you or I can really understand how deep these sports run in the blood of these families. It's their identity— in their own eyes, and among their social circle. Winning and their standing in the rankings matters as much as any business deal or how much is in their bank account. It's who they are."

That didn't sound particularly healthy to me, but then again, I didn't come from Charleston blue blood. Maybe Anthony would understand; his family's been prominent for generations, with a house on The Battery and one of the oldest law firms in the Holy City.

I tried to clue into my gift. Even without handling an object, I can often pick up a vibe if the piece is "transmitting" a powerful resonance. Hell, I've picked up impressions through the soles of my shoes in a location where something really bad happened. The impression I received from the exhibit was difficult to pin down. The energy felt restless, unsettled. Worried, like something bad might be about to happen. As I slowly passed the cases, fixing my attention on silver medals and red ribbons, big two-handled cups, and engraved platters, I sensed pride, satisfaction, competitiveness, and a hunger to be remembered. All very normal, and what I'd have expected if there hadn't been a problem. Yet underneath all that, I felt tension.

Then it struck me. The ghosts weren't dangerous. They were scared.

"You said Josiah seemed to be warning you," I mused. "Is there an anniversary coming up—his death, or some other tragedy?" Ghosts tend to get hung up on things like that, and finding a connection might help us understand what was really behind it all. Because it seemed unlikely a sudden spike in ghostly activity was unrelated to all the other strange goings-on throughout the city.

"Not his own death; I checked," Alistair said. "We're not quite sure who the other ghosts are, but the staffers who saw them also said they had the feeling they were being warned. They didn't think the ghosts meant to harm them."

"What are ghosts afraid of?" Teag wondered aloud. But we both could supply plenty of answers, each one worse than the next.

"What about the object that was stolen?" I looked around, but none of the cases appeared to be damaged, no smashed glass or broken locks.

"A hunting dagger, very old," Alistair replied. "Belonged to Josiah Nicholson, and it's been passed down through the family for generations. They call it their 'lucky dagger' and claim the first Nicholson brought it over from Scotland, that it was ancient, even then."

"Do you believe the story?" I asked. "Was there anything special about it, other than its age?"

Alistair considered the question for a moment. "It was a beautiful piece, even with all the wear. Celtic design on the handle, and what might have been Norse runes carved onto the blade."

"Was it valuable?" Teag and I handle a lot of heirlooms in the store, but true relics are the province of historians.

"Probably more to the family for sentimental reasons than to collectors," Alistair replied. "Although pieces that old do have value. But it was a dagger meant to be used, not a ceremonial piece set with gems or precious metals. Nice workmanship, but no provenance of being part of a famous battle, for example, or belonging to a king. So it's an odd piece to be the only thing the thief stole."

"How is the family taking the loss?" I shivered and realized that the temperature in the room had grown colder as we talked. I couldn't see any ghosts, but I had the feeling that they were listening, and very interested in our conversation.

Alistair shook his head. "Not well, as you can imagine. Yes, the piece is insured. And the museum has insurance. But it's not the sort of thing that can be replaced. And the theft makes no sense since nothing else was touched. Of course, that leads to difficult questions. The police have to consider the possibility of an inside job."

"Do you think that's likely?" Teag looked up from where he'd been closely examining the names on an old picture of a large hunting party from the turn of the past century.

"Personally? No. I can't imagine anyone on our staff doing such a thing. But the police are right to investigate. And if it isn't someone who works here, then there's no telling who it might be. Because the thief didn't leave any fingerprints or evidence, or show up on any of the security cameras."

Getting past keypads and cameras wouldn't be difficult for a powerful witch, or a creature with the right kind of magic. Not that the police would believe that. Still, that left the question of why someone wanted the dagger that badly, and how the Nicholson family had gotten quite so tangled up in the strange goings-on.

"I can ask Father Anne to come by and read a blessing," I offered. "But before that, I'd like to bring a medium back with me. Alicia's very talented. If the ghosts can tell us something, she's the one who can find out what they have to say."

Alistair gave a curt nod. "Could we bring her in before the exhibit opens—when the public isn't around? I'm afraid some of our board of directors might not be open-minded about such things."

"I'll call her and see when she's available," I said.

"Thank you," Alistair said, taking my hand. "You don't know how much this means to me. It's such a good exhibit—I don't want the theft to put a damper on it."

As we walked, I had been trying to get a "feel" for the objects in the cases with my gift. Given how important they were to their owners and how much they were valued and coveted, I expected to pick up a lot of resonance, even if it was mostly pride and satisfaction. Yet the pieces surprised me with their lack of mojo, which seemed strange. I stopped in front of a tall silver cup engraved with what must have been at least a hundred names. It gave off more of a vibe than anything else, yet it, too, felt oddly weak.

I read down through the names, speaking them aloud in the hope that would call up more of the trophy's energy. I registered a lot of positive vibrations, but instead of getting glimpses of celebrations or champagne bottles being uncorked, the persistent image was of a pitcher being emptied. I shook myself out of my intense focus and tried to make sense of what I'd seen.

"Did you pick up anything?" Teag asked.

I nodded. "The 'signal' is very weak. But I don't think it always was. In fact, I've got a suspicion that someone or something drained energy from the pieces." I looked to Alistair. "Before we leave, I want to swing by some of the permanent exhibits. I know how much juice some of those items should have—and I'll know if it's changed."

"Of course." Alistair looked startled at the thought of psychic energy being siphoned off. "What kind of person could do that?"

"I'm not sure," I replied, although I could think of a few. Psi-vampires, for one. They can steal energy from living people; I figured some of them could probably drain an object's resonance. I didn't doubt that some witches could tank-up on stolen energy, and maybe very powerful ghosts as well. But I didn't want to keep Alistair from sleeping at night, so I kept my suspicions to myself. "But we'll figure it out."

"Do you think my staff is in danger?" Alistair asked. "If the ghosts are trying to warn us, should we be worried?"

Teag gave me a look that clearly told me it was my call. "I don't think so," I said slowly. "Not unless something else worrisome happens. I don't see a threat to visitors, either. You know I would tell you—and that I have told Mrs. Morrissey when I thought a display had dangerous elements."

Alistair nodded. "I know. Thank you." He pinched the bridge of his nose as if staving off a headache. "It's not what I expected when I planned the exhibit."

"We'll keep our eyes open," I promised. "And as soon as we know anything more that could help, we'll fill you in."

Alistair thanked us again, then headed back to his office. Teag and I veered off to the Common Threads exhibit, and I didn't need to be an empath to tell how excited he was.

"Beautiful textiles always carry power," he told me. "But it doesn't have to be something big like the quilts at the Archive, or those rugs we saw a while back." Teag entered the exhibit room like a kid heading for the packages under the tree on Christmas morning. I could hear the passion for the topic in his voice.

"Oh, look at these!" He groaned in appreciation as we got a good look. Beautiful hand-embroidered tablecloths and other linens hung behind glass. Next came framed "samplers" showing off the needle-work skills of their creators. Hand-made lace filled the center case, so delicate and fragile and with such immaculate, tiny stitching that my breath caught.

The far side of the room had a video showing artists at work. The long glass case had examples of thread-making, yarn-spinning, dyeing, and weaving. A small collection of shawls, scarves, and other finished pieces showed the final outcome.

"They're all beautiful," I said.

When Teag didn't respond, I turned to look at him. He had a pinched expression, and he seemed to be gazing at nothing.

"Teag?"

"I think I know what you were feeling, out in the other room," he said. "The energy's wrong. These pieces are all masterworks. Some of them took hundreds of hours of work, and whether the maker has magic or not, there's a lot of devotion and creativity and love that goes into these. They should practically glow with energy, to me if not to you." He shook his head. "But it's gone. It feels like they're husks. Like they're missing their essence. And it's like something stole their soul."

I knew he meant that metaphorically, that objects don't actually have "souls." Then again, even a rock has energy on some level, and plenty of other cultures believe that inanimate objects have a spirit.

So maybe what Teag and I knew as "resonance" carried even more weight than I thought. That would be an interesting existential conversation with Father Anne and Lucinda over cocktails some evening, but right now, we had an energy vampire—or something —to catch.

"Teag," I whispered, and when he gave me a look, I inclined my head toward the small loom in the exhibit. The translucent form of a woman stood in front of the case, and as we watched, I saw her gesture. She held her hands out, chest high, palms out, and waved them back and forth, a timeless motion of warning. Then she looked straight at Teag and pointed directly at him, eyes filled with a silent caution. The woman glared at me, then looked back to Teag. I got the message. *Watch out for Teag.*

The ghostly woman vanished before I could figure out how to ask my questions in charades.

"Okay, I'm officially creeped out," Teag said quietly, still staring at the spot where the ghost had disappeared.

"You and me both." I walked closer to the display, and sure enough, the ghost looked exactly like the weaver whose picture hung next to her prized loom.

"Why you?" I wondered aloud. "The warning was clearly meant for you. But what was she warning you about?"

"Maybe…" Teag began, then stopped. I gave him an expectant look. "You sensed the energy drain in the other exhibit. I could feel it here. Maybe whatever drained the objects can drain energy—or magic —from people, too."

"And we'd both look like a tasty snack," I finished for him. "Damn." I ran a hand back through my hair, but I had no idea what to say. So I reverted to our original plan. "Just to be sure, let's check out those relics I mentioned to Alistair." I hated to see Teag look so sad at the psychic violence done to the beautiful textiles.

Plenty of objects on permanent exhibit in the museum carried beaucoup resonance, but there were a couple that always stood out to me like beacons. One was a collection of death photographs from the Civil War, pictures taken of the newly dead by grieving relatives, back when photography was new, rare, and expensive. While the resonance is sad, it's powerful, underlaid with devotion and love.

The other was happier, an elaborate silver tea set that had been passed down from mother to daughter for more than a century as the heirloom wedding gift. It carried the vibration of all those happy celebrations, and being near it usually lit me up inside.

Every time we visited, I could sense both collections from the far side of their respective exhibit rooms. I oriented myself on their energy wherever I was in the museum, like compass points. And now, as I stood in the entry hall, their energy was gone.

Teag trotted after me as I speed-walked from one end of the museum to the other. The physical pieces were right where they were supposed to be, safe and sound behind alarmed glass. But to my gift, they were lifeless and dull, silent and empty. I felt the loss so hard; tears filled my eyes.

"They're empty," I said, trying not to let my voice break. "Someone's taken the resonance. They've been drained dry."

CHAPTER FIVE

TURNING AN OLD MANSION INTO A FUNERAL HOME IS ALL KINDS OF stupid when it comes to psychic energy. If the place didn't have ghosts of its own already, it sure stood likely to collect some from all the dead bodies coming and going.

"You're sure this is the place?" I asked, as Teag, Father Anne, and I stood outside the Kubler Funeral Home. The white clapboard Victorian sprawled across most of a block. On the plus side, being turned into a mortuary meant someone had the money to keep the house looking like a showplace. But the trade-off lay in how the owners earned that cash, sending the dearly departed on to the afterlife pumped full of embalming fluid and covered in spray tan.

"I'm sure," Father Anne replied. "Horace Kubler showed up in my office this morning completely beside himself. Wanted me to come do an exorcism right that very minute."

"Exorcism?" Teag raised an eyebrow.

Father Anne shrugged. "It's the first thing people think of when things go bump in the night. Unless they've been watching ghost hunter TV shows, and then they're telling me how to do my job at the same time that they're begging me to come save them."

I eyed the rambling white home. The original owner must have had a slew of kids, and maybe servants, too. It definitely had more space than the normal modern family needed with its two-point-five children. If it hadn't been turned into a funeral parlor, it probably would have been subdivided into apartments or fallen into disrepair. That would have been a shame since it was a beautiful building. Even so, I dreaded going inside. Mortuaries are filled with uncomfortable resonance, for obvious reasons.

One hand went to my agate and silver necklace as I sought protection and a cleansing blast. Just touching the healing gemstone made me feel better. "Do we know what we're up against?" I asked.

"Not completely," Father Anne admitted. "That's what worries me." She had a black shirt with a clerical collar on under her leather jacket, over jeans and Doc Martens. I could see the sheath for a blessed boline knife on her belt, a weapon with some extra mojo for going up against nasty spirits. She wore a silver crucifix on a chain around her neck, and I knew she had a flask of holy water in a pocket, as well as salt and sanctified oil.

"How long has it been haunted?" Teag asked. He had his hands jammed in his pockets since the night was cool enough for a jacket. While most knives wouldn't do much against ghosts, Teag had brought his *espalda y daga* set, as well as his silver whip, an iron short sword, and a silver dagger.

"Horace says that the house had family ghosts before it became a mortuary and that those spirits don't trouble anyone. They're either oblivious to the change, or they seem to have appointed themselves the official hosts," she added with a chuckle. "He doesn't want to get rid of them, but he says that since the other spirits showed up, those ghosts seem to be hiding."

"Great. We've got ghosts that scare other ghosts," I muttered.

"What about the new ghosts?" Teag prompted.

"They're big on pranks—but some of the tricks have an edge to them," Father Anne replied. "Hiding objects is one thing. Breaking them is another. And Horace says that the new ghosts 'feel' different. Edgy, angry, maybe even dangerous. He's already had one person quit, and another started carrying salt in her pockets, a squirt bottle of holy water in her purse, and as he puts it, enough religious jewelry to put Madonna to shame. The singer, not the Virgin Mother," Father Anne clarified.

"Anything else?" I had the feeling we didn't know enough about the problem, but that might mean Horace didn't, either.

"Yeah." Father Anne looked like she deeply regretted giving up smoking. "And I don't like it. He said he keeps hearing things in the walls, moving around. And last night, one of the bodies was damaged."

"Damaged how?" I asked, although the hair on my arms rose, and I didn't think it had anything to do with the cold night.

"Chewed on," Father Anne replied. "Nothing actually missing, but Horace thinks that might have been because he made a lot of noise going into the mortuary and interrupted whatever it was."

"Chewed?" Teag echoed. "Shit. That sounds like more than a ghost."

"That's what I'm afraid of," Father Anne replied.

Horace had given Father Anne a key. He and the other workers had made themselves scarce since no viewings or services were scheduled. Father Anne let us in the back door. The security lights made it bright enough to see where we were going, although they gave everything a bluish glow right out of a low-budget horror movie. I shook the dog collar on my left wrist, and Bo's ghost appeared beside me. I kept my athame in my right hand, but I had iron shavings and salt in my pockets, a spray bottle of holy water, and an iron knife.

The main floor of the funeral parlor looked like a well-appointed private house—with five living rooms, and no kitchen or dining room. Without the bustle of a crowd coming to pay respects, I could feel how huge the old mansion was. It felt cavernous and cold, despite its designer-perfect decor and upscale furnishings.

"The upstairs are all offices," Father Anne said. "Horace said there haven't been any problems up there. Nothing in the front rooms on this floor either, although this is where the regular ghosts show up when they're active. No surprise, since they would have remembered this house as a family home."

"So the problems are in the back, where the bodies are handled," I guessed. My gut knotted. I'd been to a few morgues, but funeral homes seemed so much more personal, maybe because they were in old houses. With everything we dealt with, I knew that dead bodies weren't anything to fear. But my hindbrain wasn't listening to reason, and I hoped I didn't look as reluctant as I felt to head down the hallway to the "business" end of the mortuary.

The building felt cool when we entered, but the temperature had dropped enough between the front of the house and the back that I had goosebumps. Once we went through the doors to the section of the building that held the preparation rooms, the funeral home looked much more like a hospital or a morgue than its homey reception areas. Gleaming white tile covered the walls to shoulder height in wide corridors made to wheel gurneys to the workrooms. Compared to the tasteful decorations in the parlors, this part of the building felt spartan and empty of personality.

We moved slowly, alert for trouble. I wasn't thrilled about stretching out with my gift, but I knew that would be part of what was needed when I agreed to come along. I tuned into my psychometry, tentatively extending my senses in case Horace's problems stemmed from a cursed or haunted object that had hitched a ride with one of the dearly departed.

"Can you read anything?" Teag stayed close beside me. Teag knew I'd be vulnerable when I focused on the impressions, and he was good at watching my back.

"I don't think the ghosts are tied to an object," I said, since my spidey sense wasn't honing in on a particular location. "As for the ghosts themselves, I'm sensing less sadness than…surprise." I paused. "Everyone always thinks they've got more time, and then—wham."

"You might have given me the theme for next Sunday's homily," Father Anne said. "I bet that 'Wham—You're Dead' would make people look twice at the church's sermon sign."

I'd learned a long time ago that dark humor can get you through a lot of bad situations. But even as I cracked a smile at her comment, I felt a shift in the energy around us. Unlike a real medium, I can't summon the dead or make a connection with a reluctant ghost. My gift works best when I can touch an object that belonged to the departed, and then I can read the memories "imprinted" into its resonance. But if a ghost wants to make itself send or heard, I'm maybe a little more tuned in than the average person, and I suspect my abilities attract spirits who probably see my energy like a candle in the darkness.

The air grew even colder, and I saw Teag shiver. "You feel it, right?"

Teag nodded. "Yeah. Temperature's dropping. And I'm picking up on a vibe that's trying to make us turn around and leave."

"Dread," Father Anne said quietly. "Something is trying to keep us from going down the hall."

A breeze picked up. All the doors and windows were closed, and no air conditioner put out a gust that whipped our hair and made jackets flap. We passed a door marked "*Storage*" and heard a crash that sounded like an entire row of shelves had tipped over. When I opened up the door, a barrage of shoes, belts, hats, and other articles of clothing pelted me, hurled by invisible hands.

I yanked the door shut, catching a man's tie half in and half out. The mismatched pieces littered the floor in the corridor, and I tried to make sense of the impressions I picked up.

"They're angry," I said slowly. "But not at us. Angry at something else. Something that hurt them. I think…they're trying to tell us to turn back."

We were a few feet from the double doors to the big preparation room where the bodies were kept. That's when I heard it—a skittering, scratching sound way too loud to be rats. We all exchanged a glance, and I knew Teag and Father Anne had heard the noise, too. The loud shriek of wrenched metal clearly came from inside the mortuary room. We readied our weapons and rushed inside.

"What the hell are those?" Teag breathed.

Four pale, naked creatures looked up from where they had wrenched a steel refrigeration drawer off its track, leaving it pulled out askew and revealing the corpse inside. The creatures had the same fish-belly white color as the dead body. Their joints and spines seemed unnaturally visible through nearly translucent skin, and their heads looked overly large for their bodies. Skin stretched tightly across their faces, flattening their features, and the black eyes that turned their gaze on us were as cold as a snake's. Too-long fingers gave their outsized hands a skeletal appearance. But for as bony as their bodies were, the intruders' distended bellies looked bloated, and when their black lips pulled back in a snarl, I could clearly make out rows of razor-sharp teeth.

"Damned if I know, but they're trying to eat the bodies." Leave it to Father Anne to get to the heart of the matter.

"Ghouls." They both turned to look at me. "Pretty sure that's what they are." I'd never seen any myself, but I'd heard about them. And now it looked like we were going to have to fight them.

The creatures turned on us and hissed, which might have been their language, or a warning. They were unarmed, but their fingers ended in sharp claws and I didn't want to see their teeth close up. We faced off against them, as each side sized up the opposition. My athame dropped down from my sleeve into my hand, and Bo's ghost let out a low growl.

Everyone moved at once. Ghouls are damn fast. They scattered, not just left and right, but two of them skittered up the walls and across the ceiling. Bo dove for one of the ghouls still on the floor. I aimed my athame and sent a stream of bright, cold energy that tore one of the creatures off the ceiling and flung it across the room. It slammed into one of the stainless steel autopsy tables with enough force to have broken a human's spine, but the creature got up and shook itself off, eyeing me like a tasty morsel. They might eat dead flesh, but ghouls probably don't mind a warm meal when they get the chance.

Teag's silver metal whip snapped out, snaking across the back of the other ceiling ghoul, and the sharp, coiled blade opened up a gash from shoulder to hip that dripped foul, black sludge instead of blood. The ghoul shrieked and let go, managing to twist in mid-air like a falling cat so that it landed on its feet in a crouch.

The creature sprang at Teag, but his long knife came up fast, impaling the ghoul with its own momentum. A downward slice gutted the monster, and a hard swing sent the ghoul's head rolling.

Meanwhile, the ghoul I'd thrown against the autopsy table was ready for round two. Its squeal sounded hungry and furious, and it ran at me on all fours, like a huge, ugly attack dog. Bo was still busily harrying the third ghoul, and Father Anne was busy with her very own monster.

I sank my gift deep into the resonance of my spoon-athame and blasted the ghoul again. But this time I held the blast as long as I could; moving forward as I kept the creature pinned against the wall. The dark red stain around its mouth brought to mind images I didn't dare dwell on, and I closed the distance between us at a dead run, so I didn't have too much time to think.

My knife blade sank deep into the ghoul's chest as I ended the blast from my athame. The ghoul dropped to the floor at my feet. I swung the sturdy knife with all my strength, as its razor-sharp blade sliced through the monster's neck and the head fell to one side with a wet thud.

By the time I looked up, the fight was over. Bo had kept one of the ghouls cornered until Teag could lop off its head. For being a ghost, Bo has a very real bite, and teeth marks suggested that for once the ghoul was on the receiving end of being chomped. Father Anne stood over the body of the fourth ghoul, spattered in ichor and breathing hard from the fight.

The once-pristine preparation room looked like something out of a zombie movie, with gore sprayed across the white tile walls and black pools of stinking ooze puddling around the headless bodies. Teag navigated carefully over to the morgue drawer that the ghouls had pulled from the bank of refrigerated shelves on one wall.

"Doesn't look like they had time to start on dinner," he observed. "Other than the damage to the drawer, the body doesn't look chewed."

I turned to Father Anne. "Does the funeral home have a crematorium?"

She nodded. "Yeah. Are you thinking what I'm thinking?"

"Probably," I replied. We walked over to the big sink against the far wall and washed, scrubbing the awful liquid from our hands, arms, and weapons, and mopping at our clothing with wet paper towels.

While Teag and I cleaned up, Father Anne pulled out her phone. "Horace," she said. "We've solved your problem, but you're going to want to handle the clean up before your employees come in. I'd suggest waiting fifteen minutes, and then heading over here. If anyone asks, say that the alarm tripped. The vermin that chewed on the bodies are dead, but it would be best if you burned them…when no one's looking." I couldn't hear Horace's side of the conversation, but Father Anne smiled. "You're welcome. And if anyone asks—we were never here."

"Do you think the ghosts are gone?" Teag asked as we made our way back out to the driveway. None of the spirits bothered us as we walked through the corridor, and we encountered no strange wind or odd cold spots.

"I don't think they meant to hurt anyone," I replied, looking over my shoulder but seeing only the shadowy hallway. "They were trying to warn Horace and his people away from the ghouls. Maybe they were the spirits of the people in those drawers, who didn't want to get eaten."

"Seems reasonable to me."

"So unless the ghouls come back, the new ghosts are probably going to rest easy," Father Anne said as we put our weapons into the trunk and got into the car. Teag drove, and I slumped back against the seat as he pulled out of the parking lot without the lights on.

"Is this kind of thing happening elsewhere, and we never heard about it?" I asked.

"First time for me, too," Father Anne replied. "And since the dead rising kind of goes with my job description, I figure there would have been chatter in my professional circles if other people were getting calls for exorcisms and the like."

"So back to the idea about everything being connected," Teag said. He flicked the lights on when we were a block away and drove carefully at the speed limit.

"Explain what you mean by 'everything,'" Father Anne said from the back. We took turns filling her in.

"Ghosts going bonkers, everyone's on edge, strange break-ins and missing relics, zombies and ghouls, and something's draining energy from charged objects—how does it all fit together?" I asked as I wrapped up our tale when Teag pulled up in front of my house.

"I don't know—but there has to be an answer," Father Anne said as she got out of the car. "And in the meantime, be careful. Until we know who's behind it, we don't know where the next attack is coming. So watch your backs."

I opened my door. "Want to come in?"

Teag shook his head. "Thanks, but I'm going to head back. Anthony had a continuing education class that went really late, and if I hurry, I can clean the ghoul guts out of my hair before he gets home."

I hurried inside, greeted Baxter, and took a hot shower. Between ghouls and zombies, I was going through soap faster than usual. Usually, I didn't like heavily scented bath products, but when it comes to washing off gore and blood, I found a real use for body wash I would have otherwise considered to be overpoweringly strong.

It was only eleven o'clock, and the thought of curling up in my sweats on the couch with Baxter and watching some TV sounded wonderful—especially if that also included a glass of wine and fuzzy slippers. But as I got a treat for Baxter and poured myself a nice glass of Shiraz, my phone went off, and the ringtone told me it was Kell.

"You still up?" he asked.

"Yeah. Just starting to wind down. You?"

Kell hesitated. "We came back from a ghost hunt about an hour ago, and I'm still pretty ramped up. Want company? I'll bring snacks."

I smiled. "Throw in a bottle of wine and plan to spend the night. I'll fill you in on my day. I'd rather not be alone tonight."

Fifteen minutes later, Baxter did a happy dance at the door when Kell arrived. Baxter is the official guard dog and welcoming committee, torn between biting noses and wriggling for hugs. Kell patiently scooped Bax up, held him at arm's length until the growls subsided, then ruffled his fur and snuggled him before releasing him and turning his attention to me.

I knew from the way Kell pulled me close and the feel of his kiss that something had gone wrong. He held me tight, a gesture that seemed more protective and reassuring than romantic, and the touch of his lips felt like he wanted to affirm that both of us were still safe and alive.

"Bad hunt?" I asked, taking his hand and leading him into the living room as Baxter jumped and pranced around our feet.

"Not the worst I've been on, by any means." Kell leaned against the kitchen counter as I pulled goodies from the grocery bag he'd brought. Kell is about Teag's height, with blue eyes and light brown hair, a combination that caught my attention from the first time we met.

"Then again, you've been on the scariest hunts," he added, moving away from the counter to help me get a plate for the selection of yummy appetizers he'd picked up. Cheese, olives, crackers, spreads, and toppings along with some charcuterie made my mouth water. He opened a new bottle of Cabernet and poured himself a glass to match mine, then followed me into the living room.

"Fill me in," I said, settling into the corner of the couch with one knee pulled up, facing him. He smeared pimento cheese on a cracker and gobbled it down. I realized that he looked rattled, and my concern grew. Kell had been chasing ghosts for years, and not much shakes him up. We've seen some pretty horrific things on hunts, and he's usually pretty cool about it. So I wondered what had gotten under his skin.

"I think Charleston's ghosts have all gone mad," He said, taking a gulp of wine. "The phone at SPOOK has rung non-stop. Ghosts that never had the juice to make themselves seen are now visible. Or audible. Or able to throw things. And most of them seem disturbed about something. Jittery. Even the repeaters seem more solid and active."

Kell ran a hand back through his hair, and I noticed how tired he looked. "I thought maybe it had something to do with the phase of the moon or some upcoming obscure holiday. But...I can't find any connection. And I told myself that it was just ghosts, no one was getting hurt." His voice trailed off, and I reached out to put my hand on his arm.

"What happened?"

Kell closed his eyes and leaned his head back against the couch. "I got a call from a friend who does tours at the Old Jail. Not many of the tour companies in town will go there at night, because we all know the ghosts are real, and they're not nice. But usually if anything manifests, it's some cold spots, or a disembodied voice, or someone feels a touch on a shoulder or an arm."

He let out a long breath. "My buddy said he heard the gallows trap-door dropping open, and heard voices all around them, muttering and mumbling."

"Someone's idea of a prank?" I asked, though I doubted that was the case. "Maybe a bunch of theater majors who thought it would be fun to freak the guide?"

"I don't think so," Kell replied. "He saw orbs materialize right in the same room with them and zip around. You know those usually only show up on pictures. The guests thought it was great, until one of the orbs went right through a woman and she passed out. Then the lights went off."

I'd been to the Old Jail once. It's one of Charleston's most popular tourist attractions, but it's got a brutal history of blood and death, and the resonance reflects its past. I hope I never have to go back again because I sure wouldn't consider it an evening's entertainment.

"Those iron steps aren't great to navigate even with the lights," I said. "Did someone get hurt?"

Kell nodded. "People started shouting about being pushed. No way to know in the dark what was going on, but then others denied doing the pushing. The guide tried to call for assistance, but his phone was dead—and no one else could get a signal, either." Ghostly activity often drains electronics. The dead phones didn't surprise me.

"The guests started to panic. So the guide tried to get everyone calmed down and out of the building. But one woman fell down the steps. She's hurt pretty bad." Kell looked at me as if I could solve the mystery. "As soon as she fell, the lights came back on again, and all the paranormal phenomenon stopped. The guests who were near the top of the stairs said they felt a body slip between them, solid but cold as ice, right before she was pushed."

"Do you believe them?" I asked. "Or were they covering up being scared enough to crowd the stairs?"

Kell stared into his wine for a moment before he took another sip. "Tom, the guide, has been doing that tour for five years. He's one of two guides at his company that will go to the Old Jail at night. We always used to go out for drinks, and he'd tell me stories about things that happened and none of it ever got to him." He drained his glass, and set it aside.

"Tom quit after that incident. Says he'll go home and live with his mom if he has to while he finds another job. But he's never setting foot in the Old Jail again."

I finished my wine and moved over to snuggle against Kell. No surprise that Baxter insisted on being on Kell's lap—he's a possessive bit of fluff. Kell wrapped his arms around me, and I laid my head on his shoulder. He felt warm and solid, grounding me and letting me know I wasn't alone. I hoped my presence did the same for him.

He nuzzled my hair and gave me a squeeze. "How about your day? Sounds like you had a rough one, too."

Kell, like Anthony, knows what we really do at Trifles and Folly. Given his work with SPOOK, he usually isn't fazed by run-ins with regular ghosts. He's backed us up on outings where he's seen real magic at work, and the fact that he's still here means a lot to me. Kell helped us out in dangerous situations without demanding to know everything ahead of time, because he trusted us—he trusted me. That meant I had to trust him, too. When I explained about the Alliance, Kell wasn't completely surprised. He said that he had pretty much figured that to be the case, and was waiting for me to be ready to tell him the whole truth. It felt good to share the secret with him, and he swore that he would never tell anyone. We were coming up on our first anniversary of dating, and I had to admit that having a relationship last long enough to settle into a comfortable routine felt...nice. Very nice.

He listened while I told him about the ghouls, and heard me out without needing to throw up, which won props in my book. I went on to tell him about the other weirdness since it had been a couple of days since we'd seen each other. Kell's a good listener and curled up next to him and Baxter, I felt safe. The house is warded, I have some badass magic, and Baxter is a ferocious watchdog, so I was already physically protected, but tonight, it was really nice not to be alone.

"I wondered if your gang had been dealing with any new weirdness," Kell said, shifting so we could stretch out. "Any idea what's kicking the supernatural strangeness into overdrive?"

I shook my head. "Lots of possibilities; no real leads. I took our medium friend, Alicia Peters, back to the museum to check out their ghosts. I thought that might help. But we didn't get anything new, at least not from those spirits. A total dead end—no pun intended."

Baxter squirmed, and I figured he was getting too warm, although he didn't go far. He hates to not be the center of attention. I rustled his white fur, and he brazenly rolled over to have his tummy rubbed.

"Maybe the ghosts at the museum have something in common with the ones at the funeral home," Kell suggested. "Maybe they can sense something going on, and they're trying to warn you."

I thought back to what Mrs. Teller had said, and how people were lining up to buy Hoodoo protections. "That would make sense," I said. "Maybe it's worth making the rounds of all my favorite botanicas and New Age supply stores and seeing what the gossip is. I could use some more copal incense, sage, and High John the Conqueror root."

We didn't use a lot of special objects, despite the fact that we banished unruly ghosts, fought vampires and shifters, and dispatched the occasional demon back to Hell. Then again, we buy salt by the fifty-pound bag, and we keep a good stash of the more versatile gems, metals, plants, and roots on hand, because when we need something, it's often in the middle of the night when the shops aren't open. The stores I favor aren't the ones that look like Halloween all year round for the tourists. I go to the little shops that aren't in the fanciest part of town, where the owners and the shoppers have a spark of something extra, and we all know that magic is serious business.

"Probably a good idea. I'll hit up my regulars, and see what's being said on the other paranormal investigation sites," Kell said. "Discretely, I promise."

I stretched up to kiss him. He kissed back, and my heart skipped a beat. "We're still on for dinner with Teag and Anthony tomorrow night?"

"You mean, later today?" he joked. I glanced at the clock and realized how late—or early—it was. "Yes. Looking forward to it." Kell stretched and sat up, dislodging both Baxter and me from our comfy spot. "Come on. We should get some sleep. The ghosts will have to look after themselves for the rest of the night."

THE NEXT MORNING, I got to the shop before it was time to open, and found Teag already at work on his laptop in the break room. "Did you make it home before Anthony last night?" I asked, pleased to find the coffee pot already full and hot. I poured myself a cup, noting that it looked like Teag had already drunk a few rounds of java himself.

"Barely," he replied, not looking up from his screen. "But I did get into the shower and managed to shove my clothes in the washer before he could ask about the bloodstains. Lawyers are funny about those kinds of things."

"I bet." After I fixed my coffee, I came around to look over his shoulder. "What's up?"

Teag sat back and angled the screen so I could see it better. "Sorren left a list of names from the dug-out graves for me, and Father Anne sent me her info. I've been looking them up. And big surprise—there's a connection, but damned if I know what it means."

"Let me guess. They are all either from families featured in the museum and Archive exhibits, or they were extremely involved in those kinds of hunting sports."

"Got it in one," Teag replied with a sigh. He chugged his coffee and blinked hard a few times as if his eyes were bleary from the screen. "And here's one other little tidbit. All of them died as a result of their 'hobbies.'"

My eyebrows rose. "Really? So Alistair was right about all those gentry sports being dangerous?"

He shrugged. "Even the carriage rides downtown have a waiver on their tickets about the 'inherent dangers of equine activities.' People fall off horses or get trampled. Guns go off and hit the wrong target. Fishermen drown. Maybe it's karma for hunting Bambi. Things like horse racing or jumping hurdles is even more dangerous. I guess that's part of the attraction."

I pulled up a chair to get a closer look at the screen. "Was there talk that those deaths weren't accidental?"

"Are you looking for murder, or something supernatural, or both?" he asked.

"Not sure. Right now, we need to find out what the connection is. We know the stuff that's been going on is not random."

He agreed. "I've already looked to see if the deaths came in cycles —or waves—and there's no pattern that I can see."

I glugged down my coffee and poured another cup. The bell jangled, and Maggie let herself in. "Good morning!" She greeted, far more cheery than anyone has a right to be this early. Let it be said that I am not a morning person, so skulking around in the wee hours suits me far better than being up at the crack of dawn like normal people.

"G'morning," I managed, doing my best to fake enthusiasm. Maggie's known me long enough to recognize that I wasn't caffeinated enough yet.

"We've got a beautiful day today, so hopefully, that means a busy shop." Maggie stashed her purse and shawl in my office, grabbed a cup of coffee, and headed up front. I joined her, leaving Teag to his research. Together, Maggie and I chit-chatted as we pulled out the jewelry from the safe and put the trays in the glass display cases.

Most of our inventory is too big to lock away each night. Silver candelabra, heavy tea sets, lamps, and clocks, and odd pieces of furniture too bulky and awkward to steal. But in theory, at least, a thief could smash the window and break into a display case and grab a handful of jewelry if we didn't keep the little pieces locked up. We go through the motions to keep the insurance company happy, but the truth is, no regular thief is going to make it through the layers of magical wardings laid down on the shop over nearly four centuries.

Maggie's prediction proved true; the good weather brought out shoppers in droves. Fortunately the crabby opal lady didn't come back, and for the most part, the customers played nicely with each other. Even so, the vibe felt off to me, like everyone was wound tight for no particular reason.

Trifles and Folly attracts an eclectic clientele. That's putting it mildly. We get bargain hunters who quickly find out that while our prices are fair, we aren't giving away stuff because it's old. Collectors frequent the shop and tell their friends. Interior designers who specialize in historic restoration, funky B&Bs, or homeowners with a love of the past shop us or send us their wish lists.

Weekends—especially in the fall—bring out the antiquers, couples who love looking for the perfect piece to set off a room. Tourists get intrigued by the window display, wander in and wander out. Vintage jewelry buyers know that we not only have a beautiful selection, but the pieces always have a positive feel to them. And those in the know about supernatural things either stop by to talk shop, pass on a warning, or look for the more specialized relics and benign magical items we keep in the back.

Today seemed to belong mostly to the tourists, antiquers, and bargain hunters. Plenty of people walked in, took a look around, and walked out. Some of the shoppers had such a specific item in mind for the right spot that while I could offer alternatives, I didn't have the perfect piece. That's the trouble with antique stores—almost everything is one of a kind, and the things that aren't can't be stocked in bulk. Then again, Charleston has more than its share of antique shops to browse, so I felt confident they'd eventually discover something they could use. And the tourists? Bless their hearts.

I counted ourselves lucky that neither Alistair nor Mrs. Morrissey called with a new crisis. Neither did Father Anne, which either meant that the dead had taken a break from rising, or they were waiting until after dark.

The day passed quickly, and before I knew it, the last shopper headed out the door. Considering all the browsers who came and went, we still sold well, mostly small items like rings or necklaces. I totally understood that if you came to Charleston on a tour bus, taking back a hundred pound silver tea set might cause problems. That's why I talked one lady into having us ship her treasure home for her.

"Want to join us for dinner, Maggie?" Teag asked as we cleaned up, locked the door, and switched the sign to "closed." When all three of us put the jewelry back in the safe, we're done in less than ten minutes.

"Thank you, but my neighbor's cooking tonight, and I wouldn't miss it," she replied with a smile. "Thanks for asking."

"You're welcome to join us anytime," I added.

Maggie laughed. "Truly, thank you. But she's making one of my favorites tonight. Linguine with homemade puttanesca sauce." Then she blushed. "She's also inviting her friend. He's also retired. And single."

"Then, by all means, don't let us keep you from a hot evening!" I said. She waved, and we both watched to make sure she got to her car all right, though tourists crowded the sidewalk and the gas street lamps were still bright enough to read by.

"God, I hope Anthony and I are half that frisky by the time we're Maggie's age," Teag said, with a wistful expression.

"I can't believe you used the word 'frisky.'"

He grinned. "I can think of plenty of alternatives, but none of them are suitable for polite company." We closed everything down and headed out the back door, locking up behind us. "See you and Kell at eight?"

"Count on it. We're looking forward to a good meal and even better conversation," I promised him as we got in our cars. "See you then."

I went home, fed Baxter, and took him out in the garden, got a shower, and went through the mail. And all the while my mind churned through the weird stuff going on, trying to make sense of it. So far, no one had gotten killed—at least, that we knew of. But it's never a good idea to ignore power that can raise the dead, and I had the feeling we hadn't seen the main event yet. "Worried" didn't begin to cover it.

Bax gave me his best puppy eyes to try to guilt me into staying home. He's persuasive, but I figured that since Kell and I would be coming back here after dinner, Baxter wasn't suffering too much— especially when I knew we'd both slip him some leftovers.

We met up with Teag and Anthony at Jocko's, our favorite Italian restaurant. Everything on the menu is good, and it all comes from the owner's family recipes. I gave Anthony a hug. "Haven't seen you in forever. You work too hard." It had only been a week or so, but it felt longer, especially since these past few days had been stressful.

"Thanks for keeping Teag from getting bored," Anthony replied. Teag and Anthony make such a cute couple. They're close to the same height, but otherwise such a contrast. Anthony's blond and broad-shouldered, looking every inch the South of Broad scion that he is. Teag still rocks a skater boy haircut, and while Anthony is all Brooks Brothers, Teag's more of a jeans, t-shirts, and Vans kind of guy. Some-how, they make it work.

"Hey Cassidy!"

I turned and saw two of my favorite people, Drea Andrews and Valerie Dane. Drea runs Andrews Carriages, and Valerie is one of her top tour guides. It's rare for them to have a night out, given the type of business they're in, and even more unusual for them to be out together.

"Birthday? Anniversary? Promotion? Apocalypse?" I guessed. "How'd you two slip the leash and get the night off?"

Drea laughed. "All of the above? We're dreaming up new tours for next year, so I decided we deserved to have some fun doing it!"

"You go, girl! Can't wait to see what you come up with."

Drea gave me a knowing look. "I wasn't maybe completely joking when I agreed on the apocalypse part," she added. "And somehow, when strange things are going on, you usually have an inside track."

"What kind of strange things?" I asked. Kell slipped an arm around my waist. We had time to kill waiting for our table to be cleared, and I wondered what Drea had heard. She's usually very tuned in since her job means she's talking to people all over the city all day long.

"For one thing, the way everyone's suddenly crabby," she replied. "This city doesn't even get ruffled when we're washing away in a hurricane, and now people seem unusually grouchy. And then, there are the ghosts."

"We're thinking of suspending the ghost tours until things settle down," Valerie chimed in. "Too dangerous, after what happened at the Old Jail."

"Yeah, we heard." Kell and I answered almost in unison.

"Do you think it has anything to do with what's going on out in Aiken?" Valerie asked.

Kell and I exchanged a glance. "What's going on out there?" I asked. Aiken ranks right up with Lexington and Louisville for big money horse racing. Back in the 1800s, folks from the old money crowd from up north would winter in Aiken to get their prize horses ready for the Triple Crown.

"Prize thoroughbreds gone missing," Drea confided. "Hunting dogs, too. And we're talking expensive livestock. Those horses cost big bucks, and champion dogs aren't cheap. Plus, all those big race farms have security. It's not like horse thieving in the Wild West."

"Any people vanish?" I asked.

"Not that I've heard," Drea replied, and Valerie shook her head.

"Can you keep me posted on the Aiken thing?" I asked, as their server came to lead them to their table. "It might be important."

Teag and Anthony came up behind us. "Something going on?" Teag asked quietly.

"Maybe," I replied. "More weirdness."

The server seated us then, and conversation came to a halt as we glanced through the menu. We ate at Jocko's so often we should have had the choices memorized, but sometimes it was fun to try something new. I went for spicy seafood pasta, and Kell opted for the Chicken Marsala, while Teag and Anthony split a specialty pizza. Of course, we had to get stuffed mushrooms and bruschetta to share. Once we had our drinks in front of us, we all relaxed. Anthony slung an arm over Teag's shoulders, and Teag leaned into him. Kell and I sat hip to hip, and if my hand strayed to his knee, no one was going to mention it.

"So what's new in your world?" I asked Anthony. He can't talk about the confidential details of any of his cases, of course, but his work often yielded scuttlebutt from law enforcement agencies and local police that we might not otherwise hear. The longer Teag and Anthony are together; the better Anthony has gotten at listening for the right kinds of things, the type of details that suggest strange goings-on might be our kind of problem.

Anthony sipped his wine and let out a deep breath, rolling his shoulders like he wanted to shuck off the weight of the day's worries. "You mean, other than that the whole world's gone crazy?"

I gathered from the way Teag turned to look at Anthony that this tidbit hadn't been mentioned before. "Oh?" I prompted.

"Arrests are up for everything from bar fights to domestic violence." Anthony toyed with his wine glass as if he were already thinking about a refill. "There've been more murders in the last two weeks than Charleston usually sees in a month. 'Crimes of passion'— things that people do when their temper's running high—are through the roof. It's like everyone's lost a grip on sanity."

"Or something's lowering their inhibitions," I suggested. I had noticed some of the headlines, but failed to make the connection, in volume or in timing, to realize just how big the problem had become.

"Or feeding on the aggression," Teag added.

"Or creating a distraction so we aren't looking at the real problem," Kell chimed in.

Anthony looked from one of us to the next as if he realized he was outnumbered. "You think there's something supernatural behind an outbreak of widespread pissiness?"

"Not the strangest thing I've heard," I replied. "There are creatures that feed off strong emotion—love, hate, violence, envy. That whole 'seven deadly sins' list keys into primal human urges, and that's like the smell of fresh cinnamon rolls to some of those beings."

Anthony mulled that over for a moment, and took another sip of wine. "Honestly, that would make more sense than people just going nuts," he said. "We've had a few clients in our office have a complete personality shift, go from reasonable and pleasant to angry and awful. And as far as anyone knows, there isn't a reason. No health problems, family issues, pending divorces, or financial trouble."

Teag laced his fingers with Anthony's and leaned forward. "The people who've been getting arrested—have the police found motives?"

Anthony shook his head. "Under normal circumstances, most

motives aren't rational—at least not to other people. But the comments I'm hearing from the cops we deal with make it sound like even the people involved don't really understand what made them snap. And they don't back down easily, not until they're in custody. Then they're suddenly back to normal, wondering how the hell they ended up in jail."

Teag caught my eye. "Hex bags?"

"Maybe. But it's awfully widespread for a single spell," I replied. "And that wouldn't explain the ghosts or some of the other stuff."

"What's strong enough to affect the living and the dead—*and* their spirits?" Kell asked, and a cold feeling of dread settled in my gut. Because anything that strong was going to be a son of a bitch to stop.

CHAPTER SIX

I HADN'T SEEN SORREN SINCE THE NIGHT AT MAGNOLIA CEMETERY, but that wasn't unusual. Trifles and Folly is only one of the many fronts for the Alliance that Sorren runs all over the world, and flare-ups at those other locations can take him out of town—and off the grid—for days or weeks.

Still, Charleston is close to Sorren's heart for many reasons, and he usually keeps pretty close tabs on the city. He texted me every day with questions about the goings-on, and I filled him in. Sorren promised he was looking into the problems from his own angle, and that he would tell us everything soon. So I had to trust that the messages I'd left and the secure emails were giving him what he needed and that he would come back when he could with more answers.

In the meantime, we had work to do. The morning shaped up to be another busy day, and while customers were even more curt and impatient, they came ready to buy.

"Rough night?" I asked Teag as he refilled his coffee in the break room. He looked haggard and a little bleary-eyed. Everyone had been in good spirits when we left the restaurant, so I doubted he and Anthony had a fight.

"Bad dreams," he replied. "I can't shake them. I've smudged with sage, lit candles, cleansed my chakras, washed the sheets with lavender —nada. Last night I tried a stiff belt of whiskey, and it made me drowsy, but I still woke up with the dreams...nightmares...in the middle of the night."

"Are you dreaming about things we've seen?" I leaned back against the counter. Heaven knows we've been through some horrific stuff in service to protecting the city—and the world—from supernatural threats. I'd be lying if I didn't admit to more than my share of nightmares myself. Fortunately, Kell's a patient soul. And I knew for a fact that Anthony would walk through fire for Teag. But talking about horrors that most people couldn't fathom was easier with someone who had been there, and that meant Teag and I needed to depend on each other more than ever.

"No—or at least, not all of it," Teag replied, and he looked away. I could tell from how he shifted from me that he felt embarrassed.

"Talk to me," I coaxed. The stuff we do, like that fight at the cemetery or the ghouls in the morgue, weighs on a person. Horrors of war— that's real, even if what we're killing is already dead. "Let me help."

Teag drew a shuddering breath, and drew his coffee cup in close to his body, like a shield. He kept looking at the floor. "Sometimes I see bits of all the fights we've been in, all mashed together. I think those are the normal nightmares because that stuff is hella terrifying and I figure my mind needs extra cycles to process."

"Sounds about right," I agreed. "I get the same kind of dreams. More often than I'd like to admit."

"Lately though, it's been worse." Teag's voice dropped to a hoarse whisper. "What I'm dreaming *feels* real, but they're not my memories. They're not even always my time period." He ran a hand through his long, dark bangs. "Sometimes, I see smoke and fire and battlefields, but from a long time ago—Romans maybe, or Vikings. It doesn't look like something from a movie. I swear, the memories are real—they aren't mine."

He paused, then went on. "I see a man in the shadows, often in silhouette. He's lanky and built like a fighter, and he has a staff that's taller than he is. I can't tell what time period, just that he wears a cloak and, the weirdest thing is, he has a head like a bird." Teag looked off past me, remembering. "There is a woman, too. I can't see her face, but I can feel her power. Both of them are scary strong, old magic. I get the feeling that they're going to fight, or that they have fought, but I wake up before I see the battle."

I put a hand on his arm. "Have you talked with Mrs. Teller? Maybe someone's put a root on you, or a hex bag?"

He shook his head. "She says no, there's nothing like that. But she does see dark energy around me, and she's given me all the protections she has."

"Dark energy?" That worried me, and I remembered the ghostly warning at the museum. "Is this something we need to get Rowan to look into? Because if someone's screwing around with magic, you and Anthony are in danger."

"In a lot of the dreams I'm running away from something, trying to hide," Teag continued as if I hadn't spoken. "Something bad is looking for me, chasing me. Maybe the big man with the raven head. It's a forest at night, foggy and dark. I run as hard as I can, I've been running in the dream for a while, but it's still behind me, closing in. Searching for me."

"Can you see what's chasing you?" My voice had fallen as well, and I glanced toward the door to the front of the shop, hoping Maggie was holding her own with the customers because I couldn't leave Teag like this.

He bit his lip, then shook his head. "No. I never see a face, but I know it's bad. Deep down in my gut, I know it's a monster, and if it catches me, I'm dead. Worse than dead." He looked up at me, finally, and his eyes were wet and red. "I don't know what to do, Cassidy. Anthony's beside himself worrying about me. He wants me to go see a doctor. But I don't dare take sleeping pills. What if I take the pills and they slow me down enough that the monster can catch me?"

Teag set his mug aside, and his hand shook. "I think the dreams are real," he confided. "I'm not sure *how* they're real, but I don't believe

78

they're my imagination or from something I saw on TV. And the worst of it is, whatever's chasing me is powerful. I can feel it. Anthony wants to help, but this is so far beyond the kind of things he knows how to handle. I'm scared, Cassidy."

I took both Teag's hands in mine. "We'll figure this out. How about we start with having Rowan and Lucinda refresh the wardings around your house, and if you're okay with it, do a special warding on your bedroom. The first thing we need to do is put up a firewall around your dreams, and then we'll figure out who the son of a bitch is that's doing this to you."

He nodded, looking relieved to have finally gotten the matter off his chest. I gave his hands a squeeze. "We'll get to the bottom of this. Sorren should be back soon, and maybe he can shed some light. We'll fix it."

Just then, Maggie screamed.

Teag and I came running. The Opal Lady was back, and she had gone after Maggie right over the counter, fists flailing. Her pink shawl flapped over her back and shoulders like a weird cape, as she tried to haul herself across the display case. Maggie had a vivid red mark on her cheek from a blow that might turn into a black eye, but at the moment, she'd managed to plaster herself against the wall, out of reach of Opal Lady's clawing hands.

"Get away from her!" I shouted. "Stop this minute!"

Opal Lady ignored me. Teag lunged for her, while I moved around the counter to get Maggie to safety, shielding her from the pink-clad attacker with my body. Teag's martial arts training came in handy, and he managed to get her off the fragile glass case before it caved in and skewered her. I dialed the cops, once I'd steered Maggie to a seat in the break room. Teag had Opal Lady pinned face-down on the floor, but she kept on screaming and thrashing like a madwoman.

Several customers fled, but two women hung back, watching worriedly from the other side of the shop. "We saw it all," one of them said. She was tall and thin, in a velour jogging suit, with short gray hair.

Her companion wore jeans and a denim jacket, with graying hair pulled back in a braid. "That lady came in the door and went right after your assistant," she said. "Like she was on a mission."

The police arrived within minutes and had us all give statements. Maggie looked shaken, and the blow to her cheek had started to bruise, but she spoke to the cops calmly and recounted the attack clearly. They took the struggling Opal Lady away and said they would get back to Maggie about pressing charges. Only after they left did she slump in the chair and bury her face in her hands.

"Can I get you some tea?" I felt completely inadequate. I hadn't been able to protect Maggie inside the store. Our wardings are for supernatural threats, not crazy people. And Teag was hurting, but I didn't know how to help. What good was magic when it couldn't fix the things that mattered?

I closed the shop early, and we drove Maggie home. Maggie's strong; I knew she'd bounce back. Fortunately, the injury wasn't serious. But it's the feeling of vulnerability that comes from an attack that takes a while to fade, long after bruises and cuts had healed. And I wondered if that vulnerability didn't lie at the heart of Teag's bad dreams.

For the moment, I seemed to be the most functional of our little group. Was that a good thing, or did it mean I hadn't reached my breaking point yet?

I left another message for Sorren, updating him on the incident, and drove Teag back to get his car. The attack on Maggie troubled him.

Teag rubbed his hands together as if to scrape off unpleasant residue. "When the cops pulled Opal Lady away from me, I brushed against her pink shawl. It had a really bad vibe, maybe even cursed. I wonder if it's what made her attack Maggie."

"We need to find out who Opal Lady is, and who her enemies might be," I replied. "Because she's either pissed off a witch, or someone she knows has powerful friends."

By the time I'd fed Baxter and eaten my dinner, Teag had tracked down Opal Lady and called me to fill me in.

"Joan Tandy," he said, as I finished my last bite of chicken casserole and put my plate in the dishwasher. "I've got an address and a phone number. And even more important—thanks to social media, I've tracked down her best friends. They should know whether she's always been a loose cannon, or if this is new, or when things started to change."

"Maybe they'll also know where the shawl came from," I said, giving Bax an after-dinner biscuit. "That's what I want to know."

After I hung up, I scooped up the pile of mail I'd brought in with me from where I dumped it on the counter. I divided the envelopes between bills and junk mail and paused at the small box. I recognized the markings as a store in Charlotte where my mother often picked up little presents for me, sometimes for holidays, sometimes just because. She hadn't said anything about sending me a gift, but then again, she often doesn't, claiming that the surprise is part of the present.

"What do you think it is, Bax?" I asked, as I carefully opened the box. Bax huffed and lay down at my feet, making it clear that any gift that wasn't edible didn't merit his attention.

"Oh, wow." The lovely hand-loomed scarf lay on a bed of tissue paper. It was perfectly dyed, and the soft yarn begged to be snuggled. I figured the gift card from mom was underneath.

As soon as I moved the tissue paper and touched the scarf, the energy of the box felt all wrong. *A distraction spell?* I wondered. A spell would have to be pretty powerful for my magic not to have picked up on bad energy when I first lifted the box. I stumbled, as my head started to pound and my stomach suddenly rebelled. My balance seemed off, and my vision blurred. I knew then that whoever sent the scarf, it wasn't my mom. I dropped the box, and as I fell, the scarf fell with me.

Baxter knew something was wrong. He barked and danced around me, and I worried he might get ahold of the scarf. I ordered him to his bed, and he went, but he stared at me, whimpering.

I grabbed for my phone and managed to knock it off the table. My knees buckled, so I went down with it. Lying on my side, I reached out and hit speed dial.

"Cassidy?" Teag answered. "What's up?"

"Come quick," I panted, feeling a fever building. "I think I've been cursed."

～

I REMEMBERED FALLING, and the call to Teag. The next thing I knew, Baxter barked up a storm, and then Teag knelt next to me. "Cassidy? We're here."

"Don't touch...the scarf." I could barely get out the words. Whatever I had, it felt like the worst bout of the flu topped off with food poisoning. Even worse, from the instant I removed the tissue wrap, my gift had been screaming, seared through with the malice the sender had woven into the cloth.

We hadn't pissed off a witch. Somehow, we'd made an enemy of a powerful Weaver, and that spelled big trouble.

"Get back," Mrs. Teller ordered. I could only see her shoes until she bent down. Then she used a plastic pasta spoon to tease the scarf away from my body, and I saw her shoes head toward my sink. She dropped the cursed scarf into my stainless steel sink, murmured words I didn't recognize, and a few seconds later, I smelled smoke and burning yarn.

Meanwhile, Teag had been sprinkling salt all around me and poured a flask of holy water over my hands where I had clutched the scarf. Mrs. Teller spoke again, a rebuke to the powers of evil. I heard another voice, and only then realized that they had brought Rowan with them. Rowan was chanting and burning sage, but I picked up on other scents of plants I dimly remembered being for cleansing and protection.

Teag laid a woven blanket over me from shoulders to knees. It cooled my fever and soothed the pain that radiated from my belly, and even my headache felt bearable. I figured it was something he had woven his magic into.

"Hang in there, Cassidy," he urged. "We're going to fix this."

I lost track of time. Baxter whined, upset to not be close to me.

Mrs. Teller and Rowan spoke in low tones, sometimes chanting or speaking words of power, or conferring quietly. Teag moved back and forth, infusing the blanket with his magic and keeping me calm, or stepping over to talk with the other two. I had a Weaver, a witch, and a root woman on my side, but I wondered if it would be enough.

Even with Teag's spell-woven blanket and all the other magical preparations, I still felt awful. Under normal circumstances, I'd be begging to go to the hospital. But doctors couldn't help me. Whatever whammy the scarf put on me was beyond the reach of medicine. Magic did this, and magic would have to save me.

My view from the floor remained limited to shoes, but I heard the front door open and close, and the tread of a man's steps.

"Sorren. Thank you for coming so quickly."

"Of course." Six hundred years ago, Sorren was the best jewel thief in Antwerp. Now, it's rare to hear a trace of a Dutch accent in his voice. I've only heard it when he was hurt badly enough to kill a mortal, exhausted—or worried. The fact that I heard that accent now would have made me panic if I'd had the energy.

Sorren crouched beside me. "Cassidy, can you hear me?"

"Yeah." My voice sounded weak, even to me.

"Rowan and Mrs. Teller are working on the counter spell. How much contact did you have with the scarf?"

"Barely touched it." I licked my lips. They felt dry and parched, but my stomach probably wouldn't hold down water even if I could drink it. I hadn't felt this awful in a long time, maybe never.

"That's a good thing," Sorren replied, and I could hear the relief in his voice. "Hang on. It won't be much longer, and we should have you feeling better."

"Can we move her?" Teag asked. That's when I realized that no one had touched me. Even when Teag put the blanket over me, he never touched my skin.

"Should be fine," Mrs. Teller paused her incantations long enough to answer. "The curse was in the scarf. Can't catch it from her, and the scarf is gone."

I expected Sorren to take my shoulders and Teag to grab my feet, but Sorren scooped me up like a toddler who had missed nap time and carried me into the living room, where he laid me down on the couch.

"How bad is it, Cassidy?" Sorren asked. We've been through some horrific fights together, and I've been hurt pretty badly. But hurt is different from sick, and right now I felt like my body was on fire from the inside.

"Bad," I murmured. "Hospital bad—except...magic." Talking felt like an exhausting burden. "Baxter?"

Sorren knew what I meant, although I hadn't managed a whole sentence. "It won't hurt anything if he's with you." He went into the kitchen and came back with Bax in his arms. For everyone else, Bax is a wiggling yipper. But vampire glamoring works on dogs, and while it's totally cheating, Baxter barks at everyone now except Sorren. He set Bax down on the couch, and my little fluff ball immediately snuggled in beside me.

"I'll be back," Sorren promised. Out in the kitchen, I heard him conferring with the others. The low hum of voices felt comforting, like a memory from childhood of a house crowded with relatives after a holiday meal. I felt floaty as if I were half-asleep or dreaming, drifting and wondering if it was a good thing that I seemed only lightly tethered to my body.

Sorren's hands gripped my shoulders and shook me. "Cassidy! Stay with us. We're close. Hang on." Vaguely, I realized that his heightened senses could probably read my vital signs as closely as medical equipment, and that vampires don't worry easily.

I felt too floaty to care.

The next time I opened my eyes and roused enough to take in my surroundings, I saw the flicker of candles and smelled a mix of herbs. Cedar, chamomile, fennel, sage, and more swirled in a haze around me. Teag removed the woven blanket, and I shivered.

"It's drawn out a lot of the poison, but not all," Teag said, and I saw the corner of the blanket flap as he held it up.

"I'll burn that," Mrs. Teller said, and her footsteps retreated to the kitchen. I hoped she didn't set off the smoke alarm, and then couldn't remember why I cared.

"Drink this." Rowan pressed a cup to my lips and helped me sit up enough to sip. The mix tasted bitter and strong, and I tried to push her hand away.

"You have to drink this, Cassidy." Rowan wasn't one for coaxing. Her voice was stern, like someone in charge, and I thought maybe I should listen, but my mind felt so foggy.

"Drink," Sorren spoke, and the fog lifted. I wondered if that was his vampire compulsion, something he'd never used on me, but saving my life might have made him fudge on his promise. I needed to have what the cup held. Rowan kept me from spilling in my haste. When I finished, I wanted more.

"Rest." Sorren's voice let me relax, and I sank back down into the couch.

"How long will it take?" Teag must have been behind the sofa because his voice seemed close. I shivered, missing the blanket. Teag leaned over and laid a thinner strip of fabric down the length of my body. Even floaty, I recognized it as the protective stole he often wears under his shirt when we go up against a big bad. Teag's magic and personal energy are woven deep into that stole, and it comforted me like a balm.

"It's complicated magic," Mrs. Teller replied. "It'll take what it takes."

I zoned out again, and when I woke I had to blink to make sense of what I saw. A shimmering light surrounded me, glistening like a soap bubble in the sun. But not soap…energy. *Am I dead?* I wondered, but I didn't really care.

Voices rose and fell—Rowan, Mrs. Teller, and Teag. The candle flames flickered, rising higher than they should have, or maybe it was a trick of the light. The soap bubble got brighter, shifting from iridescent to blinding. I shut my eyes, and the light made my eyelids glow red. I felt the buzz of energy against my skin, and in my imagination I saw tendrils of the bubble stretching down to touch me, boring through to my core, drawing out the poison.

And when it hurt too much to stand it anymore, I screamed.

~

"CASSIDY." Teag's voice sounded hesitant.

"Erm." I couldn't manage more, but at least he'd know I heard him.

"The curse broke," he said, sounding ragged and hoarse. "Fever's gone. You're probably tired as hell, and you should be from fighting off that bad magic, but that's all it is—tired. Sorren says he can tell, and you're going to be okay."

"Everyone...okay?" I felt groggy, like waking up after a potent sleeping pill. Bits and pieces came back to me, the scarf, pain, magic.

"You gave us all a run for our money," Teag replied, with a rueful chuckle. "That scarf packed a wallop." His tone grew serious. "Whoever sent it wasn't fooling around."

"The box—"

"Sorren took the box and packaging," Teag said. "He's going to see what he can make of it, try to figure out where it came from. But the bigger question is, why?"

I wanted to care. Deep inside, I knew this was important, but I was too damn tired. Teag seemed to recognize that conversation was beyond me, and he patted my shoulder. "Go back to sleep. Mrs. Teller and Rowan finished up, and I got them settled into your guest rooms." He paused. "I hope you don't mind—I called Kell. He's going to be over soon to sit with you, because I've got to crash, too."

"Thank you," I murmured. "All of you. Sorry to be a bother."

Teag's grip tightened on my arm. "Cassidy—if you hadn't called me, and if we hadn't come right away, you wouldn't have made it. Someone intended to kill you. So don't be sorry about calling. Not at all."

He rose to answer a knock at the door. Baxter barely moved, raising his head and giving a low growl without any heat behind it. I heard Kell's voice, and Teag answering questions, and then Kell sat on the floor beside me and took my hand. He kissed the back of it, then held my palm against his cheek.

"I'm okay." We both knew it was a lie, but I needed to say something.

"I'm here," Kell said. "And I'm not going anywhere. So sleep. I'll take the first watch." He slipped his fingers between mine and held on tight. I closed my eyes, and let myself sink into the darkness, knowing that this time I wouldn't lose my way back.

CHAPTER SEVEN

"You've got to believe me. She wasn't like that." Patricia Cullins twisted her rings nervously, looking so bereft I wanted to comfort her. Instead, Teag and I had come to try to figure out why her friend Joan—Opal Lady—had attacked Maggie, and see if we could learn anything about who tried to kill me.

"When did she start to change?" Teag kept his voice quiet and reassuring. Two days had passed since I'd nearly been done in by a scarf, and I was only starting to feel back to normal. I let him take the lead.

Pat frowned as she thought. I guessed her to be about Joan's age, somewhere between late forties and late fifties. Pat had blond hair cut in a wedge, and a pair of reading glasses with bright blue frames hung from a beaded lanyard around her neck. Her pink lipstick and matching nail polish made her skin seem too pale in comparison.

"About two weeks," Pat finally said. "She wasn't having any health problems—at least nothing she told me about. No big upsets." She looked up at us, and I caught a hint of defiance in her face. "Joan and I have been friends since high school. Thirty years. We tell each other almost everything. So if she'd had something bad happen in her life to send her off the rails, I'm sure I would have known."

Pat shook her head. "Joan didn't get belligerent when she was

88

angry—she broke down in tears. She sucked at being angry. I mean, she couldn't even give what-for to a rude cabbie."

"Can you think of anything that was different around the time that Joan started to change?" I probed. I figured that the shawl was behind Joan's sudden personality swing, but I thought I'd better lead up to that slowly. Not everyone easily buys into the ideas of cursed objects. And besides, I might learn something important if I gave Pat a chance to give me her side of things. "She had come into the store the day before, and she got really angry about us not having opals."

Pat chuckled. "She liked opals. Her husband bought her one when they started dating, and she always said it was lucky for her. But that's not something she'd get worked up about—as much as she ever got worked up over anything."

"We want to figure this out because we don't think Joan was responsible for her actions," I said, hoping Pat felt she could trust me. Maggie hadn't pressed charges against Joan, but she did have a restraining order issued.

"You mean like someone might have slipped her a roofie?" Pat's eyes went wide.

I smiled. "Not exactly, but maybe a little."

"I saw this show on TV where a guy hypnotized people and made them steal things," Pat confided. "Maybe that happened to Joan."

If a cursed object or hex bag lay behind Joan's sudden changes, Pat's guess might be closer to the truth than she'd ever know. "Did she buy anything new or get any presents right about the time she started to act differently?" Teag asked, since what we both wanted to know was how Joan got the pink shawl. "Maybe something she inherited, or a gift from someone?"

Pat looked into the distance, searching her memories. "We went out that weekend, to do a little shopping, have lunch, get a mani-pedi. Girl's day out, you know?"

"Where did you go?" I urged. "It's important."

"We got fancy coffee, and started off at the spa," Pat said and named a nice salon on King Street. "Then we had lunch." Their destination, a popular brunch spot, seemed like a low risk for curses or hexes. "And since it was such a nice day, we walked through the City Market."

Teag and I exchanged a glance. We'd run into troublesome items finding their way into the open air market that lay at the center of the Historic District. Mrs. Teller and Niella usually kept an eye out for problems, since they had a permanent location for their sweetgrass baskets at the doors to one of the buildings. Still, the City Market rambled through several buildings, and they couldn't keep watch on everyone.

"Did she buy anything? Handle something unusual? Or did you pick up a funny vibe about any of the vendors?" I asked.

Pat seemed on board with playing detective, so if she found my questions odd, she didn't say anything. "We both bought things," she said, with a faraway look that told me she was replaying the day in her mind's eye. "I picked up some pretty cutwork place mats and a set of coasters, plus an adorable bib for my grandbaby."

"And Joan?" Teag asked.

"She bought some okra chips from that healthy snacks place and a Christmas ornament. It was cute but mass-produced, and I tried to talk her into something handmade, but it struck her fancy."

Until witches figure out how to run assembly lines, I could probably rule out the ornament, and the food seemed an unlikely culprit. "What about a pink shawl?" I asked. "Was that new?" Joan wore a bright pink handmade shawl when she went off on a rant about the opals, and she had it on when she attacked Maggie. And Teag had mentioned it had a bad vibe, so it was maybe cursed.

Pat gasped and put a hand to her mouth. "Yes. I almost forgot. How did you know?"

"Did she buy it that day?" I asked, conveniently side-stepping her question. I didn't want to put words in her mouth. And while I didn't think Pat was in on it, I thought I'd still give her enough leeway to trip up.

Pat nodded. "She got it at one of those stalls in the Market. I didn't remember seeing that vendor before, and she had a lot of pretty things. Joan wanted me to get a shawl, too, but I didn't."

Teag gave her a questioning look. "Why not?"

She hesitated. "I'm not sure. I…they didn't appeal to me." Pat's body language told me what she couldn't quite find the words to express. On some instinctive level, her intuition had recognized something wrong, and that reluctance probably spared her sharing a cell with her buddy.

"Could you go to the market with us, and take us to the stall where she bought it?" I asked. "I'd like to talk to the vendor. If there's some kind of chemical in the clothing that caused this, we don't want other people to be affected."

"Oh dear." Pat looked so distressed; I doubted she was faking her reaction. "Do you think that might be it?" She glanced at the clock. "If you want to follow me, I don't mind driving into town. I know right where the table was, because I always stop at the photographer's booth beside it, and that's why I knew the shawl seller hadn't been there before."

"We'd be very grateful, if you can spare the time," Teag replied.

"Sure," Pat said. "Anything to help Joan." She looked up at us, searching my face and then glancing to Teag. "She really isn't a bad person. So whatever I can do…"

We thanked her, and followed her to her car, then let her lead the way through the streets crowded with tourists who didn't know where they were going. Getting a parking spot felt like a minor miracle, but soon enough we were following Pat through the busy market. When we got to the second building, Pat stopped in front of an empty booth.

"I swear, it was right here," she said, staring at the wooden tables. I believed her, because this wouldn't be the first time someone intent on causing mayhem found an unsuspecting audience at the Market. People like that generally didn't fill out all the paperwork or pay a deposit, either.

"Let's ask around," I suggested. Pat stuck with me while Teag headed down the other row, and together we canvassed all the merchants in the building.

I recognized nearly all of them as long-time vendors who had been in their spots for years. As we talked to the other merchants, I expected to get an earful about "squatters"—unlicensed sellers who swooped in if a booth's owner was temporarily absent and set up an illegal shop. The other merchants watch out for each other, and they'd be quick to report someone who did that, but oddly enough, their memories proved vague.

"How can no one remember any details?" I ranted once we got outside. "The person had to be there for at least a whole day!"

"Please believe me," Pat begged. "I want to help Joan. There was a person there selling woven items—shawls, scarves, ponchos, even men's ties. They were all nicely done, but I guess I wasn't in the mood to try anything on," she said, with a little shiver that I picked up on even if she didn't seem to notice. Intuition can be a powerful protector.

"We do believe you," Teag said. "Scam artists are very good at not being memorable." I was betting more on witchcraft than larceny, and I figured Teag felt the same, but his answer seemed to satisfy Pat.

"What now?" she asked. "I'm sorry I wasn't more help." She looked crushed, and I empathized with wanting to help a friend in trouble.

"Here's my card," I said, handing her one from the shop. "If you think of anything—or you see the vendor somewhere else, call me. Don't try to approach the merchant yourself. We need to get the proper authorities." Pat might think I meant the cops, but I was thinking about Sorren and Rowan.

"Sure," Pat replied. "I'll keep an eye out." She swallowed hard. "Do you think Joan will be all right?"

"I'm sure she'll be released very soon," I replied. "But if the police give her back the shawl—don't let her keep wearing it. See if you can get it away from her, but don't touch it—we don't want it affecting you."

"This is why I don't trust chemicals," Pat said, shaking her head. "They're in everything. Probably something in the dye. Like that food coloring a while back that they said caused cancer."

A malicious Weaver witch was more likely the cause, but I couldn't tell her that. "Thanks for all your help," I said, and we walked Pat back to her car. After she left, Teag and I headed back to find Mrs. Teller and Niella in their usual spot.

"You're looking better," Mrs. Teller observed, sparing a glance from her weaving. "Gave us all a scare."

"Scared me, too," I admitted. "Did you hear anything about a squatter up in Building Two a couple of weeks ago?"

Niella's eyes narrowed. "You think it's connected?"

I shrugged. "It's the only lead we've got."

Mrs. Teller stared down at the basket in her hands, fingers flying as the braid took shape. "If a person with real strong power came to the Market, I'd know it," she replied. "Unless that person was strong enough to hide what they are. If that's the case, we're in for trouble."

"Maybe the person with power had a minion," Niella suggested. We were all carefully avoiding words like "magic" or "witch" because the Market was crowded and we had no way to know who might be listening.

"Someone who could handle things and not be affected?" Teag asked.

Niella nodded. "Maybe a charm of some sort for protection. It's a possibility."

"Too many possibilities, and no answers," I said with a sigh. "But if the squatter sold anything like my scarf, I'd hate to be the minion taking chances touching those things."

"They wouldn't dare sell something that strong here," Mrs. Teller said, and I saw anger in her gaze. "I guarantee people would notice if someone bought a scarf and fell down sick." She looked back down. "No, it'd be subtle. Maybe build over time, so when the reaction came, that buyer'd be well away from here."

That made sense. Even people who didn't believe in magic could follow a short chain of cause and effect. If a customer bought a shawl and immediately got into a fist fight, people would make a connection.

"I do remember something, and I bet it's related," Niella said. "That one day, everyone seemed so out of sorts. Pretty day, but oh my, people were in foul moods."

"I do recall," Mrs. Teller said. "But it didn't affect us, and I know why. We've held this corner for a long time, Niella and me. I put down salt and goofer dust, and say a blessing every week. Say a prayer for protection and good fortune. Draw down some white light. Do that kind of thing every day for years and years, and bad things keep their distance."

We thanked Mrs. Teller and Niella and headed back to Trifles and Folly. I couldn't help feeling that we had spent all morning and had nothing to show for it.

"What about those botanicas and New Age shops?" Teag said as we pulled into traffic. "We could hit one or two and see what people are saying."

Maggie had assured us she could handle the store, so I figured a detour wouldn't be amiss. I drove to a little shop on a side street in an older part of town that missed out on gentrification. Most of the signs were in Spanish, and so was most of the store's clientele, but Marcella, the owner, catered to everyone who needed plants and herbs for healing or rituals.

"*Hola*, Marcella," I called out in greeting as we entered.

Marcella looked up and grinned when she saw us. "Hiya Cassidy. What brings you out here?" With her dark hair pulled back and her makeup perfect, Marcella looked like she walked out of a *telenovella*. And whether it was magic or good genes, she also looked too young to have a kid in high school and two more graduated and out on their own.

Teag grabbed a basket and started to make the rounds, picking up supplies. Spending money earned goodwill, and, besides, we went through a lot of protective plants and herbs.

"The usual. Need to stock up. How's it going?" Marcella's shop always put me to ease. I figured some of that had to do with the smell of sage, sandalwood, and copal from the incense and candles, and some from good energy vibes.

Marcella came from a long tradition of *doulas* and *brujas*, women who healed, delivered babies, and watched out for the people in their communities. Her magic wasn't flashy, but it had quiet power. The glass case held a collection of saints' medallions, as well as rosaries and jewelry made with protective gemstones and silver. Behind her, shelves held all kinds of prayer candles. Some had the image of Catholic saints on the glass holder, but closer inspection also revealed Voudon Loas, Wicca ritual candles, and Hoodoo symbols.

Beneath the other counter was a display of spices, herbs, powders, roots, and dried plants used for magic or medicine. On top of the counter were trays of gemstones and crystals. Behind me, tall shelves held books, liquids I couldn't begin to identify, Tarot cards, and ritual materials. Marcella stocked the good stuff, and her customers appreciated it.

"You didn't come just for supplies," Marcella said, tilting her head and eyeing me carefully. I suspect she's a bit of a mind reader, or maybe an empath. "What's up?"

"We do need some supplies," I said with a nod toward where Teag explored the shelves. "But I'm really looking for information. Have you had a run on any particular kind of thing lately?"

She gave a boisterous laugh. "You mean the way protection candles and charms have been practically flying off the shelves? Oh yeah. Don't know what's going on, but people are feeling it. Haven't seen folks this scared since the last big hurricane warning." Marcella leaned over the counter. "You know something?"

"A little, not enough," I confessed. "Someone was selling cursed clothing down at the Market. Now the vendor can't be found. And it's like there's something in the water—people's moods are off without any good reason."

Marcella nodded. "I hear you. I didn't know about the cursed clothing—that's a real shame. Stuff like that's bad to mess with. The community needs to find that person and shut them down." I knew when Marcella said "community" that she didn't mean the Chamber of Commerce. She meant the magical community, a close-knit network that operated under the radar, present but out of sight.

"No argument from me on that," I agreed. "Have people said what they're worried about—any particulars?"

Marcella shrugged. "Everything and nothing. What it comes down to is dread. My customers come in saying they have this feeling like something bad is coming, bad things going to happen, but when I ask 'is it your relationship' or 'is it your job' they say no. It's in their gut," she said, putting her hand over her midsection. "Like when animals know there's going to be an earthquake or a storm, and they leave, get to shelter. Only my customers, they can't leave, so they buy candles and incense and make offerings at their shrines, and hope for the best."

"You have any theories?"

Marcella's dark eyes held old secrets and deep wisdom. But now, she looked worried. "I wish I did, Cassidy. I've done the Tarot time and again, looking for insight, and I've cast corn and read the omens from eggs. Even when I've tranced, it's the same. There's a big threat, a storm, a danger, but all I see is the image of a woman with dark hair, and a tall man. I can't see their faces. But the woman is angry. And the man…his head is the wrong shape. Like a large bird." She dropped her voice. "My customers are scared. Normally, I find peace in my magic, but all I get are more questions and a warning. If you know something, I'd sure like to hear it."

"I've got all the same questions, and none of the answers," I replied. "But whoever's behind this has power—and they're danger-ous. The magic is dark—and it's strong enough to kill."

CHAPTER EIGHT

"I THINK YOU OUGHT TO SEE WHAT WE'VE FOUND." RYAN ALEXANDER said, catching up to Teag and me as we were ready to close up shop for the night. Maggie had already headed home, and Ryan slipped in right before I flipped the sign to "closed."

"Ghosts or cryptids?" I asked.

Ryan, aka the "Nikon Ninja," is a photographer who leads a group of Urban Explorers that likes to poke around in abandoned buildings, forgotten infrastructure cubbyholes, and other interesting places that aren't open to the public. Given how often Teag and I ignore things like trespassing or breaking and entering when it comes to busting supernatural bad guys, I can't get too upset that some of Ryan's expeditions border on illegal. We just don't mention that to Anthony.

"Neither," Ryan replied, leaning against the counter in the break room. The coffee was long gone, and the carafe for the drip brewer sat cleaned and drying in the rack. I offered Ryan a soda from the fridge, but he shook his head. "Thanks anyhow. I wondered if you'd be up to coming with us tonight. Something strange is going on, and I think it's your kind of weirdness."

"Thanks—I think," Teag said. "What's up?"

"We've been exploring the new drainage tunnels they put in a few years ago around the City Market," Ryan replied. "Remember?"

"Sure," I said. "That's why the Market doesn't flood ankle-deep every time it rains anymore."

"Exactly," Ryan confirmed. "They're one hundred and forty feet deep, and they run all around the Market. They're drains, not sewers. And they're big—nine feet top to bottom and side to side."

"How big are the rats?" Teag quipped.

Ryan rolled his eyes. "Big enough. Although we don't see many down there. I think it's too new—not enough easy ways for them to get in."

"But your folks found a way," I said.

"Make of that what you will," he replied with a grin. "We got in, and the rats didn't. And since the tunnels are new, it was more about the thrill of documenting them than thinking we'd find any cool secrets. After all, the news crews filmed the site during construction, but no one's gotten good pictures since the tunnels were completed. So we decided to tackle it."

"So what did you find?" I asked. "Bones? Hidden treasure?"

Ryan looked uncomfortable, like we might not take his discovery seriously. "It's a little stranger than that. There are pieces of…clothing…scattered around the tunnels. They weren't there the first time we went down a month ago, but then we went in earlier this week, and there they were."

Teag and I exchanged a look. Ryan doesn't know nearly as much about our "extra services" as Kell does, but we've helped him out of enough scrapes with supernatural trouble that he considers us his own friendly neighborhood ghostbusters.

"What kind of clothing?" Teag asked.

"Ponchos. Big scarves. Shawls. They're not dirty or in bad condition, so I don't think it's a homeless person making camp," Ryan said.

"Why does that sound like it's up our alley?" I asked, knowing that there was something Ryan was holding back.

He rubbed his neck and looked flustered. "My team gets along really well," he began. "We've been doing this for a long time. And you know the kind of stuff we run into—we've got to have each other's backs. So we're tight. But when we went down into those tunnels, a couple on my team freaked out. They got angry over nothing, and one of them took a swing at someone else on the team. It was bad."

"What do the people who got angry have in common?" I probed. "And how are they different from the rest of you who didn't?"

Ryan quirked his head as he considered my question. "They're probably the two people on the team who are wound the tightest, if you know what I mean. They get upset faster, stay mad longer, hold a grudge. The rest of us are laid back, by comparison."

I hadn't considered that items like Joan's cursed shawl might affect people differently, but then again, Pat had avoided the items at the Market, while Joan rushed in.

"Were any of you wearing protective items?" Teag asked.

Ryan smirked. "We always use protection."

I rolled my eyes, and Teag groaned. "You know what he meant."

Ryan grinned. "Sorry. Couldn't help myself. But the answer is yes —physical and spiritual. This wasn't going to be a dirty crawl, because the tunnels are fairly new, and they're carrying storm water, not sewage. But still, since you never know what goes down a drain grate, we've got waterproof boots, coveralls, gloves, and respirators. As for the other kind of protection, I always carry the agate and onyx you recommended, and most of the others have their own amulets or charms."

"And the ones who were affected?"

I could tell from Ryan's expression that he made an unexpected connection. "Probably not. They're our resident skeptics. Pretty much agnostic about everything in life. Very much on the 'I have to see it to believe it, and maybe not even then' side of things. So no, I doubt it."

"That might have made a difference, along with their personalities," I mused.

"And if the tunnels run near the Market, maybe those pieces of clothing are causing the general grouchiness we've noticed," Teag said.

"How does clothing cause mood swings?" Ryan looked perplexed.

Teag let out a long breath. "Someone's been weaving curses into fabrics. One of those pieces almost killed Cassidy. And the lady who attacked Maggie was under the influence of another piece."

"You're not kidding," Ryan said quietly, looking from one of us to the other. We shook our heads solemnly. "Damn."

"I think you suspected something like this when you came here," I replied.

Ryan frowned. "I thought you'd tell me I was being silly, and that we probably had a stripper vagrant loose in the tunnels."

"I wish I believed that," Teag said. "But I don't." He and I exchanged a look of silent agreement. "So when can you take us down? We need to get rid of those pieces of clothing and do a cleansing."

"I don't suppose you mean with bleach."

I shook my head. "Nope. But if we can neutralize those cursed garments, it might make the whole city breathe a little easier, and prevent a raft of assaults."

"I'm in," Ryan said. "I'll pull the team together. We can go later tonight if you're up for it."

Teag moved to make an excuse on my account, but I shook my head. "That works—unless Anthony will be home early."

Teag shook his head. "His continuing ed program has a three-day retreat. He won't be home until the weekend."

I tried to sound more confident than I felt. "All right. Let's do it."

THE FIRST HURDLE was getting into the tunnels without being seen. But by three in the morning, Charleston's closed up tight. Ryan and his team knew their way around, and I wouldn't be surprised to find out that they might even have a few friendly cops who look the other way.

The hardest part was getting a steel box down with us. Teag and I agreed that whatever else we did to break the curse on the fabric in the tunnel, the garments would ultimately need to be burned, and we didn't think that was a smart idea to do down below. So we planned to use his blessed wood walking stick to pole the cloth into the box, haul the box away to somewhere less noticeable, and take care of everything.

"You really need that box?" Ryan eyed the container skeptically.

"Yes. Unless you want us to light them up in the drain," I replied.

He winced. "Okay. I see your point." He helped us lower the box on a rope. It was awkward, but not heavy. I really hoped Ryan knew where the traffic cameras were located, because anyone watching would probably think we were planting a bomb.

We climbed down a long metal ladder and finally dropped onto a concrete floor. The only light came from the headlamps on our hard hats, and the glow barely penetrated the darkness. My breath rasped in the respirator, and the face mask made me feel claustrophobic. The protective coveralls gave me plenty of room to move, but they felt baggy, and I missed my regular jeans and jacket.

It had been a while since we were out with Ryan and his team, so he reintroduced the gang once we were in the drain and out of sight of passers-by.

"Hey everyone. You remember Cassidy and Teag."

They nodded, some with more welcoming expressions than others. "This is Tandy," he added with a nod toward a woman with short, pink hair and several eyebrow piercings. "And Jason," Ryan gestured toward a tall, thin man with dark hair caught up in a man bun. "Penny," he said with a nod toward a dark-haired, petite woman who carried herself like she had been in the military. "Karen," acknowledging a blond with a short, pixie cut and freckles that were jarringly at odds with the no-nonsense look in her eyes. "And Kurt," Ryan added. The fourth member of their group, a red-headed man with wire-rimmed glasses and nervous blue eyes, gave me a wave.

I tried to take comfort in the lack of rats. Ryan hadn't said they'd seen evidence of any supernatural creatures. That beat finding the half-eaten remains of a ghoul's dinner, or a black dog's chew toys.

"What's so special about some rags?" Penny asked.

"We think they're connected to missing persons," Ryan replied, repeating the cover story we'd come up with together. He didn't like misleading his team, but we didn't dare bring them in on the whole truth. After all, the witch who made the cursed cloth was still at large, and we didn't want to put any of Ryan's people at risk. In a way, the people who'd been affected by the malicious Weaver magic were "missing" in that they weren't themselves. We were stretching the truth, but it wasn't a total lie.

"How are you going to turn them over to the police without turning us in?" Tandy demanded.

"We've got friends on the force," Teag replied. Again, we were shading the truth. These particular items would be burned after they were cleansed, so bringing in the police was never part of the plan.

"You'd better not get us arrested," Karen warned.

"We won't," I promised.

"Lighten up," Ryan told his team. "You brought your amulets?" Everyone except Penny and Kurt nodded. "Good. Let's go."

I listened with my gift as we made our way through the tunnels, and tried hard not to think about how far we were underground. Unlike in a haunted place, I didn't pick up on any resonance from the structure itself, and when I'd glanced at the news articles about the tunnel project, I hadn't seen any deaths mentioned related to the construction. At least we wouldn't have extra complications.

"The first one should be just ahead," Ryan said. I knew when we came into range when Teag staggered.

"Shit," he muttered, and I moved to steady him. "I'm warded to the gills, and whatever's up there feels like a bath of raw sewage and roadkill."

"What do you need?" I asked.

Teag set down the steel box and opened it, then sidled around to get a better look at the cursed cloth. Our headlamps revealed a finely woven piece of fabric that looked more like a table runner than a scarf.

I didn't dare get too close because I had no intention of touching the item. Even from several feet away, I picked up turbulent, negative emotions. I consider myself a pretty even-tempered person, but I'm human, and I can get plenty angry when the situation warrants. I felt the pull of the cloth and raised one hand to clasp the agate necklace at my throat. The tug receded, but I could still feel the power probing me, looking for a weak spot.

My left hand slid into my pocket and closed around the old polished spindle whorl. The instant my hands touched the smooth stone, I felt an invisible shock wave blast between me and the fabric.

"What did you do?" Teag asked, glancing at me.

"Nothing," I said, but I gave him a look that meant "not now."

"Whoa—what was that?" Ryan asked. He knows about my psychometry, but not about Teag's Weaver magic, and he hasn't really seen us go up against a big bad.

"Don't let your imagination get to you," I said, not sure what the fabric's reaction to the relic meant. "I'm picking up a very bad vibe."

Teag had carried his staff down in a sling on his back. He could fight with it like a real badass, and it was a formidable weapon. But the runes carved along its ash wood length imbued it with magic, as did the woven cords fastened at one end that stored his power. He'd refreshed the blessings and protections on the staff and charged up the cords with magic and intention. If anything could lift the cursed cloth into the box safely, his staff could do it.

"It's just an old bit of fabric," Jason said and started forward.

"No!" I flung out my arm, blocking him at chest height. "Let Teag handle it."

Jason looked at me like I had gone crazy. "Sure. Anything you say."

"That is a nasty piece of work," Teag murmured as he dipped the end of the staff beneath the cloth and carefully maneuvered it into the box. Inside the container lay a layer of protective powders made from plants good for warding off evil and canceling negative mojo. We'd also included some iron filings, salt, and a liberal sprinkle of silver dust. As soon as the cloth connected with the inside of the box, I immediately felt its power weaken, and gave Teag a nod.

"That's one," he said grimly. From the set of his jaw, I wondered what he had felt as he poled the cloth into the box, and made up my mind to ask him later.

Teag moved on to the next bit of cursed fabric, along with most of the team. Ryan lingered behind with me. I edged my way close to where the item had been, picking up a low-grade resonance from the concrete beneath my feet.

"What are you going to do?" Ryan asked. "I'd rather you not leave behind clues that we were here."

I pulled out a bottle of holy water and a canister of salt. "I don't think anyone will notice the salt, and the water will dry."

"You buy holy water by the gallon?"

"Nah. Got a friend who's a priest. Easier that way." I kept back from where the cloth had actually lain on the concrete, but made sure that the salt I sprinkled and the water I poured hit dead on. I gripped the spindle whorl again, and in my mind's eye, I felt the residue of malicious power vanish like smoke.

"Let's catch up," I said. "This spot is clean now."

We moved through the tunnels like that, making a circuit of sorts around the Market. Teag picked up twelve pieces of finely woven linen. I had expected something knotted like Joan's macramé shawl or a rough weave like a blanket. Instead, these were the exquisite pieces of a master weaver. For all their beauty, I knew how deadly the power behind them could be. We were lucky that the Weaver had wanted to sow discord. If he or she had wanted to kill large numbers of people, I knew how easily it could have been done. I thought of Marcella's vision of a tall man and a dark-haired woman and wondered which of them brought the cursed cloth down here.

"That's all of them," Ryan confirmed. I poured a layer of salt over top of the last piece of fabric and sprinkled some holy water for good measure. Then Teag closed the lid and secured the latches, binding it with spelled cord for good measure.

"Let's get out of here," he said, sounding weary, and I wondered what toll the dark magic had taken on him, despite his precautions. "We've still got a bonfire to light."

WE PARTED company with Ryan and his crew once we got back to our cars. Ryan promised to call if they found any more of the spelled cloths, and we assured him we'd let him know if we turned up any information that might affect the safety of his group.

Teag and I drove into the countryside, to a cabin out on St. John Island that Sorren keeps as a safe house. We were far enough away from other people that no one was likely to call in some smoke, and if anyone did show up, we could blame it on the fire pit.

We poured lighter fluid over the cloth, and Teag tossed in a match. The flames leaped higher than my head, blood red and stinking of sulfur. The burning fabric curled in on itself, writhing like a living thing, and an inhuman shriek sounded from the cursed linen.

Teag cried out in pain, holding his head, and sank to his knees. I shook the dog collar on my left wrist, and Bo's ghost materialized to protect us. The athame slipped from its arm sheath, in case the fabric's scream called its maker.

"Teag? Talk to me. What's going on?" I wanted to go comfort him, but I couldn't afford to leave us unprotected. Teag was vulnerable, so I had to stay on watch. Bo immediately oriented on the burn pit, lowering his head and raising his hackles as he stared into the flames.

"I can feel the power in the fabric being torn apart," Teag replied through gritted teeth.

"Try this." I took his hand, and slipped the agate spindle whorl into his palm, then closed his fingers around it.

A white light flared from Teag's fist, making me look away. The fire in the pit streaked upward, like a bloody scarlet gash in the night. Teag fell to one side. Bo barked in warning, and I could have sworn I saw faces and figures in the red flames. Then with a *whoosh*, the fire was sucked back into the fire pit and went out, leaving only black ash.

"Teag!" I knelt next to him, as he pushed up on his elbows in the grass. Bo remained staring at the fire pit for another few seconds until he assured himself the flames were truly gone. Then he turned to me with a doggy grin, wagged his tail, and vanished. I kept my athame in my hand, in case the threat hadn't completely gone away.

"I've got a hell of a headache," he groaned, accepting my help to get to his feet. He opened his clenched fist and gave me back the spindle whorl. It felt warmer than it should have been just from his hand. "Let's finish up and get out of here," Teag said, "and I'll tell you all about it."

We soaked the ashes in holy water and covered the fire pit. I texted Sorren and figured he and Donnelly could figure out how to dispose of what was left.

Together, Teag and I made it back to my RAV4 and sat, but I didn't start the car yet. "When we lit the fabric, I felt the power lash out. It knew I was a Weaver, Cassidy; I'm sure of it. I shielded myself to keep it out and drew on my amulets, but it felt like a battering ram on the side of my head."

"Trying to get in?"

He shrugged. "Maybe it wanted to tap into my magic to sustain its hold, or to break free. I don't know. I pushed back. And then you gave me the spindle whorl, and that light blasted the curse away." Teag turned to look at me. "That magic didn't come from inside the whorl. There was sentience behind it. How much do you know about that charm and where it came from?"

I took the agate disk out of my pocket and looked at it as I turned it in my fingers. It had a hole bored into the middle, to weight the spindle for hand-spinning thread. Centuries of use had worn the stone smooth, and the agate shone with a deep luster. Yet in all the time I'd carried the whorl, I had never sensed a mind behind it, though its protective power had saved me more times than I could count.

"Sorren gave it to me. He said it had belonged to a Norse Weaver witch, someone he and his maker, Alard, ran across back in Belgium. Sorren said it carried her protection, but he never said anything about her…haunting…it."

Teag looked up sharply. "That belonged to a Norse *Seiðr*?" He eyed the whorl like it had turned into a nuclear warhead.

"Yeah. And…?"

Teag pushed his hand through his hair, though his skater-boy bangs fell back into his face. I put the whorl back in my pocket, started the car, and headed home. "The Norse *Seiðr* were incredibly powerful witches. This woman—" he began.

"Secona." I remembered the name Sorren had told me because it was so unusual.

"You know her name?" Teag said, eyes going wide. "That means you have a claim on her power."

I spared a glance as I drove. Almost no other cars passed us. We were too late for the party crowd and too early for rush hour. "Teag, the whorl is close to a thousand years old. This 'Secona' is long dead."

"Sorren's not," he challenged.

"Sorren's a vampire."

"Donnelly's got to be over a century old—maybe more. And he's a necromancer."

"Secona would have to be a lot more than a regular witch to live that long." I'd never considered that my magic might extend my life. Given the dangers of our work, I figured the opposite.

"If she really was a Norse *Seiðr*, she was much more than a 'regular' witch." Teag slumped into the seat.

"You want to crash at my place?" I asked. He nodded, and I figured his headache hadn't miraculously vanished.

"A Viking *Seiðr* was a sorceress," Teag continued, and his voice held an edge of pain. "She wasn't just a *Volva*—a witch—or a *spa*—a prophet. She was also a shaman who could use spells and incantations to work magic—and her special type of sorcery was Weaver magic."

"What about male *Seiðrs*? Weren't any of them men?"

"Not for long," Teag replied. "Being a male *Seiðr* was punishable by death."

I frowned. "Why?"

He sighed and squinched his eyes closed, likely fighting his headache. "Because the Vikings were really hung up on gender roles, and weaving was woman's work. So any magic that had to do with weaving belonged to women. And if a man possessed that magic, then he was considered to be gay. And the Vikings killed gay men—at least, the ones who were 'catching' instead of 'pitching.'"

"But Secona's whorl protected you—twice," I said, pulling up in front of the house in my spell-protected parking spot. We got out, locked the car, and headed inside. At this hour, even Baxter declined to make much of a fuss, bothering to raise his head to see that it was us before going back to sleep on the foyer carpet.

"I don't know what to make of that," Teag said, following me into the kitchen as I put water on to boil to make us herbal tea. I reached for a bottle of ibuprofen and shook two out for Teag. "Maybe since Sorren gave the whorl to you, she's extending protection to me as a professional courtesy."

"Or maybe not all Vikings agreed on things, like people don't nowadays," I replied. Exhausted as I was, I still felt too jazzed by the events of the evening to fall asleep right away, and so I counted on hot chamomile tea to do the trick. Within minutes, Teag and I settled at the table with steaming mugs, and for good measure, I put out a plate of lemon benne wafers, a Charleston specialty.

"We need to find out more from Sorren about Secona," Teag said. "Because if she does hold traditional views, then I'm in trouble."

"We won't let that happen," I vowed, snapping a crisp benne wafer and letting a fine spray of powdered sugar dust the top of the table.

"If she's a full-powered *Volva*, we might not have the mojo to stop her."

I put my hand on Teag's wrist. "Teag, you know Sorren. He wouldn't bring someone—something—into this if he thought they'd make us a target."

"The real question is, if Secona didn't weave the cursed cloth, then who's behind the malicious fabric? And what does all this have to do with the amped-up ghosts and all the other weirdness?"

"I don't know, but we'll get to the bottom of it," I promised. "And our whole gang together—we're pretty formidable, with or without a *Seiðr* on our side."

CHAPTER NINE

"FIND ANYTHING?" I MADE IT INTO THE KITCHEN AROUND TEN IN THE morning, practically feeling my way to the coffee maker. A text to Maggie assured she'd cover for us, and I promised we'd be in after lunch. She was used to us being somewhat nocturnal, given the demands of our "other" job, and I knew she'd have coffee ready when we showed up.

Teag not only woke up before I did, but he'd already made a pot of coffee. Bless him. Teag stays over often enough that I consider one of the guest bedrooms to be his. I noticed that he had already stripped the sheets and left them in the laundry room. When I got downstairs, I saw his laptop open on the kitchen table. I wondered how many cups of java he'd already drunk.

"I hacked into the police evidence logs," Teag said, looking up. He hadn't shaved, and the stubble looked good on him. "I'm trying to cross-check what personal items were on the people who've been booked for violent crimes in the last two weeks."

"Hold that thought," I said, grabbing a jacket from a peg on the wall and taking Baxter out into the garden for his morning business. We came back in, and I finished fixing my cup of coffee.

"And?" Baxter danced around my feet, ready for breakfast. I filled his bowl with kibble and gave him fresh water. Then I opened a box of muffins I'd bought from Honeysuckle Café the day before and set them on the table in front of Teag and sat down on the other side of the table, hunching over my coffee to let the smell waft around me and wake me up.

"Slow going," Teag said with a shrug. "But so far, every one of the people they arrested who didn't have a previous criminal record had some sort of woven fabric on them or in their possession at the time they were apprehended."

"So those are most likely to be the people influenced by the cursed cloth, right?" I said, picking up on his line of thinking. I snagged one of the muffins, and chomped into it, then washed the luscious bite down with coffee.

"That's my theory," Teag confirmed.

"What kind of woven pieces did they have?"

Teag snaked out an arm and grabbed a muffin, polishing it off in two bites. He finished off his coffee, then poured himself another cup. "Shawls, scarves, men's ties, vests, even some woven bracelets," he replied. The photographs suck, but from what I can tell, most of them look pretty new."

"So they might have come from that stall at the Market."

He nodded. "And since the 'weirdness' has been building for a couple of weeks, we can't be certain that it began with the Market stall vendor. For all we know, this Weaver popped up at flea markets, or craft shows, or manipulated people to give the clothing as gifts."

"And we have no idea how many other garments are out there." I gulped my coffee and filled the cup again. "Can we tell if the hospitals have had a run of suspicious, sudden deaths?" I thought about the cursed scarf that had nearly killed me. If I hadn't known about magic and had friends who were powerful witches, would my death have been explained away as a fluke allergic reaction?

"That's going to take longer," Teag said. "Hospital databases are better protected. But I don't think we'd find a spate of strange deaths." He looked up and met my gaze. "I believe that the Weaver meant to kill you. I don't think it was random. Someone sees you as a threat."

"So the *Seiðr* saves you instead of killing you, but another Weaver has it in for me? That doesn't make any sense."

Teag took a second muffin and polished it off. "It does if Secona is on our side for some strange reason, and the other Weaver thinks you pose a danger to her plan."

"You're sure the bad Weaver is a woman? Marcella said she sensed both a man and a woman." I tried to savor the muffin instead of cramming it into my mouth. I eyed the last pastry and then grabbed it, figuring that ganking ghosts had to burn off calories.

"No. No reason to assume that. What are the odds that two immortal Viking sorcerers show up in Charleston?"

Slim, I hoped. But knowing our luck, probably not impossible. "I left messages for Sorren about last night, and another one about Secona," I said, with a mouth full of muffin. "He hasn't answered, except to tell me that he's working on things and to keep the spindle whorl with me at all times. I don't know where he's been going, but I think he and Donnelly may be up to something."

"If he's with Donnelly, then the question isn't 'where' Sorren is, it might be 'when' he is."

Archibald Donnelly oversees the Briggs Society, a club for adventurers who find themselves misplaced in time. The building appears and disappears, and apparently travels throughout the centuries, although I haven't been along for one of its trips. Inside the Briggs Society is a highly "eclectic" collection of relics and curios, many of which are cursed and dangerous. Donnelly takes some of the worst items off our hands at Trifles and Folly, so he's as much curator and warden as he is the head of the society. The only other person I've ever seen in the Briggs Society is Higgins, Donnelly's valet and bodyguard who looks like a butler and fights like a ninja.

"I guess he'll tell us when he thinks we need to know." I wondered for a moment what it would be like to have a normal job, like Anthony, where the answers existed in textbooks and continuing ed classes. Boring, I answered myself. But a whole hell of a lot safer.

"What have you told Anthony?" I asked. I put my cup aside and stretched.

"He knows about my magic, so the idea of weaving spells into cloth isn't new to him," Teag replied. "And if you can use something for good, someone else could make it a weapon. I told him about Joan's shawl, and the scarf you got. So he won't be opening any strange packages that come in the mail or get left on the doorstep."

"Did he have any insights?" Anthony might not have magic himself, but he's a smart guy, and he wouldn't be a hotshot lawyer if he wasn't good at putting puzzle pieces together, something we credited to a spark of intuition mighty close to magic.

"His first comment is always 'follow the money,'" Teag said with a laugh. "But I can't figure out how anyone stands to gain from what's been going on. Ghosts attacking tourists don't boost anyone's business, and neither do black dogs chasing people down the street. The pieces that have been stolen from the museum and the Archive were valuable, but not like a Picasso painting. And the ghouls and zombies? None of it makes sense."

I leaned back, knowing I needed to go take a shower and stalling because I wasn't quite awake enough to face the prospect. "Maybe those aren't features, they're bugs," I mused.

"Huh?"

"Maybe some of the things that have happened are side effects, not the Weaver's main purpose." I toyed with my coffee cup. "Maybe the Weaver is doing something that throws off extra power, and so calling the ghouls and black dogs or raising the zombies is spill-over."

"Maybe," Teag agreed, sitting back and frowning as he considered the implications. "But why would someone throw around that kind of power? What do they want to achieve? And why the cursed fabrics that affect random people? Other than your scarf, none of the victims appear to be chosen intentionally—or to be part of the supernatural community."

"We're missing a piece," I said, finishing my second cup and pushing it aside. "I'm sure it makes sense to the Weaver, so now we have to figure out what the puzzle looks like. We're looking at this wrong."

Teag sighed and closed down his laptop. "We probably won't

figure it out right now. Go get your shower. I'll clean up in the bathroom down here."

Teag spends enough time at my place that he knows where to find
everything, and he's got a stash of clothing for emergencies. Baxter
followed as I trudged upstairs, and made himself comfortable on my
bedroom rug as I showered and dressed for work. When I came down,
Teag was already waiting for me.

"Aw, you shaved," I teased. "You were rocking that scruff."

Teag grinned. "Did Anthony put you up to that? Because it's a
weekend thing, and he's always sad when I shave on Monday."

"Hey, I never said you had to," I assured him as I made certain
Baxter had what he needed for the day, then locked up when we
headed outside. "It's not part of the Trifles and Folly dress code."

"I'll think about it," Teag replied. "It's only been in the last couple
of years that I could even grow a decent beard, without it being patchy.
So maybe I'll work up to it."

The afternoon crowd at Trifles and Folly kept us hopping, so I
didn't have much time to brood. Sorren still hadn't responded in detail
to my messages, meaning he was probably off chasing his own leads. I
figured he'd get back to me when he had the chance, but I wanted to
know more about Secona, and so waiting drove me crazy.

When my phone vibrated, I thought it might be Sorren, but saw
Kell's number pop up instead. "Hi Cassidy. What are you doing
tonight?"

I chuckled. "Is this a date or a ghost hunt?"

"Isn't it usually a little of both for us?" he asked, and I liked the
warm sound of his voice. Not everyone would take the demands and
dangers of my life in stride, let alone be supportive and protective.
Personally, I thought Kell and I were a good match.

"Yeah, you're right. What's up?"

"The scarf problem got me thinking, and I realized that one of the
sites SPOOK monitors is an old textile mill," Kell replied. "We check
back on 'hot' locations every quarter and try to measure how the manifestations or energy readings vary. I thought maybe if you're dealing
with magic that's woven into cloth, there might be a connection. And,

bingo! We did a quick drive-by, and the EMF readings were off the charts. Big change from last time."

"And you want to go in and see what's made it jump?"

"You bet," Kell chuckled. "Then how about you bring your team and I bring mine, and afterward, you and I slip off for a drink?"

Teag overheard the conversation and nodded. Anthony would still be at his retreat, so that freed us both up. "Sure," I said. We worked out the details and agreed on a meeting place before I ended the call, then I put the phone back in my pocket, deep in thought.

"You said 'yes,' but you don't look happy about it," Teag observed as we finished up for the day and said good-night to Maggie.

"Something's obviously going on, or the old mill wouldn't have leveled up its mojo," I said, heading for the office to grab my jacket and purse. "Maybe it's spill-over like we talked about earlier—a side-effect of something unrelated. But that could still be dangerous, and Kell's folks aren't really equipped for dealing with powerful, malicious ghosts."

"They've started bringing salt canisters with them, and Kell bought them all iron knives," Teag said with a grin. "Plus that shotgun with rock salt pellets he started carrying. So they're not entirely helpless."

"None of them have magic," I countered as we walked out together. "So that might hold off regular ghosts, but what if there's something like ghouls or zombies? Or souped up spooks? I don't want them to get hurt."

"I'm not arguing," Teag replied. "And I'm on board with going along. Until we know what's going on and who's behind it, I consider ghost hunting to be a high-risk activity."

By the time I went home, took care of Baxter, grabbed a quick bite to eat, and changed clothes, it was time to go. Teag drove this time since Kell usually had a car full of gear for a ghost busting session.

The old Edwards fabric mill sat in a forlorn industrial park that had seen better days. For many decades cotton drove the Southern economy—both growing the crop and turning it into cloth. Then times changed, and a lot of the textile mills moved overseas. The Edwards plant opened in the late eighteen hundreds and modernized through the years, but it couldn't compete with cheap labor, and finally shut down in the 1990s. I'd heard plans bandied around more than once for what to do with the huge factory, everything from turning it into pricey loft apartments to a big entertainment complex, but nothing ever seemed to happen.

If the place *was* haunted, that might explain why the building renovation plans kept falling through.

Kell and his team were waiting for us in the parking lot. At night the old industrial park looked dark and creepy. Half of the overhead lights had burned out, and the rest looked likely to die at any minute. Crumbling asphalt and faded lines made it clear that the parking lots were long abandoned. A rickety chain link fence made a half-hearted attempt to keep trespassers out of the Edwards plant, but from the way it had been cut, trampled, and twisted, the effort was largely symbolic.

"Hi Cassidy, Teag," Kell said as we joined his group. "Take a look at this." He pulled an EMF meter from his pocket and turned it on. Even though we were probably thirty feet from the mill's entrance, the meter squealed loudly and pegged the needle, red lights flashing.

Ghosts give off unusual energy, especially electromagnetic frequencies. And that's what the EMF reader measures. A reaction like Kell's meter was showing can be caused by non-paranormal causes—like an electric power surge—but I suspected that the old mill's electricity had been shut off years ago.

"Can you localize the disturbance?" Teag asked, eyeing the huge plant. "That's a lot of square footage to cover."

The enormous plant sprawled in every direction. We'd gone around back, to where the loading docks sat unused and empty long after the last trucks packed up and pulled out. The huge glass windows were cracked and broken, some gaping open like empty sockets.

"We think the readings are coming from the center of the plant, where the machinery would have been." Calista, a perpetually dour young woman who handled the computer analysis for SPOOK, pointed toward a wing of the mill. Tonight, Calista rocked bright blood-red hair, only partially hidden beneath her black hoodie. Heavy eyeliner and dark nail polish were a nod to the Goth librarian vibe she favored.

"From what we found online, the plant had a terrible safety record." Drew, SPOOK's video and tech expert, often doubled as the group's historian and main researcher. His jacket seemed to hang on his rangy frame, and the ripped jeans, faded concert t-shirt, and pony-tail made him look like a college student. "Back in the early 1900s, a fire destroyed one wing and killed several workers—badly burned a few dozen others. They rebuilt, but the plant was dogged by bad luck. A heavy rain collapsed the ceiling in one area, crushing three mainte-nance workers. Even by the standards of the time, the mechanical looms were man-eaters. Losing fingers, hands—even arms or legs—in the big looms or fabric rollers was common. And the automated cutting machines pulled more than one worker in and spat them out in little bits."

"Yikes," I said.

Pete, SPOOK's sound guy, didn't chime in, but he was busy fiddling with his microphones and recording equipment. Short and wiry, with muscles like a welterweight wrestler, Pete had a hat jammed down over his unruly ginger hair. All of the team wore hats with action cameras, in addition to the professional grade video cam Drew fussed over. Calista ran everything through a tablet computer when they weren't staking out a location for the whole night.

"Oh, and did we mention the big union fight back in the 1930s?" Kell added. "Turned bloody between the striking workers and the scabs. The mill owners brought in private security—bully boys—and started cracking heads and taking names. When the dust settled, four workers were dead, twenty more were in roughed up and jailed, and the strikers lost their jobs and got run out of town."

"So there's plenty of bad mojo to go around," I summarized, looking askance at the towering dark building.

"Just the kind of place you love," Teag murmured.

"Yeah, right."

"Here's the map we made the last time we came here," Kell said, and we all gathered around him. "I started with what I could find online of a blueprint and then added the new modifications that weren't on the old plans. If we go in here," he said, pointing to the docks, "we can cut through the administrative wing, and then into the oldest section of the factory. That had the most activity, although we ran into orbs and cold spots in all of the working areas."

I snapped a photo of the map with my phone, in case we got separated. Teag did the same, although I knew we'd all stick close together. Still, better safe than sorry.

I noticed that Kell's team wore their iron knives in belt sheaths. Kell had his shotgun, and I checked before we went in that everyone had protective charms. Teag and I came armed with iron, silver, holy water, and salt, as well as the lighters and fluid back in the car. I had my athame plus Bo's collar, and Teag had his silver whip and a few other surprises that I hoped we didn't need.

Graffiti covered the loading docks. The side door had an easy lock to pick, and then we were inside. Kell had passed out the night vision goggles before we went in. Our flashlights barely made a dent in the cavernous space.

"Wow. They didn't clean up much when they left, did they?" Pete observed. The huge storage room would have housed crates and pallets filled with cloth, ready for shipment. Now, broken crates littered the cement floor, and mildewed bolts of faded cloth spilled from bins and carts. It looked like everyone walked out and left things where they lay.

Kell turned from side to side, but the EMF meter remained quiet. "Nothing in here," he said. "Come on. The last time, we got the hottest readings in the actual factory."

I couldn't help looking around as we plunged deeper into the darkness. I'd always assumed that when companies go under, someone comes along and sells off anything of value. The Edwards mill offices had desks, chairs, and filing cabinets, all covered with a thick layer of dust. Whoever had tagged some of the walls in the loading dock must not have thought the offices interesting enough to vandalize.

The stone and brick walls held the cold. The offices were in the oldest wing, dating from the original mill back in 1872.

"Can you feel it?" Kell asked, turning toward me.

I nodded. Given the level of spirit activity, I figured everyone in the group sensed that we weren't alone. But I picked up more than ghost vibes. The Edwards mill had enough imprinted tragedy to redline my psychometry like Kell's EMF meter.

Desperation echoed down the corridors and reverberated in shadows. Textile workers were often women, children, or immigrants, paid a pittance and exposed to dangerous machinery and chemicals. Even the men who worked in these factories didn't command the pay of those in the steel mills in the north or other types of manufacturing. The sense of constant worry, of living one paycheck from disaster clung to the bricks and settled into the concrete like a permanent stain.

I fought to keep from being overwhelmed by the lingering despair, and touched my agate necklace and the spindle whorl in my pocket to ground myself, separating my own thoughts from the resonance all around me.

"Yeah, I feel it," I replied after Kell shot me a look that said I'd been silent too long. "We must be coming to one of the areas where there had been a disaster. The desperation is shifting to fear."

Kell nodded. "This is part of the wing that was rebuilt after the fire."

I staggered as new impressions overwhelmed me. Teag caught me by the arm, steadying me. Out of the corner of my eye, I saw fleeting movement in the shadows and bobbing orbs. Pete and Calista remarked on the strength of the manifestations. I felt echoes of the mortal fear that overwhelmed the workers trapped by the fire, flashes of pain and terror that spiked my heart rate and quickened my breath.

"Cassidy?" Kell asked. "Are you okay?"

"Yeah," I lied. "I'll be fine. Just strong impressions. Keep going." Personally, I couldn't imagine how anyone with even a hint of psychic sensitivity could have stood to work in the building. The poor workers who died in the fire had left indelible energy shadows, even if their souls no longer remained behind.

We opened a set of double doors and stepped into a huge, high ceilinged room as cavernous as the loading dock. But as Kell and the others let their flashlights sweep the area, I saw that the massive industrial looms remained in place, waiting for the next shift of workers who would never come.

"Those are huge," Teag murmured.

I nodded, fighting the growing sense of dread in the pit of my stomach that I couldn't quite put a name to. Instead, I focused my attention on the looms. Each one was easily the size of a compact car, a complex marvel of levers and jointed metal. Several of the machines still had hundreds of strands of rotting thread leading down to the mechanisms like ghostly webs. The thread hung heavy with dust and would probably fall apart at the slightest touch, but in the stillness of the night, it gave an eerie impression that the looms still awaited their weavers, dead or alive.

The whine of the EMF meter cut through my thoughts. "Shit," Drew muttered. "There's too much going on at once. I need everyone to turn around and let your cap cams pick up the phenomena."

"Orbs, incoming!" Calista shouted as glowing bubbles materialized out of nowhere, hovering and zooming all around us. As pretty as they were, my intuition told me we were in for trouble.

Teag must have felt the shift as well, because I saw him reach for his iron knife, and take out a canister of salt from his bag. I caught glimpses out of the corner of my eye of women in long, old-fashioned dresses moving around the looms, thin-faced and pale. Their energy felt resigned, as if they had been unable to free themselves from their indenture to the mill in life, and had lost all hope of freedom after death.

But something nearby felt dark and angry, a spreading stain on the resonance. I turned slowly, obliging Drew's request, and the limited glow of my flashlight caught a hint of motion to one side. I stared into the gloom, and saw the images again, the sudden crash of ceiling and roof coming down, a surge of panic, then pain and death. A repeater, but a strong one. I looked away as the old disaster replayed.

"Are you getting any of that?" Kell asked in a hushed voice to his team.

"Trying," Drew confirmed. "But there's a lot of interference."

The EMF meter screeched, and the temperature in the room plummeted. I felt the resonance shift again, and Pete gasped as a voice on the audio feed spoke clearly above the white noise.

"Get out."

"Holy shit," Calista said, pivoting to hone in on the source of the voice.

I didn't need to have skin-to-surface contact to know that a dark tide of ugly energy seeped into the room like overflowing psychic sewage. And it headed straight for Teag.

"Watch out!" I yelled, and Teag spun toward my voice at the same time that the shadows rushed at him. He hurled salt, and the darkness parted where the crystals landed, but the mass swept toward him, relentless.

I heard a metal screech, the yielding of age-old rust and disuse, and then a hum and clatter as the hulking looms around us came to life.

"This can't be happening," Pete yelped, crossing himself.

The darkness headed for Teag once more, enveloping him, and I knew it intended to hurl him into the moving guts of the massive looms, the tangle of metal parts that had chewed up and mangled so many workers.

I shook my left wrist, jangling the old dog collar, and Bo's ghost barely had time to materialize before he leaped snarling into the roiling shadows. My athame fell into my hand, and I leveled it, but before I could send a blast of cold power to loosen the hold of the darkness, the boom of a shotgun deafened us.

Kell reloaded, firing another salt round off center, and I took aim on the other side, channeling my gift and the resonance of the athame into a bolt of white energy. The darkness withdrew like a wounded predator, releasing Teag, who fell to his knees far too close for comfort to the possessed loom.

"Come on!" I yelled as more and more of the old looms woke from their slumber, filling the huge room with the rumble and roar. I wondered how the workers had stood the noise, so loud it made my bones vibrate, and my ears ring. I realized the others couldn't hear me, so I grabbed Teag's wrist and yanked him to his feet, then started to drag him back the way we had come.

If we made the trip to validate ghostly activity, we had what we came for, and then some.

Kell shot into the malicious shadows once more, the report of his gun barely audible above the din of the looms.

I glanced over my shoulder to make sure that Kell and the rest of his team were with us, and saw them keeping up. Kell brought up the rear, ejecting the spent shells and loading as he ran. My head throbbed with the noise, and my ears buzzed. I burst through the double doors with Bo's ghost at my side and Teag stumbling along a step behind me. The others tumbled out into the darkened hallway seconds later, and the doors clanged shut.

Abruptly, the looms fell silent.

"What…in the bloody hell…was that?" Calista panted.

"That would be ghosts, amped up by something or someone," I replied.

Teag shook his head at my worried glance, assuring me that he hadn't been hurt, although from how pale he'd gone and his wide eyes, I could see how scared he was.

"Come on," Kell said, reloading his shotgun. "Let's get out of here, before anything else happens."

Bo stayed beside me until we got back to the parking lot, then he wagged and vanished. Pete stared at the space where the ghost had been.

"You have a ghost dog," he said, as the rest of the team eyed me with suspicion and a little bit of fear.

"It's a long story," I said. "And one I'd rather not see on the evening news."

"We're not investigating Cassidy and Teag," Kell told his team, warning clear in his voice. "They're allies, not test subjects. So whatever you think you saw stays between us."

"That white stream of light—what did you do?" Drew asked, sounding more curious than awed.

"I can read the history of objects by touching them," I said matter-of-factly. "And if the resonance of the memories is strong enough, I can use it to defend myself. It's redirecting energy."

"That's cool," Pete said. "Weird and a little freaky, but cool."

Teag and I had been on many ghost hunts with the SPOOK crew, and more than once we'd used our magic to save our collective asses from an other-worldly threat. But until now, our abilities managed to escape notice. I felt uncomfortable having more people know about us, and still, I trusted Kell and his group to keep our secrets.

"We won't tell anyone," Calista said. "Thanks for whatever scary-ass thing you did back there."

I grinned. Coming from Calista, that was high praise. "You're welcome," I said. "Let's go home."

CHAPTER TEN

THE DAY AFTER OUR NEAR-FATAL ENCOUNTER WITH THE HAUNTED looms at the Edwards mill was blissfully normal. Plenty of traffic at Trifles and Folly meant we had little time to dwell on our brush with danger, and the day passed smoothly enough for us to take a mental break from the ongoing weirdness and catch our breath. No new cursed objects, no rabidly angry customers.

So the knock at the door while I fixed dinner caught me by surprise. With the wardings, only a short list of trusted friends can come all the way up on the porch without being escorted, so that cut the number of possible callers down to a select few, none of whom I was expecting. My surprise heightened when I saw Anthony.

"May I come in?" he asked, looking like he felt very self-conscious turning up on my doorstep.

"Of course," I answered, stepping to the side to let him in. "Is something wrong? Is Teag okay?"

Anthony walked inside, hung up his jacket, and dropped onto my couch. I saw the fine lines around his eyes from worry and sleeplessness. "Teag's not hurt," he said, leaning forward onto his thighs and clasping his hands in front of him. "He's at his lesson with Mrs. Teller. But he's not okay."

"Bad dreams?" I hazarded a guess.

Anthony nodded. "At first, I figured it went with the kinds of things you see with what you do. I only know a fraction of it all, and what I've seen is enough to cause nightmares. But there's something really wrong, and I don't know what to do."

I sat across from Anthony. "Tell me what's going on."

Anthony sat straight and leaned back against the couch, then closed his eyes. "The dreams changed about three weeks ago. Before that, I'd have said they were normal, considering. I mean, once in a while, Teag would have a nightmare, and when I'd wake him up, he'd tell me that it had to do with some creature you'd fought off. Except that in his dreams, everything went wrong, people got hurt, and the good guys didn't win."

I shrugged, knowing those kinds of dreams too well myself. "Yeah. I know what that's like. Can't say that those are 'normal,' but they're regular nightmares." Recurring, traumatic, and terrifying, but still nothing supernatural.

"The new dreams are coming more often, and it's harder to wake him out of them," Anthony confided. "Like they don't want to let go of him. When he's dreaming, he's really in the dream. His whole body thrashes, he kicks and fights—nearly gave me a black eye more than once—and he cries out."

Anthony opened his eyes and met my gaze. "Something's hurting him, Cassidy. I see welts appear on his body after a dream that weren't there when we went to bed the night before. I've heard him scream, and seen bruises form, with no one touching him. No one that I could see."

"What else does he say about the dreams, when he wakes up?" I asked.

"He says he doesn't remember them," Anthony replied. "At least, not much. What he's told me is spotty, but I believe him. I can't figure out how he could be so scared and involved in the dream and supposedly have almost no memory of it minutes later."

I got up and made us both a cup of tea. Baxter begged to be picked up, and Anthony lifted him onto the couch, where Bax settled up beside him like a good little therapy dog. Anthony took the tea gratefully, and I sat down again facing him.

"And you think it's more than PTSD?"

Anthony nodded. "I mean, I'm not a psychologist. I've heard about night terrors, and from what I've read online, those can feel real and be horrific. But something about these new dreams raises the hair on the back of my neck. There's a wrongness to them I can't explain."

"Then trust your instincts," I replied. Teag and I both think Anthony has a bit of clairvoyance, although he'd never admit it. "If your gut thinks there's something wrong, you're probably right." I frowned. "Sorren strengthened the wardings recently on your house. I can make sure Rowan stops by to juice up the protections on your bedroom. Did you bring any new objects home that might have carried a curse or a hex?"

Anthony gave me a look. "If you mean, did we suddenly redecorate with ancient relics from pilfered tombs, the answer is no."

I returned the side eye. "You know that's not what I mean. But this sounds personal, like someone has it in for Teag. So that could be a small item he might not have even noticed, tucked into a pocket or slipped into a bag."

"Like a reverse pickpocket? Planting something instead of stealing your wallet?"

"Exactly. It could be a charm, a hex bag, something that looks like a bit of twigs and twine," I said. "Have you let anyone inside the warded area recently, someone who isn't usually around, like a repairman or a new lawn worker?"

Anthony thought for a moment. "We had a plumber come to take care of a problem with the upstairs bathroom," he mused. "I was home at the time, but I didn't follow him around and watch his every move."

"Someone you'd used before?"

He shook his head. "No. We use a service company, and they send whoever's on duty. He had the right uniform and ID. I always check."

"That's where I'd start," I said, and paused to sip my tea. "Go through all your pockets—even the stuff in the back of your closet. Look in corners, in the far end of drawers, and if there are access panels in that bathroom, check inside. And if you're really worried, I know Rowan would be willing to do a sweep and see what her magic picks up." I shrugged.

Anthony nodded, and I could see how much concern for Teag wore on him. Anthony's a good looking guy, and while some of that comes from pretty eyes and killer cheekbones, he usually exudes confidence, and that's damn attractive, especially when it's not cocky or arrogant. Now Anthony had dark circles under his eyes, and he seemed off his game.

"It's really hard to see him suffer and not be able to do anything," Anthony said in a raw voice just above a whisper. "I know what he does, what all of you do, is important. I get that you've saved Charleston—hell, the world—a few times." He ran a hand back through his thick, blond hair. "This is the part they leave out of super-hero movies," Anthony said with a wan smile that didn't reach his eyes. "What it's like for the lover, dealing with the PTSD."

"As I recall, superheroes are pretty lousy with relationships." I reached out to lay a hand on his arm. "So this is one case where real life needs to beat the movies."

Anthony swallowed hard and nodded. "I'm in it for the long haul, Cassidy. He knows that. I love him. And I'm so proud of what he can do, even though I don't understand all of it. But it's hard seeing something hurt him, and I can't help." He spread his hands in frustration.

"If this were some kind of blackmailer or stalker or hitman, I've got resources. I know how to use the law as a weapon, and I've got connections with law enforcement. I could protect him. If things got bad enough, there are ways to disappear."

Anthony had to be plenty spooked to be talking like this. I could see the desperation in his eyes, and in the way his hands shook. Not being able to protect Teag wasn't just scaring Anthony; it had him questioning whether he could do right by the man he loved.

"I think you're getting ahead of the problem," I said gently, giving him my most reassuring smile. "No one needs to disappear. Sorren and Donnelly are working on an angle of their own. Mrs. Teller and Lucinda and Father Anne are all tapping into their contacts. We're going to figure out what's behind all this, and we'll figure out a way to protect you and Teag."

Anthony nodded, and I hoped he believed me. I felt like a shitty best friend, not noticing how much the lack of sleep wore on Teag, or figuring the signs I saw were due to the usual worry that went with our work. "What do I do, now, besides not letting anyone else into the house?"

I nodded. "That's a start. We'll figure this out," I promised. "How about if I come over and help you search?"

"Good," he said, still sounding worried and distracted. "Thanks. I'm out of my element, you know? Every time I think I've got my mind wrapped around this magic stuff, there's something new, and it throws me."

"Believe me, I understand," I assured him, since even though I was part of 'this magic stuff,' there always seemed to be something new and even more terrifying right around the corner.

He stood and walked his teacup back to the kitchen, then turned and gave me a big hug. I threw my arms around his waist and squeezed back. "We'll protect him, Anthony. And you, too."

I followed Anthony back to the house he and Teag shared. I sensed the buzz of wardings at the edge of the property, so those protections were still active. When we walked into the foyer, I paused and closed my eyes.

"Everything okay?" Anthony asked.

"Trying to see if I can feel anything amiss," I told him. I picked up traces of Rowan's magic upstairs and figured those were her spells around the bedroom. I wondered what kind of protections Rowan had used, and how the malicious magic got through her wardings.

I opened my eyes and followed Anthony through the house, moving room to room, first downstairs, and then up the steps to the second floor. I frowned as I walked into the master bathroom.

"Something isn't right here," I murmured to myself, keying in on a jagged energy almost too subtle to notice.

"Can you tell where it's coming from?" Anthony asked, staying in the doorway.

"Not yet," I replied. I closed my eyes again and let myself focus on my gift. Like a magical game of Marco Polo, I moved first in one direction than another, waiting to feel when the unsettled energy grew stronger.

Now that I sensed the bad mojo, I felt it strengthen as I moved back toward the doorway that led to the bedroom. I held out one hand in front of me like a dowsing rod and stopped when I bumped into the wall.

When I opened my eyes, my palm was against a small, framed picture of a sailboat on the ocean. I recoiled, as the sinister magic seemed to reach for me.

"Cassidy? Did you find something?"

"Can you get me some tongs? I don't want to touch the picture."

Anthony hurried down to the kitchen and returned with a pair of metal cooking tongs. I found a pair of rubber cleaning gloves in the bottom of the linen cabinet and put on a glove to further insulate me from the harmful energy, then gingerly lifted the picture with the tongs and set it in the sink, with the back of the photograph exposed.

"There," I said, pointing to a tangle of what looked like twigs, dry leaves, and hair. "It's a hex, and I bet it has something to do with Teag's bad dreams. I need a lead box, and salt. Lots of salt."

"Hang on," Anthony said and ran from the room. I could hear doors opening and then the rustle of paper, and in a few minutes, he returned with an empty portable safe and a canister of salt. "Here," he said. "Will this do?"

"I think it'll be perfect," I said. Even with the buffer of the tongs and the rubber glove, I winced at the roiling malice given off by the hex charm. I felt like I had a poisonous snake in my grip, trying to evade its sharp fangs. It took only seconds for me to rip the hex free of the back of the photo, drop it into the safe, and douse it with salt, but I knew I would need a shower and a sage smudging to strip away the psychic filth I felt from the contact.

Anthony slammed the safe door shut and spun the lock, and the lead box smothered the malignant energy. He looked up, worried and hopeful. "Do you think that will stop the dreams?" he asked.

I made a sweep of their bedroom and found nothing else. Then again, I didn't expect to, since Rowan had warded the space. "I think it will help," I said cautiously. "Rowan's wardings had a weak point at the bathroom door, and whoever planted the hex knew it. Whoever did this has power. Some of what Teag's picking up on might be that malicious energy, and that's harder to ward against because his own abilities are feeding him the images. But with the hex gone, it should reduce the strength of the dreams."

"What about this?" Anthony asked, looking down at the safe.

"Let's put it in my trunk, and I'll get Sorren to take care of it, after Rowan and Lucinda have a look at the charm. Maybe they can make out something about the witch that made it, to help us find out who's behind all this."

Anthony carried the box like it was full of rattlesnakes, and deposited it in my trunk. I threw a silver-infused net over it, just in case. He thanked me profusely and promised to have Kell and me over for supper soon. I gave him a peck on the cheek and sent him in to get dinner ready for when Teag got home.

I worried about the box in the trunk, but it remained silent as I drove home. When I closed the door, I leaned hard against it, and took several deep breaths. Then I took a shower, lit some sage in an abalone shell incense burner, and headed for the couch. I wrapped Baxter up in my arms and hoped like hell we could figure out how to keep Teag safe and get to the bottom of whatever power lay behind the weirdness. The longer this went on, the worse it got, and I had a sinking feeling we'd only seen the previews, not the main attraction.

THE NEXT MORNING, my cell phone rang before I even got to the store. "Sorry to catch you so early," Valerie, the top tour guide at Andrews Carriage Rides, greeted me. "But I need your help."

"What's going on?" I asked, envisioning black dogs chasing tourists or more injuries from rogue ghosts at the Old Jail.

"Thoroughbred horses and hunting dogs are vanishing out of

locked barns," Valerie said. "Security cameras were on and recorded no one entering or leaving the stables. The gates were locked, and the gatekeeper saw nothing. Security guards patrolling the area reported no unusual incidents. So how in the hell did three two-ton horses—each worth close to half a million dollars—just vanish into thin air? And half a dozen champion hunting dogs, too?"

I parked behind the shop, although I had a sneaking suspicion that I wouldn't be staying long. "It sounds more like something for the police," I said, not wanting to leave Maggie with the store again.

"Cassidy, they found really strange markings in the stable, and in the dog kennel. You know about these kinds of things."

"How did you get involved?" I asked, knowing that my protests staved off the inevitable.

"My cousin is married to the son of the stable owner," Valerie replied. "This could ruin them."

"The insurance company is not going to accept 'magic' for an answer," I warned her.

"No, but if you can figure out how they disappeared, maybe there's a way to get them back," Valerie said. "I'm desperate, Cassidy."

I pinched the bridge of my nose and felt a headache coming on. "Okay. Fill me in," I said, and leaned back in my seat, knowing it was going to be a long day.

Teag gave me a look when I walked in fifteen minutes later. I was late, but he'd probably heard me park behind the shop. To my relief, he actually looked rested.

"Sleep a little better last night?" I asked.

He gave a wan smile. "Much. Just normal nightmares, but not like it had been. Anthony told me about what you found. Thank you. From both of us." He nodded toward the phone in my hand. "Something up?"

"How do you feel about a trip out to Aiken?" I asked. "Valerie called. There's been some seriously strange goings-on at a horse farm, and she didn't know who else to ask for help."

"Don't worry—I've got the store covered," Maggie volunteered, bustling out from the break room with a fresh cup of hot tea. "Run along and save the horses."

"Horses?" Teag asked, raising an eyebrow. He went to collect his laptop and messenger bag from my office. I poured more coffee into my travel cup for the trip.

"And hunting dogs. I'll fill you in on the way," I promised. Then I turned to Maggie, contrite and grateful. "Thank you."

She shooed me off with a gesture. "It's my contribution to saving the world," she said with a grin. "Make sure you tell me all about it when you get back."

Ten minutes later, Teag and I had everything we needed loaded into my SUV and were headed out of town. I told him about Valerie's connection to the owner of Harrison Stables, their thoroughbred hunting horses and championship hunting dogs, and what she'd passed on about the animals' disappearance.

"How the hell do you make three horses disappear?" Teag asked. "I mean, the dogs would be a challenge. But horses? They're huge!"

"There's got to be a connection," I said. "Everything that's happened has revolved around fox hunting, hounds, sporting events. And if you're going to steal prime horseflesh, Aiken's the place to go."

Whether the goal was fox hunting, polo, or racing, Aiken knew horses. It had the best stables, jockeys, hunt coordinators, vets, and breeders outside of the Kentucky bluegrass region, and the people behind Aiken's longstanding success came from old money.

We had a drive ahead of us, so Teag pulled out his laptop and went to work. "Harrison Stables is quite an enterprise," he said, after giving an appreciative whistle when he read the search results. "Plenty of their horses have won big races, all the way up to being Triple Crown contenders," he said. I wasn't a "horse person," but even I knew that the Holy Grail of horse racing was the Kentucky Derby, the Preakness, and the Belmont. It took serious money to buy, maintain, and train elite racehorses and to hire the staff required to make it to the top races. And that didn't count the money wagered on those events, or the lavish social affairs centered on watching the race in style.

"Valerie said that Aiken also is big with steeplechase races, and polo—plus hunting," I added. "Everything 'horse.'"

"There are at least ten major fox hunting events held every year, and plenty of pedigree hunting hound breeders in the area, too," Teag said, reading down through his search results. "Those poor foxes don't stand a chance."

Personally, my sympathies were also with the foxes. Racing and polo didn't bother me, as long as the horses were treated well and found good homes once they no longer competed. But I'd never been a fan of fox hunting, which struck me as cruel and unnecessary. I had plenty of friends who went deer hunting, and shooting pheasants and other game birds was a big deal in the Lowcountry. But at least you could eat what you shot. Fox hunting was about the thrill of the chase, the excitement of running your target to ground, with the quarry hopelessly outnumbered. Maybe someday they'd invent an artificial intelligence fox that could lead the hunters on a merry run, but until then, I wasn't in favor.

"Aiken's got quite the history," Teag remarked. "People with names like Vanderbilt and Astor spent their winters here and brought their money with them. As for the Harrisons…now that's interesting."

"Oh?"

"Would you be terribly surprised to find out that the Harrisons of Aiken are related to the Nicholsons of Charleston?"

I sighed. "No, not really. So the plantation with the ghostly hunting hounds has a connection to the missing horses and dogs?"

"Uh huh. One of the Nicholson daughters married into the Harrison family after the Civil War," Teag recounted, condensing the history he scrolled through on his screen. "According to this, the Harrisons—like the Nicholsons—found a lot of financial success, but were followed by personal tragedy."

"Or possibly, cursed?"

Teag's raised brow confirmed my suggestion. "Quite possibly. Unfortunate racing accidents, gunshot wounds on hunts, some questionable deaths that might have been suicides or something even stranger, and a couple of notable disappearances." He made a face.

"Not to mention at least one guy who got trampled to death by his horse in its stall, and another man who was apparently mauled and eaten by his pack of hunting dogs."

"Eew."

"So if a long-ago Nicholson made a deal with the devil—or something like him—they didn't bargain well," I said. "Or they managed to piss off a really powerful witch." Curses—the gift that keeps on giving. "Anything else?"

Teag frowned as he scanned the screen. "I recognize some of the organizations that sponsor the races and the hunts. No big surprise—they cater to the well-off. Investment banking firms, wealth management advisors, high-end car dealers, luxury goods. Some of the sponsors are celebrating over a hundred years of involvement."

"So we've got a small group of people with big money playing some high-stakes, dangerous games," I recapped. "They've been tight with each other for generations, probably heavily intermarried and involved in each other's business affairs, maybe even more so than the Charleston norm—and that's saying something."

Charleston's upper crust was notoriously cliquish. Teag and I flitted around the very edges by virtue of Trifles and Folly's long history and the kind of heirloom goods we handled. Even Anthony's family, with their South of Broad social circle and Battery address weren't at the center of the local power brokers, though they were closer. Sorren had moved among that crowd in his very long life, and both Mrs. Morrissey and Alistair McKinnon came from old blood. Aiken sounded even more clannish, and that kind of exclusivity usually didn't bode well for uncovering secrets. I wondered how far Valerie's family connections would get us into such a tight-knit community.

We drove into downtown Aiken, a picturesque small town that obviously drew a well-heeled tourist trade, not unlike Charleston. Local boutiques, bistros, and bars lined the sidewalks. The old brick buildings with their colorful awnings were well-maintained, with window boxes and planters for a dash of color. Fancifully-painted statues of horses were everywhere. If Valerie hailed from around here, her love of all things horse-related came naturally.

"Valerie is meeting us at the bed and breakfast where she's staying," I relayed. "She'll go out to the stables with us."

The charming downtown and the many lovely B&Bs made me decide to add Aiken to my mental list of places to take Kell on a getaway weekend. From the way Teag noted the restaurants and commented on a few of the shops, I figured he had the same idea for a mini-vacation with Anthony. After we settled all the strange goings-on, we'd both need some time off.

Valerie waited on a porch swing on the wide veranda of a beautiful white Victorian clapboard turned into the Bluebells Bed and Breakfast. A well-managed cottage garden in the front sported color and blooms, and pretty decorative flags fluttered as wind chimes made bell-like sounds in the breeze.

"Teag! Cassidy! Thank you so much for coming." Valerie hopped down from the swing and headed for us before we'd barely gotten out of the car. She looked worried, and between the strange apparitions causing problems for the tours in Charleston and now trouble for a family member, I imagine she'd been under a lot of stress.

"Of course," I reassured her. "We did some research on the way, and I brought Teag up to speed after our phone call. What now?"

Valerie managed a tired smile. "Ronnie Harrison, my cousin's husband—and the owner of the stables—is meeting us for lunch out at the clubhouse. He's eager to meet you. I told him a little bit about your gift, but since he's a big donor to a lot of local history non-profits, he already knew Mrs. Morrison and Alistair from the museum, and they've sung your praises."

"I hope we can help," I said. Our abilities went far beyond what Valerie or the others knew, but with luck, none of those "extras" would be necessary.

"If Ronnie's married to your cousin, isn't he a bit young to be running such a big operation?" Teag asked as we drove.

"Ronnie's the public face for the stables, but everyone knows that the real power lies in his grandfather, Norris. The man is ancient. He outlived Ronnie's father, and he'll probably outlive the rest of us," she said. "Mean as a snake. He'd still be running the business if he could, but he's had a series of strokes and can't get out of bed."

"So Ronnie handles the day to day stuff—" I started.

"But the big decisions—and the real money—goes through Norris," Valerie confirmed. "No one sees him except Ronnie and the nurses who care for Norris. And from what I've heard, no one misses him, either."

When we drove through the wrought iron gates at the end of the long driveway to Harrison Stables, it felt like entering another world. An allée of live oak trees hung over the winding drive, leading up to the big house with white pillars that was the original Harrison home and now served as the clubhouse. Off in the distance, down another gated road, I saw the new—and even more grand—homestead. Betting on the track might be for suckers, but apparently owning the horses paid big.

I followed Valerie up the steps into the club. Inside the atmosphere was dark wood, leather chairs, and paint the color of the felt on a pool table. In other words, it felt like a rich man's den, minus the cigar smoke.

A tall, dark-haired man came striding toward us as if he owned the place, and I figured him for Ronnie Harrison. "Valerie!" he called out, greeting her with a hug. He turned to me and extended his hand. "You must be Ms. Kincaid."

"Cassidy," I replied, shaking his hand.

"And Teag Logan," Valerie added, leading to another round of handshaking.

"Ronnie," he answered. He stood aside and waved us past him into what I guessed was his office. "Come on in. Thank you for coming." He motioned for us to sit in the very comfortable leather chairs in front of his desk, while he sat in his expensively ergonomic office chair.

Ronnie's office smelled like tack oil and bourbon. Paintings of horses and fox hunters covered his walls, and I noted that they all appeared to be original oils. Crystal decanters on an antique mahogany stand held liquor, with engraved silver tags to mark the types. Ronnie's burled wood desk had to be at least a hundred and fifty years old, fine craftsmanship, famous maker.

"The desk's been in my family for a long time," Ronnie remarked, noting my interest.

I grinned. "Sorry. Antiques are my business, and I can't switch off my mental appraisal."

"No offense taken," he assured me. Ronnie's voice sounded deep and smooth, with the softened consonants and easy cadence of the old patrician South. "Valerie's told me a lot about you. I'm so glad you came."

I cleared my throat. Willing as I was to help out Valerie's friend, I needed to be honest. "I'm not a detective, Ronnie. I run an antique store. I'm glad to help any way I can, but surely there are people who are better qualified."

Ronnie leaned forward, resting his forearms on the desk. "I've already talked to those 'qualified' people, Cassidy, and they've drawn a blank. Local police, state police, even the FBI because of the dollar amount involved, and no one's turned up anything. We went so far as to ask them to check into the possibility that organized crime might have had something to do with the horse theft, because of track betting. Nothing."

He met my gaze. "This isn't about the money. We run a family business, and that includes the horses and the dogs. Their bloodlines go all the way back with ours, and there's a bond there at least as strong as what most people feel for their pets, maybe stronger. We raised those horses from foals, put a lifetime of knowledge and effort into training them, caring for them. Same with the dogs. To have them gone, no idea what happened or whether they're all right," his voice broke. "I can't let it go."

I liked Ronnie, and his grief over the missing animals made my decision for me. "I'm a psychometric. I can read the memories and...energy...of objects by touching them. Not all objects have resonance—imprinted images. Most don't." And that was a good thing, or I'd probably go mad. "The pieces that have the strongest resonance either are connected to vivid memories of important events or were part of a tragedy." I decided to leave out curses and magic for now.

"All right." Ronnie didn't bat an eye at my revelation. "Valerie didn't give me that much detail, but she told me you've uncovered evidence to solve crimes, and I'm desperate, Cassidy. I went to a Tarot reader my assistant swears by, and she told me the cards spoke of secrets, curses, and old grudges. So my takeaway is that the answers aren't going to be conventional."

He sat up, grief etched on his face. "I want my horses and dogs back safely. But if that's not possible, I need to know what happened."

I didn't need to know anything about horse racing to appreciate the sentiment behind his words. "I'll do everything I can to try to give you that," I replied. "Just as long as you realize, I can't promise."

"That's enough," Ronnie said.

He placed a call, instructing someone to meet us at the barns, and then stood. We followed him back outside, and as we crossed the yard toward the nearest barn, Ronnie constantly waved or smiled at the people we passed who hailed him by name. Ronnie chatted as we walked, filling us in on the essentials of the racing season. I listened in fascination since I knew nothing about horse racing. At the same time, I kept my Gift near the surface, casting out my senses as I walked, alert for anything that felt off.

Teag walked beside me, and I wished we had enough privacy for me to ask for his take on what he saw. He'd been quiet in Ronnie's office, and since Valerie didn't know about his Weaver magic, he didn't volunteer any insights. Maybe she and Ronnie thought he was there for backup, but I knew in my gut that all the weirdness going on had something to do not only with Weaving, but with Teag himself. I didn't want to let him out of my sight unless I handed him off to Sorren or someone with even stronger magic than mine. So the reality was, we were watching each other's backs, as usual.

All around us, the stables hummed with activity. The air smelled of horses and feed, straw and worn leather. Trainers led horses from one place to another, and the animals were beautiful enough to be swoonworthy. I could believe each one was worth a small fortune, not for their prowess on the race track, but because they were magnificent creatures, all sleek muscle and sinuous power. Maybe I'd take up watching the Derby, I mused. If nothing else, it offered the opportunity for Mint Juleps and fancy hats.

"Cassidy, Valerie, Teag, I'd like you to meet Corbin Hahn, our head groundsman," Ronnie said as a man stepped out of the stable to greet us. Hahn was a sturdy man in his middle years, with a shock of white hair tucked beneath a cabbie hat and bushy gray eyebrows over piercingly blue eyes. He defined "craggy," a weathered face with plenty of character, a strong jaw, and fine lines around his eyes from squinting at the sun. With his tweed shooting jacket, Wellington boots, and a shotgun broken open across his left arm, Hahn might have stepped out of central casting from the BBC.

"They're here to see if they can shed some light on the disappearances," Ronnie said. Hahn raised an eyebrow, but if he wondered how, exactly, he said nothing. "Can you tell them what you saw the night things happened?"

Hahn cleared his throat. "I'd gone to check on the horses," he said, and I only realized I'd been expecting an English or Scottish accent when he spoke with a Texas twang. "We bring them in every night, of course. I'd gotten out to the north paddock ahead of the handlers, and while I don't deal with the horses myself, I've got the keys and codes to all the gates." He jangled a large ring at his belt. "For security reasons, very few people have access."

"And the horses were fine when you got there," Teag prompted.

Hahn nodded. "Yes. I'd been nearby all day, overseeing some crews trimming up the cemetery over the rise from there and clearing away brush from the access roads. But I keep an eye on the horses, and on the kennels too. We all do. We're all rather protective of them."

I understood. I suspected that everyone who made a career with Harrison Stables cared about the animals—except for, perhaps, the foxes.

"What then?" Teag asked.

"The trailers were due right around dusk. I went down to open the gate for them," Hahn recalled. "I had a bad feeling, like something was wrong." He gave a wry smile. "My mother would have said 'someone walked over your grave.' So I was antsy, looking around waiting for something to happen."

We stayed quiet, letting him tell the story at his own pace. "The wind picked up, which was odd because it had been still all day. And then I heard hounds howling nearby, which I knew wasn't right. The kennels can be noisy, and sometimes the noise carries, but it wouldn't have sounded that close."

Hahn looked away as if he expected us to doubt his story. "That's when I heard hoof beats. I thought maybe something spooked the horses I'd come to get, and they were running toward me. But when I looked out across the pasture, I could see them still toward the middle, and no others in sight." He paused. "The hoof beats got louder, like a whole herd heading for me, and the wind almost knocked me over. The dogs barked and howled like crazy. I was worried about the horses, that we might be having some kind of freak microburst storm and they'd get hurt."

"What happened?" Teag asked.

"One minute, the horses were there. And the next—the pasture was empty," Hahn said, leveling a look at us that dared us to contradict him.

"Just, gone?" Valerie asked.

Hahn nodded. "I couldn't believe it, either. The wind died down, and so did the barking. I ran out across the pasture. I thought maybe that the horses had been knocked over, or lay down to get out of the wind. But they weren't there. The hoof prints stopped, and there weren't any more. Just gone."

"Do you have any theories?" I asked.

Hahn hesitated and then shook his head. "No. But I can tell you nothing normal took those horses—or the dogs."

"The kennel master tells a similar story," Ronnie said. "The dogs started barking like they'd lost their minds, and when he went back to check on them, some of the hounds were missing, even though the lock was in place, the fencing hadn't been tampered with, and he and his staff had been there all night."

"We definitely need to see that pasture," Teag said.

"I've got a truck ready for you, Mr. Harrison," Hahn said. "I'll meet you out at the north paddock." He looked relieved, I thought, to have the storytelling over with.

I nodded toward the shotgun he carried. "What's that for?"

Hahn shrugged. "Coyotes, mostly. Raccoons, sometimes. They make a mess of things. And groundhogs."

"Groundhogs?" Teag asked. I was puzzled, too. They didn't strike me as much of a menace.

"They're the worst," Hahn said. "Burrow under the ground, and then a horse puts his foot down, and the surface collapses, and you've got a broken leg."

I could understand how, at a horse farm that would make groundhogs into Public Enemy Number One.

We got into the truck with Ronnie, and Hahn waved us off. I sat up front with Ronnie, while Valerie and Teag climbed in the back. I looked over at Ronnie. "Do you believe Hahn, about the horses?"

He nodded. "I believe it's what he saw, or what he can remember," Ronnie said. "But there's got to be something else because horses don't vanish into thin air."

The north paddock was a distance from where we'd come in. Flat pastures stretched out in all directions, with neat, white wooden fences dividing them into sections. Feed bins and watering troughs awaited the next horses to enjoy an outing. Teag and I scanned the horizon. We were miles from nowhere, on roads that only ran within the farm, far from public thoroughfares. It shouldn't have been possible for anyone to be able to spirit off three huge horses without a trailer or, hell, a military helicopter.

Ronnie parked on the road, and we climbed the steel tube gate, leaving it locked. I bent to examine the fastening. No scratches or signs of forced entry, or of a recent lock replacement. I looked down along the fence line, and the wood appeared sturdy and undamaged.

"Over here." We followed Ronnie as he strode toward the center of the paddock. Ronnie wore the same high Wellington boots as Hahn, but the rest of us picked our way carefully, mindful of the piles of horse manure.

"According to Hahn, the horses were right in this area," Ronnie said, coming to a stop about two-thirds of the way across the paddock. "And he was back by the gate."

I looked toward where we left the truck and wondered when Hahn would join us. The distance between where we stood and where we parked wasn't terribly far; certainly close enough for someone on the road to have a clear view of horses standing where we were. Behind the road rose a slight ridge with a few trees on top, and I thought I made out the edge of an old cast iron fence.

"Is that a cemetery up there?" I pointed.

"Yes, but not for people," Ronnie replied. "Ian Harrison, my great, great-grandfather buried his hunting dogs up there. He was quite fond of his dogs, and said they'd like a nice view of the paddocks, so they could stay close to the horses and hear the wind in the trees. So that's where generations of Harrison hounds have their final resting place. The kennel is about half a mile off to the left," he added, pointing.

The day had grown gloomy, with clouds dimming the light, making it seem much later than it was. It felt colder than when we left the club-house, and I looked around at the pasture, alert for trouble, and saw nothing. Teag also had tensed, and I saw him scan for danger, then return his attention, scowling as if he had missed something.

"There isn't much to get a reading from," I said, looking at the ground around our feet. "I usually get a clearer image from an object, but I'll try." I'd picked up on resonance from the ground before, but that was most likely to happen when something truly terrible had occurred in a location, like a murder or a catastrophic accident. Still, Ronnie and Hahn seemed so worried about their horses and dogs; I had to make an effort.

"You haven't found any strange pieces of cloth around, have you?" Teag asked. Both Valerie and Ronnie looked perplexed.

"No. Why?"

Teag shook his head. "We've had some unusual things happen lately in Charleston, and then found odd bits of fabric nearby afterward that shouldn't have been there. Don't know what it means, but thought it might be part of a pattern."

"Sorry, no," Ronnie repeated. "My people would have brought something like that to me immediately, because it would suggest there'd been trespassers. And with the disappearances, everyone's been on edge. We wouldn't take unauthorized visitors lightly at any time, for the safety of the animals, but now, our security guards are armed."

I tuned out their conversation, and focused on my gift, concentrating on the ground around me. I walked slowly, moving back and forth across the area until something pinged my inner sight. When I felt the tug at my energy, I closed my eyes and gave it my full attention.

Fear, primal and panicked, shot through me. I felt my heartbeat spike and my breathing speed up. I saw the wind whip through the grass, raising dust. Dogs barked, warning of intruders. Then I caught a glimpse of something I couldn't completely process. A dark, fleeting shadow barreled right at me, and I felt as if I stood in front of a stampede. Nothing could withstand its power, dark and ancient, and while part of my hindbrain rightly feared this energy, another part wanted to be swept away in its wake.

As quickly as it came, the vision vanished, and I realized I was shivering. The temperature had plummeted, and my breath misted, although the day hadn't started out nearly that cold.

"Did you see anything?" Teag asked, stressed enough that I knew he was still on guard.

"Yeah, but let's get out of here. I'll tell you all about it back at the clubhouse." Instinct told me we needed to get the hell out of there.

We headed back to the road, going through the fence gate a short distance from Ronnie's truck. I heard a low growl, and then the wind carried the smell of rotting flesh. Teag and I moved in front of Ronnie and Valerie as a dozen nightmarish hounds came over the hill. Their howl sent a chill down my back, and for a moment I thought we might be facing zombies. Then I realized that I could see through their ghastly, emaciated bodies. The ghost hounds' skin sank between their ribs and pulled tight across their skulls. Eyeless skulls turned toward us, fixing us by scent, or maybe our heartbeats.

The ghost dogs came at us in a gray horde, rushing down the hillside from the cemetery, heading straight for us. I let my athame drop down into my hand, and sent a blast of force, scattering the hounds, but only for a moment. Teag snapped his silver whip, but iron worked better against ghosts, and the specters barely slowed.

"Oh. My. God," Valerie gasped, her voice trembling. "Those are ghosts. Real ghosts."

"What the hell is going on?" Ronnie demanded, and I figured anger covered his fear. "What are those things?"

"Dangerous," I replied. "Stay back and let us handle this."

The ghostly dogs snapped their teeth and lowered their heads, and while I wasn't sure how solidly they could manifest, I didn't want to find out close-up. I blasted them again with my athame, and hurled a handful of salt, forcing them to slow their advance. Teag laid down a salt line between them and us, but the revenants were between us and Ronnie's car, so trapping us in a circle wouldn't do much good.

The boom of a shotgun made me jump. I heard the slide of the reload, and then another blast, right into the thick of the ghost hound pack. The spirits vanished, leaving behind nothing but a spray of iron buckshot.

Hahn came tromping down from a path near the dog cemetery. He glared at the empty place on the road where the dogs had been, as if to dare them to re-materialize. When they did not, he lowered his shotgun but did not break it over his arm. "Get in the truck," he ordered, planting himself between us and the cemetery, gun in hand.

Teag and I hustled Ronnie and Valerie into the truck. Valerie looked dangerously pale and her hands trembled. Ronnie had gone gray, but the set of his jaw and the spark in his eyes told me he had channeled the fear into anger at the mistreatment of his precious animals. Hahn jumped into the bed, and we roared out. I kept checking the mirrors, expecting the spectral pack to give chase, but to my relief, the road remained clear.

"What the hell happened back there?" Ronnie demanded. He had a white-knuckled grip on the steering wheel, and from the tension in his jaw and how rigidly he held himself, I suspected he didn't like not being in control.

"The kind of stuff Cassidy and Teag deal with all the time," Valerie replied before I had a chance to speak. Her voice quavered a little, but I heard steel beneath the fear.

Ronnie glanced at me. "Really? This is normal for you?"

I grimaced. "I'd say 'common' more than 'normal,'" I replied because being chased by rotting hounds wasn't really "normal" in anyone's experience. "And we've seen worse."

"Why did they go away when Hahn shot them? I didn't think you could hurt a ghost."

"Iron buckshot," Teag replied. "Something about iron seems to scramble the 'signal' for ghosts. Salt can do it, too, but we didn't have enough of it."

"Why did something disturb the dogs?" Ronnie's anger had begun to fade, and now he seemed genuinely distressed over whatever had interrupted the animals' final rest.

"I think it's all connected." I was hesitant to say too much without having an answer. "The missing horses, the strange noises and odd winds, the vanishing hunting dogs. Some very unusual things are going on—here and in Charleston, maybe elsewhere. We're trying to put the pieces together to stop whoever's doing this before it gets even worse."

"The horses and the dogs—do you think we'll get them back?"

I could tell from his voice that Ronnie cared about more than the animals' dollar value. "If we're lucky," I replied, although I thought the odds were against it. "We'll do our best to find them."

He gave a curt nod, and I figured that he knew their chances were slim. "Thank you." He paused. "How do we protect the others?"

"I've heard that horse folks are superstitious," I ventured. "Is that true?

Ronnie chuckled. "Oh, yeah. The colors riders wear, how many white 'stockings' a horse has, how horses are named…the list of super-stitions goes on and on. Why?"

"Because some people might consider the kinds of protections we can put down to be 'superstitious,' but they've been handed down through generations for a reason. They work," I replied.

"What kind of things?" he asked, and Valerie leaned forward to hear.

"Tell me, too. Drea and I can use them at the barn to protect the carriage horses," she said.

"Go buy some big canisters of table salt. Set down a line across the doors to the barn, and across the stall doors," I said.

"Iron buckshot works on the ghosts, but so do shells filled with rock salt," Teag added. Normally, he'd have offered to leave behind some spelled cords or pieces of cloth with magic woven into them. But now, with the possibility of a rogue, malicious Weaver witch, calling attention to any link with his magic might increase the risk.

"Silver and agate are protective," I continued. "Agate is pretty easy to get in bulk, especially if you've got a shop nearby that caters to people who make jewelry for a hobby. Those stores sell gemstones by the strand. If you can put some silver and agate on each of the horses, it could help. Might protect the people guarding them, too. And if you can't put a charm on the dogs' collars, then at least put something on their kennel."

Ronnie laughed. "As superstitions go, those are pretty tame. Do you think they'll help?"

I sighed. "I think that whoever's behind this is very powerful. But I've seen salt and charms stop some very scary things, so while it's not foolproof, you'd be better off than you are now."

"We'll do it," Ronnie promised. "I'm sure right now my folks will do damn near anything to protect the animals and keep people from getting hurt."

"Drea and I will make sure we put all that in place back at the barn as well," Valerie promised. "Thank you both."

"You're very welcome," Teag replied. "And when we stop whoever's behind this, you'll be the first to know."

CHAPTER ELEVEN

"FIND ANYTHING NEW?" I ASKED AS I CAME INTO THE SHOP IN THE morning. Teag was already at the break room table intent on his laptop, and the smell of fresh coffee wafted to me as soon as I opened the door.

"Actually, yes," he replied. "I did a little hacking after work last night before Anthony got home, and I found out that Harrison Stables isn't the only place missing a few horses or hunting dogs under mysterious circumstances. Not only that, but there's been a spike in missing persons' reports around Charleston in the last month."

"Oh?" I poured myself a cup and came to sit next to him.

"Yeah. And when I looked at what the victims have in common, they're all men, all from families of some prominence, and all equestrians—different kinds of riding, but especially fox hunting."

"Surprise, surprise," I murmured, and sipped my coffee. "So what's the link between our Weaver witch and the horse thief? Or between that dark-haired woman and tall man Marcella saw in her vision? I don't get the connection."

"Neither do I—yet," Teag replied, and I could tell from the look on his face that he was taking this whole thing personally because of the Weaver connection. Since Teag had recognized his magic and begun to hone his craft, he'd come to see it as an extension of himself, something almost sacred. Watching someone do harm with that power or use it for the wrong purposes, made him determined to stop them.

"Drea and Valerie put all the protections in place at the carriage horse barn," I reported. I'd stopped by the night before to check over their preparations. Their barn holds such positive resonance; I didn't have any trouble using my own mojo to juice up the power of their charms.

"Any word from Sorren?"

I shook my head. "No, and his voicemail must be full from my reports. All I can think of is that he's onto something, and he's chasing down his own set of leads."

Teag leaned back and stretched, yawning wide.

"You look beat."

He shrugged. "I was up late. Mrs. Teller and Niella and I have been working overtime to weave pieces to replace the cursed fabric Ryan's been finding, and put some good mojo back in circulation."

"There's more?"

He nodded. "Yeah. Didn't you check your email?" At my chagrined look, he tutted in mock judgment, like we didn't have enough going on. "Ryan and Kell have been finding bits of funky cloth in odd places, and getting rid of the pieces like we showed them." He pushed the laptop to face me, and tapped a few buttons, revealing some recent news articles. "I think it's working. It's even made the nightly news that the 'grouch flu' as they're calling it seems to be going away."

"Grouch flu?" I rolled my eyes. "Anything for ratings, right?" I considered Teag's comment as I savored my coffee. "So you and Mrs. Teller and Niella have been weaving replacement cloth?" Teag nodded. "What's to keep our phantom Weaver from swapping them out again?"

Teag shrugged. "Technically, nothing. But I think the discord was either a diversion or a way to gin up some cheap negative energy that could be siphoned off to give the spell caster a quick power boost. The cursed cloth would have slowly lost its power over time, although that could have taken weeks."

"Tell that to the people in jail for assault thanks to cursed pieces like Opal Lady's shawl," I replied.

"Speaking of which, there've been several new arrests for everything from bar fights to domestic violence—all with bits of woven fabric found on the people who started the brawl."

I ran a hand through my hair. "We've got to figure out what's going on. And I can't shake the feeling this is the warm-up to something a lot worse."

"Yeah, me too," Teag agreed. "On the bright side, I slept better last night," he said. "Anthony told me what you did. Thank you again."

I squeezed his hand. "Anything to help. Glad it made a difference. Rowan stopped by and took the safe, so she might be able to make something of the hex charm before Sorren gets back."

I pulled an old book out of my bag and flipped it open to a picture. The pen-and-ink drawing showed a cavalcade of spectral riders and ghostly horses led by a frightening cloaked figure, with a terrifying pack of hellhounds running alongside. "I keep looking at the evidence, and it always brings me back to this."

Teag looked up and met my gaze. "The Wild Hunt?"

"It fits," I replied, wishing I had a better suggestion. "Missing people, taken by the Master of the Hunt. Horses and dogs snatched away into another realm, and a destructive force of incredible power, unleashed to bring a 'reaping' down on a helpless population."

Teag knew the myths as well as I did. The Wild Hunt showed up in a number of Western European legends. Some claimed it was led by Odin, others said Perchta, while still more tales claimed the Erlking or other notables among the Fey. The Hunt harvested souls—willing or not—to ride with them in the Afterlife, and showed up periodically to wreak havoc during autumn nights. As threats went, the Wild Hunt rated up there with a natural disaster as a destructive force.

"But why?" Teag wondered aloud. "And why now? Someone's going to a lot of trouble to call down the Hunt, and we know damn well it's not an every-year occurrence. So who benefits? And what's the goal?"

"There's got to be a reason this all connects back to those prominent families," I mused. "And when the same names keep coming up, odds are good that someone back in the day really did make a deal with the Devil—or some other supernatural power."

"Do you think Mrs. Morrissey would know where to find the dirty laundry about this?" Teag asked.

"I bet we could narrow it down if we look at the families involved." I paused to finish my coffee, then stood to pour myself another cup. "And if it is the Wild Hunt, then it might have been summoned before. So we need to look for patterns."

"But what does a Weaver have to do with the Wild Hunt?" Teag asked. "And why would someone want to call up the Hunt? If someone wanted revenge, there are a lot easier ways to get it."

"Maybe we need to have pizza night at my house, and pull out the big whiteboard," I suggested. "You, Anthony, Kell, Maggie. Lay everything out on my dining room table and then tape the pieces up on the whiteboard when we find patterns."

"Works for me," Teag said. "It was my turn to make dinner, and I don't feel like cooking. I was probably stopping for take-out anyhow."

The rest of the day proved uneventful, although the store stayed busy. Maggie had the day off, well-deserved, but she insisted on coming over for pizza to help look for some clue to what the hell was going on. I still had a knot in my gut telling me we hadn't seen the worst yet. So far, we'd assembled a lot of puzzle pieces, without any idea of what the big picture was supposed to be. I couldn't shake the feeling that we were missing the key, the heart of the problem, and once we figured out what it was, the rest would all fall into place.

Now I had to hope that once we figured out what was going on, we still had time to stop it.

I EXPECTED AN UNEVENTFUL EVENING. We closed up on time, agreeing to meet back at my place in an hour to map our findings on the whiteboard. Teag headed in one direction, and I turned in another, intending to pick up some snacks to add to the pizza.

A large, solid object fell from the sky into the oncoming lane of traffic. I jammed on my brakes, as did the driver coming my way. I heard the screech of tires and smelled burning rubber, then looked up to see the pale, panicked face of the driver through the windshield.

Shit. Whatever fell had been big. I got out of my car and looked up to see clear sky above me. No overhead wires, no skybridge, or even a passing airplane in sight. But the thing that dropped out of the sky had looked much larger than a bird, even if an eagle somehow had a heart attack and died over downtown Charleston.

Then the screaming started.

I moved around my car door, as the other motorists crowded closer. My stomach lurched, and I felt very glad I hadn't eaten yet.

Sprawled on the asphalt was a body, none the better for having fallen to the ground from a height.

"Do you think he was alive when he hit?" A woman asked from beside, morbidly curious.

"No. I'm sure he didn't feel a thing," I assured her. I could offer that opinion in confidence, because given the advanced decomposition of the splattered corpse, I'd say the poor fellow had already been dead for a long time.

Traffic snarled since we couldn't exactly go anywhere without driving over the remains. Sirens wailed, and the onlookers had started to pull out their cell phones to snap photos or upload video. I got back in the car and called Teag.

"I might be late for pizza," I told him.

"Something wrong?"

"A dead man just fell out of the sky in front of my car."

I heard Anthony's voice in the background give a startled yelp and call for Teag. A few seconds later, Teag returned his attention to my call. "Um, you're not going to believe this—"

"Try me."

"You're not the only one. It's on the news. At least three bodies reported so far, and more calls coming in."

"I can guarantee you, this guy didn't hide in the wheel well of a passing jetliner," I said, recalling an incident in the headlines a few years past.

"How do you know?"

I sighed. "He's been dead longer than disco."

"So you're stuck 'till the cops clear the area?"

"'Fraid so," I replied. "And a little longer, because I'm not coming home before I drive through a car wash."

It took more than an hour for the police to cordon off the area, take the statements of those with a front-row seat, and get the situation under control. In the end, since I couldn't move my car without driving over gobbets of fallen dead guy, the cops impounded my car and the other car that had been right up front, told me to call the station in the morning to see when I could get it back, and sent me on my way. Teag came to pick me up, waiting on the outskirts of the blocked-off area.

"Wow. That's pretty rank," Teag said as his eyes teared up when I opened the passenger door.

I'd doused a tissue with potent hand cream so I could hold it against my nose to overpower the smell, but even that couldn't cover the stench. "Yeah. And worse, it's so strong it's a taste."

"Ewwww. Any idea what happened?" Teag asked as we drove away. The influx of police cars and news vans made it impossible to move quickly.

"I wasn't scanning the sky at the instant he fell," I admitted, "but I can't come up with any non-supernatural explanation. So I'm pretty sure this is our kind of problem, and odds are, it's connected to the rest of the weirdness."

"Pretty sure you're right," Teag agreed, then cursed under his breath as a news team car cut him off, gridlocking the intersection. "Oh, and right before you called, there was a segment on the news about animal control getting a flood of phone calls about howling dogs."

"Dogs?"

He nodded. "People have been calling in from all over the area about packs of dogs barking and howling, and how someone needs to do something about it. Only when the animal control people get there, they can't find any dogs—or wolves, coyotes, or anything else. Not a sign of them."

"Curiouser and curiouser," I mused. "So here's my question—if the police can identify the splattered dead men, want to bet they match names on your missing persons list?"

"IDing them isn't going to be easy, between the decomp and the impact," Teag replied. "If they hit hard enough, even dental records could be a challenge."

"If they've been missing long enough, dental records might not even be an option," I pointed out.

"It's going to take time for the forensics teams to match anything," Teag said. "We may not have the information soon." I knew he was thinking what I'd been thinking—that everything seemed to be accelerating toward some warped grand finale that we were guaranteed not to like.

"And we've got no idea what the timeline is, or the game plan," I answered, leaning back in the seat and closing my eyes. "Shit. Is it bad that right now I care more about getting a shower and lighting incense to make the smell go away than I do about saving the world?"

Teag grinned. "Seems logical to me."

While I showered, Teag used my laptop. By the time I came back, clean and drenched in perfume, he met me with a triumphant grin. "Well?" I asked. "Don't look smug. Share with the class."

"It's not much, but I picked up some chatter on the police radios," Teag replied. "A couple of the bodies had wallets on them. Both names match missing men on my list—ties to prominent families, horse enthusiasts, missing for two years and six years, respectively. I haven't heard anything on the other bodies, but I'll keep checking."

A knock at the door prompted Teag to put away his laptop since he didn't want to explain his unauthorized access to Anthony. Everyone showed up one after the other, and all anyone could talk about was the bodies falling out of thin air.

Even the delivery guy who brought the pizzas had to ask if I'd heard about the dead guys. I dodged the question, gave him a nice tip, and sent him on his way. Most people would avoid talking about something so gross over dinner, but not my friends. We debated possible methods and motives, tried to figure out whether the locations where the bodies fell held a hidden meaning and brainstormed why the corpses would be "released" now as opposed to any other time.

When we finished eating, I dragged out the whiteboard and markers. We all voted Maggie the official artist since she had the best handwriting. She sat on a chair next to the board, while Teag, Anthony, Kell, and I took up the rest of the couch. Baxter moved from lap to lap, trying to con everyone out of treats.

Maggie organized our information into lists and marked key locations on a big map of Charleston that we taped up on the wall. She drew lines to connect related items, and I couldn't help thinking about all the TV shows I'd seen where the FBI agent—or the obsessed killer —papers his walls with clippings and printouts and builds a web of yarn and pushpins to tie the evidence together.

"That looks more like spaghetti," Anthony observed after a few hours, looking up at the multi-colored scribbles on the big whiteboard. He sat on the floor, leaning back between Teag's knees as Teag sat on the couch. The board was vivid proof that while we had a lot of information, we were still missing the "glue" to make it stick together.

I looked away from the whiteboard to the big map. Maggie had dutifully marked the cemeteries where the zombies and ghouls had risen, the sightings of black dogs and phantom hounds, as well as the Nicholson plantation. Smaller dots noted where Ryan and Kell's groups had found cursed fabric, and where the dead men dropped from the sky, as well as the Museum and Archive since they'd been part of this whole mess, too. Harrison Stables, off in Aiken, was a red "X" in the corner of the map.

"Hand me a pencil," I said, as I studied the map. Everyone watched me expectantly as I walked over and drew a big circle around the locations of the phenomena. Then I took a green marker and made a dot in the center.

"What's in the middle?" Anthony asked, shifting to have a better view.

I met Teag's gaze. "Trifles and Folly," I replied. "We're the epicenter."

"How is that possible?" Maggie asked, looking troubled. "We haven't taken in any super strange pieces lately, have we?"

Teag and I shook our heads, equally perplexed. "In fact, I'd say that we've gotten in fewer items with bad mojo in the past couple of weeks than usual." Fortunately, only a small number of truly dangerous items came into the shop, but those were doozies. Most of the items that we dealt with either carried very negative energy or had a tragic history. We cleansed them when we could, and got rid of them permanently when we couldn't.

"The Museum and the Archive had pieces stolen that hailed from the same time period—the Viking invasions," I mused aloud.

"So we're back to the Norse *Seiðrs*," Teag muttered. "Great."

I came back to my seat and looked at the whiteboard. "Someone's charged their power by draining energy from pieces at the Archive and Museum that had good juju. They got another boost from creating the 'grouch flu.' And if making the racehorses and hunting dogs disappear means someone is gearing up for the Wild Hunt, then what about the guys who fell out of the sky today? Did they get bumped from their spot in the hunting party to make room for fresh meat?"

"That doesn't match the stories about the Hunt," Kell replied. I could count on him to know his ghost lore. "Most stories associate the Hunt with the harvest season, but the timing is at the choice of the Master of the Hunt, who isn't mortal. The legends all deal with how to stay away from the Hunt so you won't be taken. I don't remember reading anything about being able to summon it—or why you'd want to."

"And what does the Wild Hunt have to do with Weaver magic?" Teag asked. I knew the connection bothered him, and while I wasn't going to mention his dreams in front of the others, I could see the strain in his eyes. "The *Seiðrs* were sorceresses and prophets. How are they involved?"

I looked at the "spaghetti" mess on the whiteboard and felt a pang of hopelessness. We had organized and reviewed lots of data and dispelled the "grouch flu," but we didn't seem any closer to the heart of the problem than when we started.

My phone buzzed, and I saw that the new text was from Sorren. "He says that the Viking connection is important, and to keep our distance from Secona or anything to do with the *Seiðrs* until he can chase down the lead he's following. And he agrees that Weaver magic is at the heart of the situation and that Teag needs to be especially careful," I read the message aloud.

By eleven, we all agreed we'd done as much as we could with the information that we had, and decided to call it a night. I couldn't avoid feeling frustrated, because the answers were important and they remained out of reach. Gradually everyone drifted off, even Kell, who had an important interview with a TV producer involving a possible new shoot about SPOOK early in the morning. Finally, only Teag, Anthony, and I were left. We all pitched in to pick up any remaining glasses and dishes, avoiding the whiteboard like it was the elephant in the room.

My phone chirped as I walked toward the door with Teag and Anthony. Teag turned toward me as I answered, and when I saw that Alicia Peters, our medium friend, was calling, I gestured for them to wait.

"Alicia? Are you okay? What's up?" I put the call on speaker.

"Cassidy? I tried to ignore them, but they won't leave me alone." Alicia's voice sounded ragged, and I exchanged a worried look with Teag.

"Who won't leave you alone?" I asked, worried.

"The ghosts," Alicia replied, dropping her voice as if afraid to be overheard. "They're all stirred up, but that's not the worst of it." She paused to steady her voice. "I can feel a presence out there, something big. And it wants to speak through me."

"Can you tell whether it's friendly?" Teag chimed in, as Anthony hung back, waiting to take his cue from us on what happened next.

"No. I mean, it says it wants to help, and maybe that's true, but it's really strong. I don't dare let it in on my own."

She didn't have to explain. I thought that being a medium sounded terrifying. Being contacted by restless ghosts, allowing those spirits to speak to you either out loud or telepathically, or in the case of a séance, permitting another person's consciousness to slip into your body and control your words and actions. I couldn't begin to imagine the courage it had to take to handle that kind of a Gift, or what it must have been like growing up with that power and vulnerability. My own psychometry had its drawbacks, but I wouldn't trade my abilities for Alicia's for all the money in the world.

"How can we help?"

Alicia spoke quietly as if she were afraid someone might overhear. And maybe she was—only that "someone" was already dead. "Come get me. Please, can I stay with you? You've got the strongest wardings. And if Rowan and Donnelly are with me when I open the channel, I won't be afraid of losing control."

That Alicia, as strong as she was with her abilities, was afraid that she couldn't send a spirit packing after delivering its message made my stomach tighten. Then again, having a powerful witch and an immortal necromancer around for back-up would certainly boost confidence.

"We'll be there as soon as we can," I promised. Teag nodded in support, and Anthony shifted, stepping closer, silently letting me know he was coming, too. "Hang in there. We're coming."

I ended the call, then dialed Sorren and left a new message, in case Donnelly was still with him. As we grabbed coats and headed out the door, I texted both Rowan and Donnelly, asking them to come over to my house as soon as possible, that Alicia needed our help. Then we headed out to rescue one of the most powerful psychics I knew from an entity she feared might be even stronger.

CHAPTER TWELVE

ALICIA LIVED IN A MODEST WHITE CLAPBOARD NORTH OF DOWNTOWN, A quiet neighborhood that didn't look like a magnet for ghosts. I felt sure Alicia had put her own wardings and protections around her home—most practitioners did—but Sorren had seen to it that the wardings around my house and Teag and Anthony's home were exceptionally strong. Maybe it was time to think of expanding that level of protection to our friends.

"What does she mean, she's afraid of losing control?" Anthony asked as Teag drove toward Alicia's house. My car was still impounded for evidence and covered with dead-man guts.

"A medium communicates with the spirits of the dead," Teag replied. "To do that, she has to make herself vulnerable. Instead of raising her mental barriers to keep ghosts out, she has to lower her 'shields' to let them in so they can give her messages or speak through her."

Anthony looked horrified as if he had never thought about the mechanics of how a medium's gift actually worked. "You mean, the ghost possesses her?"

"Sometimes," I replied. "That's what happens in a séance. The medium calls for the spirit of the dead person, and then the ghost takes over to do the talking and answer questions."

"How can you be sure the ghost will let go when it's done?" Anthony asked, wide-eyed. "Can spirits lie?"

"Ghosts can lie," I assured him. "In most cases, the medium is strong enough to force the ghost out, or it doesn't want to stay once the message has been passed along. But there have been situations where the spirit tried to hijack the medium's body. Let's just say; it doesn't go well."

"Does it win?" Anthony pressed. "Can it force the medium out of her own body, or take over?"

Anthony had come a long way in his willingness to believe in the supernatural since he learned what Teag and I really do for a living. His fierce love for Teag made him open to accepting things others might find unbelievable. Still, I hated to see him lose his innocence and realize how dirty and dangerous it was to be, as he once termed it, a "supernatural vigilante."

"It can," Teag replied, never taking his eyes off the road. I sat in the back seat, leaning forward between him and Anthony. I saw the worry on Anthony's face, automatically translating any paranormal threat to figure out what risk it posed for Teag.

"That's why most mediums tell people not to mess with things like Ouija boards," Teag went on. "Because gifts usually come with some level of natural protection, an instinctive ability to shield, for example, and we learn to strengthen those barriers for self-preservation. But most people don't have that extra protection. So it's not good to be calling up strange spirits and inviting them in when you don't have the means to make them leave."

"I thought those things were just children's games," Anthony replied, stunned. "I mean, they sell them in the toy aisle."

"For most people, they probably are. But if you get someone with a little bit of talent and no training, and they happen to get the attention of a spirit with bad intentions—there can be problems."

Anthony stared out the passenger window in silence for a few blocks. "You said that Alicia's very powerful. So if she's afraid—"

I nodded. "Then she's sensing a very strong entity, one she's not sure she could control on her own. It's smart to call for back-up."

"Entity?" Anthony asked, turning to look at me. "Not 'ghost?'"

I shrugged. "The spirits of the dead aren't the only conscious presences out there. Some used to be human; some never were. That's where you get stories about angels and demons, gods and monsters. We're lucky that most of the time those old creatures leave us alone. But sometimes they wake up, and that's when trouble starts."

Teag double parked in front of a fire hydrant. Anthony's pained expression let me know that he noticed the infraction, but given the late hour and the urgent nature of our errand, he didn't mention it. At least Teag put on the four-ways.

"Stay here," Teag said, laying a hand on Anthony's shoulder. "When I get out, climb over to take the wheel. We might need to make a quick get-away."

"That's me. The wheelman," Anthony said with a sigh. He reached up to grab Teag's wrist. "Be careful," he said, with a glance to include me in the warning.

"We're here to walk her out," Teag assured, though his eyes held less confidence than his voice. "Come on, Cassidy. The sooner we go get her, the sooner we can be done for the night."

We came prepared. In addition to our usual protection charms—even Anthony carried onyx, agate, and silver on a regular basis now—we brought weapons. I had my athame and Bo's collar on my left wrist. I also had a big container of salt, and my plan was to lay a "salt carpet" down between the front door and the car, with some iron filings sprinkled in for good measure. That way, she could walk out protected against most ghosts.

Since we didn't know what this "entity" was, we brought some extra supplies. I had a squirt bottle of holy water and an iron knife. Teag had his silver whip as well as his spelled staff that tonight had a special iron cap, to dispel ghosts. Against most threats, that would have been overkill. I hoped it would be enough.

Anthony kept the car running. Alicia's home had a small yard and a white fence surrounding the property. While the fence might have looked decorative, I sensed the protective runes carved into the wood, the powdered plants and roots mixed in with the paint, and right behind it, the hedgerow of shrubs chosen for their protection against evil. Alicia hadn't been sloppy with her magic, and I worried about the kind of presence that could make her feel insecure behind her wardings.

My concern that the sentry spells might not allow us to enter eased when we were able to pass without harm. We hurried to the door. I kept checking over my shoulder, unable to shake the feeling that we were being watched.

Alicia was waiting for us, with her purse and a small overnight bag. "Thanks for coming," she said, glancing nervously one way and then the other as she stepped out onto the porch before locking the door behind her. "Sorry to invite myself over, but—"

"Any time," I assured her. "Let's go."

The feeling of being watched grew stronger as we crossed the yard. I couldn't tell whether the watcher was friend or foe, but I felt certain someone was out there, and that we'd drawn their attention. From the stiff way Teag held his shoulders and the tension in his body as he readied for a fight, I knew he sensed the same threat.

"Almost there," Teag said as we reached the gate. "We laid down salt and iron. Stay in the center. We'll flank you. It's only a few feet from the gate to the car. It's gonna be all right."

I felt a shift in the energy around me as Teag swung the gate open, breaking the warding. We stepped outside onto the wide swath of white crystals and dark metal flecks, and the air seemed to crackle. The gate closed behind us.

Everything happened at once.

An opaque, black cloud settled over us, so dark that I couldn't see the house or the car, though I knew they were only a few feet away. I couldn't even see Teag or Alicia, but the crunch of their feet on the salt gave me courage. The night air grew frigid, so cold I thought it might draw the warmth out of the marrow of my bones.

The air stirred. Teag let out a cry of pain and surprise, and I heard a struggle.

"Teag!" I yelled, stepping in front of where I knew Alicia stood, grabbing for Teag's shirt. I latched onto his arm, but I felt the tension in his body as something pulled from the other side. A shake of my wrist called Bo's ghost to my side, and my spectral protector materialized, glowing bright blue despite the unnatural darkness. In his light, I saw a form made out of the blackness that enveloped us, and that creature intended to drag Teag away.

I dove, gripping my iron knife, and slashed at the darkness. Teag fought back against his attacker, wielding his staff and jabbing the iron-tipped end into the shadows.

"Alicia! Get to the car!" I yelled, intent on keeping Teag from being spirited off, although I had no idea how I was going to prevent that.

Bo leaped at the dark form with a fearsome growl, teeth snapping. The darkness took scant notice of our defense, drawing back only a little but maintaining its grip on Teag.

I squirted the holy water where I guessed the entity's "face" might be, but the blackness absorbed the stream of liquid without reaction. Bo harried the dark form, but though I knew he could bite and maul a physical creature even in his ghostly state, his attack made no difference.

In the distance I heard the blare of a car's horn. What did this look like to Anthony? Had a curtain of darkness appeared from nowhere to swallow us? I knew we were only feet from safety, but that distance felt like a canyon.

The temperature had grown cold enough for me to see my breath. I heard Alicia chanting, and I guessed she called out to friendly spirits to come to our aid. We needed reinforcements, because at best we had a stand-off, and I doubted we could hold Teag's would-be kidnapper at bay all night. How the game had suddenly changed from a threat to Alicia to become a grab for Teag, I wasn't sure, but right now, we were losing.

I heard a man's voice roar out a word of power, and the dark presence drew back, releasing Teag. A burst of wind tore away the utter blackness that surrounded us, but the creature remained, and now without the dark, I saw the featureless form of a man.

A bright flare of light almost blinded me, and I heard a woman call out a command. In the next instant, Sorren appeared beside me, his vampire speed and stealth giving me no warning of his approach.

"We've got to get you to the car," he said, gripping my arm and reaching for Alicia.

"Not without Teag!"

"Donnelly and Rowan will protect Teag. You can't. Now move!"

I shook my wrist, and Bo's ghost faded. As Sorren hustled us toward the car and the darkness around us thinned, I spotted Archibald Donnelly and Rowan only a few feet away. Sorren threw open the car door and shoved us inside. "Stay here!" He ordered, shutting the door behind me. I slid over to the other side and Alicia scrambled behind me, then I gripped the door handle on the passenger side, ready to fling the door open for Teag to dive inside.

"What is that thing?" Anthony's voice stayed steady, but I heard the undercurrent of fear. He'd have been a fool not to be afraid.

"Is that the presence you called about?" I asked, not wanting to take my eyes off Teag, but needing to look at Alicia.

She shook her head. "No. It feels completely different. The presence I felt wanted to speak through me, control me. It felt...female. Whatever's out there is something else—and it's not after me. It came for Teag."

Outside, the fight shifted quickly with Sorren, Donnelly, and Rowan in the mix. I heard Donnelly bellow a command, saw another flash of light I guessed to be Rowan's handiwork, and the dark creature vanished. Sorren accompanied a very shaken-looking Teag to the car and pushed him into the passenger seat.

"Go straight to Cassidy's house," he told Anthony. "No detours, and as few stops as possible. We'll meet you there."

He was gone before anyone could begin to ask a question. Anthony pulled out so quickly, I expected him to burn rubber, and while he kept to the speed limit, he didn't dawdle. When we got to my house, Rowan and Donnelly were already waiting, obviously having ignored speed limits. I knew Sorren had to be close, although I couldn't see him. Then he emerged from my garden door, and I knew he had checked the walled backyard and porch, even though the wardings should have kept out any strangers.

"It's clear," he reported.

Rowan walked to the car to escort Teag. Donnelly remained near the gate, on watch. Sorren came around to the other side to shepherd Anthony, Alicia, and me. No one spoke until we were all safely inside the house.

"What in the hell was that all about?" Teag asked, as Anthony stepped next to him and slid an arm around his waist. Teag leaned into the touch, obviously shaken.

"Let's all sit down. We have a lot of pieces to put together," Sorren said. I headed into the kitchen and returned with a pitcher of iced tea and a tray of glasses. Donnelly glanced at the tea and went right for the sideboard, where I kept the bourbon. He brought the bottle over without being asked, and poured a liberal shot for Teag and me. Anthony shook his head, probably figuring he had to drive. I had the feeling he wouldn't be leaving anytime soon. Alicia and Rowan opted for the tea, but I wasn't surprised when Sorren declined.

"We went to protect Alicia. How did Teag end up in danger?" Anthony asked. His fear for Teag's safety made him bold enough not to mince words with a vampire and two powerful witches

"It's more like you went to stop a carjacking, and got caught up in a kidnapping," Donnelly replied, sipping his bourbon. He'd smoothed down his hair so that he no longer looked quite so wild, but I knew better than to think Archibald Donnelly was ever truly relaxed.

"Two entities, with possibly conflicting agendas," Rowan added. "One that wants to speak through Alicia, and the other focused on Teag's magic."

"I'm willing to open myself to the entity that wants to use me to speak," Alicia clarified, "but I thought it would be best to have you all with me, in case it goes wrong. I can tell it's much stronger than a regular ghost. Perhaps even one of the Old Ones."

At that, Sorren's head came up, and he frowned as if Alicia's words triggered something for him. But before I could ask, Teag spoke.

"I don't know what attacked me, but it wasn't human," Teag replied. "Where it touched me, I could feel it draining my magic."

"Like the artifacts at the Museum and Archive," I supplied.

He nodded.

"Can you please stop talking in riddles?" Anthony growled. "Just answer the question—what's going on?"

Sorren had been studying the whiteboard that sat off in the corner, forgotten in the midst of more urgent matters. "We're missing a player," he said, glancing at Donnelly and then to Rowan. "He won't come back without a big payoff. I think he's been summoned."

Before any of us could ask again, Sorren turned back to us. "I promise, I'll explain what I can. There are still gaps, but I think Archibald and I can fill in most of the story, and Rowan can tell us what we need next."

Anthony pulled Teag close. I snuggled back into the corner of the couch and lifted Baxter into my lap. Alicia wrapped her arms around herself, with a look on her face that made me wonder how much she really wanted to hear what Sorren had to say.

"It's an old story, one I had hoped I wouldn't have to tell," Sorren said. He clasped his hands behind his back and paced. "It begins before the year one thousand, not only before I was turned, but before my maker, Alard, received the Dark Gift."

I knew that Sorren had been turned back in the fourteen hundreds, a true Renaissance man in the flesh. He had spoken occasionally of Alard, the man who rescued him from a bad situation and gave him both immortality and a purpose for living. At that time, Sorren had been the best jewel thief in Antwerp, before he became a vampire. Since then, his work with the Alliance had saved the world more times than probably even he could track.

I leaned forward, intrigued. Sorren rarely spoke about the old times, although I hung on his every word when he was in a mood to talk. History always fascinated me, so having the chance to get eyewitness accounts from someone who had lived through all those turbulent events was a dream come true. But I had quickly learned that reliving the past still pained Sorren, a reminder that those who had experienced history's turning points did not survive unscarred, even if they were immortal.

"Alard's maker fought a Norse rogue, a raider named Holmgang, three hundred years before Alard was turned. Holmgang was also a powerful sorcerer, and for that forbidden magic, he was outcast," Sorren said.

"Wait—he was a Viking?" Anthony's eyes were wide. "A *real* Viking?"

Sorren nodded. "Yes. They were the scourge of Europe in their day, and Holmgang was one of the worst," he replied. "Holmgang used his magic to become immortal, but Alard's maker broke Holmgang's army and defeated him. Holmgang destroyed Alard's maker, and tried many times to find and destroy Alard as well, in retaliation," Sorren added. "When Alard met the Final Death, Holmgang transferred his hatred to me."

"You said he was immortal. How come he hasn't been back since then if he's out to get you?" I asked.

"Right after Alard was destroyed, Holmgang challenged me to a ritual duel. I beat him, barely, and he was bound by his own rules to leave me alone. That was back in 1565, when I was still new in the Dark Gift," Sorren replied. "I thought we had taken care of the problem permanently. It appears that I was mistaken."

"If you beat him once, can you do it again?" Anthony looked torn between fear and incredulity.

Sorren gave a sheepish smile. "I won because I cheated a little. Although technically it was within the letter of the rules—but not the spirit of the game. I got lucky. I don't think even after all this time that I could best him alone with brute strength. And while I have advantages over a mortal, I can't work magic." Sorren had told me many times that vampires couldn't *do* magic, their Dark Gift *was* magic.

"So he's back? What made him change his mind?" Teag asked. "And he's the reason for all of this?" Anthony eyed him worriedly, but Teag gave a barely visible shake of his head. An unspoken conversation passed between them, and Anthony sat back, trusting that Teag was recovered enough to manage.

165

"I don't know," Sorren replied. "I'm convinced someone else is involved, someone who's gotten Holmgang's attention and offered him something he wants. Donnelly and I have been off trying to find out if anyone had been interfering in the old spells, or if we could find proof that Holmgang might be stirring."

"And what did you find?" I couldn't help being equally fascinated and frightened.

"Someone has definitely been mucking around where they didn't belong," Donnelly answered, and his bushy gray eyebrows gathered together like storm clouds. He might sometimes look the part of a Victorian explorer—pith helmet and all—but beneath the appearances, he was one seriously scary man.

"If you know there's a dark witch, can't you track his—or her—magic?" Teag asked, glancing to Rowan.

"She's a capable practitioner," Rowan replied with a shrug. "I doubt she's got the power to control Holmgang for long if she can actually summon him, but she's more than able to shield her magic. We're not even sure where to begin looking."

"Do you think she was the one draining power from the objects at the Museum and Archive, and stoking bad energy with the cursed bits of cloth we found all over the city?" I asked.

"Very likely," Rowan answered. "That sounds like the kind of thing a witch like that would do to enhance her power."

"The items that went missing from both places were supposed to have a Viking heritage," I added. "A ceremonial dagger and a brooch. They both had a strong resonance, although I'm not sure either were magic."

"They might have meaning to Holmgang, or to someone wanting to gain his support," Sorren said. "I doubt that their disappearance is a coincidence."

"I've had dreams of a man in an iridescent black cloak, with a head like a raven," Teag said, dropping his gaze. "A big man, with a long wooden staff. I see him loosen the knots of the cords tied to his staff, and dark spirits come out of the knots. Did I imagine it?"

Sorren shook his head. "No. That is Holmgang, as I last saw him.

The raven head is an illusion, the hood of his cloak. He enjoys inspiring fear. His power is in his staff and in the cords where he stores magic and traps the land sprites he's bent to his will." He looked at Teag with concern. "You dreamt of him? When did this start?"

"It's been a few weeks since the dreams have gotten bad," Teag admitted. "Worse than nightmares. Very vivid, and always the same. I see men and animals hanging from trees, high on a hill in a barren, rocky land. The man in the black cloak with the hood is there, in charge of the sacrifice. I can sense his power. And then he turns around, and he's looking right at me, and I swear that even though it's a dream, he can see me for real. I start running, and he follows me into the fog. He's about to grab me when I wake up."

Teag was trembling, and his voice had grown tight as he recounted the night terror. "I'm always afraid that one of these times, he's going to catch me."

Donnelly nodded. "You're right to be afraid. That's not a dream. That's a sending. You've caught his attention, and that's not a good thing."

"Go back to the part about the land sprites," I said. "They sound like they could be trouble."

"The *Seiðrs* were from a people who lived very close to the land and its energies," Sorren replied. "Their magic is tied into rock and water, trees and wind. Primal. Elemental. The good *Seiðrs* found sprites and other spirits who worked with them willingly. But men like Holmgang feel the need to break and control everything they touch."

"Are the sprites dangerous?" I asked.

"Extremely."

"So what can we do about it?" Anthony asked. "The dreams, and this Holmgang person?"

"I've gathered some items that might be of help," Sorren replied. "A chalice for scrying, a bone wand carved with runes, and the agate spindle whorl that I entrusted to you, Cassidy."

My hand closed around the smooth stone in my pocket. "Several times now, the dark Weaver magic reacted pretty violently when I drew on the spindle whorl," I said. "That's something I haven't seen before."

"Alard left me that spindle whorl, along with the bone wand, when I inherited his possessions," Sorren replied. "He'd also left me a very helpful protective vest, but it did not survive six hundred years of use. The chalice I came by through other means, though it is Viking-made, and carved with runes and sigils."

"Holmgang was a *Seiðr* —does that mean he was also a Weaver witch?" Teag asked.

"Yes. That's how he was able to store energy and bind the land sprites in his knotted cords," Sorren said.

"So why would he want me? I'm not strong enough to be a threat."

"If he can sense your power, then he may see the potential for you to become a threat in the future," Donnelly said. "Or he might hope to take you and break you to serve him, letting him draw from your magic to add to his own."

Anthony tightened his arm around Teag protectively. Teag's expression suggested he had already considered those possibilities. "So that's what he wanted tonight? To kidnap me and use my magic?"

"It's a logical guess," Rowan said. "Holmgang is used to taking what he wants."

"The last time I fought him, I had a powerful ally," Sorren said. "A sorceress—a *Volva*—named Secona."

"Secona?" Alicia looked up. She had been quiet, listening to the conversation around her, but now her expression was urgent. "That's the spirit who wants to speak through me."

CHAPTER THIRTEEN

Everyone stopped and stared at Alicia. Sorren's look of surprise struck me as amusing, despite the gravity of the situation, because my vampire boss always seemed completely in control.

"Can we be sure it's really Secona?" Sorren asked, glancing at Donnelly.

Donnelly frowned and turned his attention to Alicia. He stared past her as if finding the space surrounding her to be utterly fascinating. "I see a woman in a blue cloak with a black and white fur headpiece. She has a long mantle, set with what look like jewels, and strings of glass beads around her neck. The staff she carries has cords wrapped around it, and her spirit radiates power, even in the afterlife."

"That's Secona," Sorren replied. "Exactly as I remember her."

Alicia's expression revealed both caution and determination. "If I let her in, will she leave?"

"One person can never guarantee the actions of another," Sorren said. "But she showed great honor, in my experience."

"I can dispel a spirit that overstays its welcome, though the process is unlikely to be pleasant—for you or for the spirit," Donnelly replied.

"She says she understands," Alicia answered.

"If you can speak for her, why does she need to possess you?" Teag asked, concerned.

"Because she can advise from a distance, but she needs a body to work her magic," Alicia replied.

"And are you willing to be possessed?" Donnelly asked, regarding Alicia thoughtfully, as if taking her measure.

"If it will stop what's going on." Alicia raised her head defiantly. "Although I want my body back when we're done. Preferably undamaged."

"Has she given you her word that she will depart when the danger is over?" Sorren questioned. "She is bound by her oath."

Alicia went silent, and her eyes took on a far-away gaze as if deep in thought. "Yes," she responded. "I have her vow."

"It's up to you," Teag said.

"I accept."

One moment, Alicia was herself, quiet and reserved. In the next moment, everything about her changed, from the expression on her face to the way she held herself, to an ineffable "something" that made it clear that the being in charge of Alicia's body was no longer Alicia.

"Your friend is unharmed," Secona spoke with an air of authority, drawing herself up straight and lifting her chin imperiously. "If we must fight, I cannot assure she will not be damaged, but my presence will not injure her, and I have no desire to stay beyond my welcome."

Sorren clasped his hands in front of him and gave a shallow bow. "Secona. It's good to see you again."

Secona's gaze swept over Sorren, and a smile touched her lips. "Sorren. You look much the same."

"Thanks to the Dark Gift."

Secona grew somber. "We must talk about Holmgang."

Sorren and the others found seats or brought in chairs and gathered 'round. Donnelly remained nearby, quietly monitoring. I sat beside Alicia/Secona on the couch and fought the disquieting sense that while she looked like my friend, my instincts told me this was a very different person.

"What brought him back?" Sorren asked. "When I bested him in the duel, I thought that settled the matter between us; the grudge left over from Alard's win."

"You did. By one of the few traditions Holmgang still held sacred, he was honor bound to walk away, and pursue the matter no longer."

"Then why—" Teag began.

"He was summoned," Secona replied. "Holmgang had grown weary, as most immortals eventually do. He withdrew to a place of solitude, and I hoped he would remain there. But now, an accomplice aids his return. I believe a witch sought him out, and I fear what his goal may be once he has regained his strength."

"Can you find the witch?" I asked. Secona's eyes were ancient, and I wondered how much of Alicia remained aware inside.

"She is protected," Secona answered. "The magic shielding her is clever, difficult to track. I pick up glimpses, but not enough to identify her or know where she is hiding."

"What of the Wild Hunt?" Teag asked. "How does that connect?"

Secona paused, deep in thought. "Even at full power, Holmgang alone cannot hope to conquer and rule. But if he bound a force of chaos to his bidding, he could draw more energy from its magic and wield it like a weapon against his enemies. So he may benefit from the Hunt, but I don't believe he calls to it."

"So someone else, perhaps the one who summoned him, is controlling the Hunt?" Rowan asked.

"A possibility," Secona replied. "Although I don't believe anyone can control the Wild Hunt except for its master. The Hunt has always existed, and it always will. It is a force of nature, like the tides. But the wind and tides can be harnessed, by a ship or a windmill, and used in service of a goal. We must look more closely at the Hunt. I believe it will provide the link we seek to find out who has woken Holmgang, and why he has been called."

"How is it possible for a witch to hide from all of you?" I asked. Donnelly and Rowan were practitioners are exceptional power. Secona, now able to channel her magic through Alicia's human form, also had very strong magic. I couldn't imagine how the witch summoning Holmgang could hide that kind of expenditure of energy.

Rowan shrugged. "Regular criminals learn how to distract notice from their activities. They hide a van with stolen goods in a fleet of cars, bury illegal financial transactions in a slew of honest ones, ship a single crate of contraband on a freighter filled with thousands of identical boxes. My guess is that she—or he—is doing the magic at times when enough energy 'noise' makes it difficult to parse out a single signal."

"The phases of the moon. High and low tide. Or strong 'natural' magic like the passing of the Wild Hunt," Teag replied, looking up to meet Rowan's gaze. She nodded.

"Exactly. Because those occurrences bring a natural energy surge, it's like trying to pick out a single voice in the crowd at a loud concert. Difficult, especially when you're not sure exactly what to look for," Rowan said.

"Earlier this evening, something tried to grab me," Teag said, addressing Secona. "Was it Holmgang? What would he want with me?"

She gave him a pitying look. "His magic would be far more powerful if he took a hostage that already possessed power of its own. To use as a container in which to store extra energy for a big salvo."

"Oh, hell no!" Anthony replied, holding tight to Teag's hand. "That's not going to happen. He's not going to turn you into some kind of magic battery."

Rowan started to speak but stopped as she looked at Baxter, who had risen to his feet and growled, then barked an ear-splitting alarm. I picked him up to sooth him and realized he was trembling despite his defense. The lights flickered, and it sounded as if a hurricane wind buffeted the house, banging the shutters and whistling around the eaves.

Sorren moved to look out the window, standing to the side so he did not present an easy target. "It's not the real wind," he reported. "Nothing in the garden is moving. But something is testing the wardings, pushing against them to see if they'll break."

"Will they?" Anthony flinched as something else clattered outside.

I felt a prickle of energy up my spine, but felt no fear, because the power rising came from the potent protections that had been raised around the house and reinforced week after week, year after year.

"Oh, they'll hold," Donnelly assured him. "Individually, the wardings are strong. Woven together, reinforcing each other—it would take more than Holmgang to undo them."

"We don't dare let Holmgang get his hands on Teag," Sorren said, ignoring the howl of the assault outside. "Just like we must not permit Holmgang and his accomplice to tap the full power of the Wild Hunt for their own purposes."

"How do we keep Teag safe?" Anthony asked. I knew he cared about the big picture, saving the world, but I also knew that for him, none of it mattered if Teag came to harm.

"Until we stop Holmgang, I suggest that Teag remains here, within the wardings," Donnelly replied. Teag moved to argue, but Donnelly held up a hand. "Anthony, too. He would make a tempting hostage."

"I can't stay inside while the rest of you take risks to stop the threat," Teag countered. "Surely there's another way."

"When the time comes for battle, my magic would be stronger if I inhabited the body of a true Weaver," Secona said. "This host is willing and healthy, but her magic does not amplify mine the way yours would."

"Is that possible?" I asked. "Teag isn't a medium." The furor outside had grown loud enough that I had to raise my voice to be heard. I'd weathered hurricanes in this house, and I'd heard the wind roar by like a freight train, or the rain lash against the walls in deafening pulses. But the power that besieged us now was different, unnatural. I realized that Rowan had begun to chant quietly under her breath and that Donnelly's eyes had taken on a glassy look as if his thoughts were elsewhere. *They're reinforcing the wardings,* I thought. *Despite their assurances, they're hedging their bets.*

"It could work," Secona assured. "He must be willing, and lower his mental barriers to permit me to enter him. All my promises would remain, that I would not outstay my welcome." Her lip twisted. "I would find such a host less…comfortable."

I took her meaning immediately. In her time, a male *Seiðr* had been anathema, and she might feel that taking on a man's body somehow sullied her power. As if she guessed my thoughts, Secona turned to me.

"I long ago moved beyond the prejudices of my people," she said. "Holmgang is evil because he wishes to control and dominate, not because he is a man with magic. The gods give power to whom they choose. I am comfortable as a woman, and being 'other' feels strange to me, like wearing someone else's clothing. Sufficient to the task, but not something I would care to do indefinitely."

I saw Anthony bristle at the thought of someone else's spirit slipping inside Teag as casually as trying on a suit or a coat. Anthony opened his mouth but stopped as Teag twined their fingers together and met his gaze.

"I don't like it either," Teag said quietly. "But it makes sense. And if it can stop Holmgang and his witch, it seems like a huge payback for a little bit of discomfort."

"You won't be you," Anthony said quietly.

"Just for a little while. Only when we face him. Not for long, I hope. We can do this," Teag replied, turning toward Anthony and dropping his voice. "Trust me."

Outside, the assault stopped as abruptly as it began. I felt the shift like a change in air pressure as if my ears would pop. I looked up. "Is he gone?"

Rowan stopped murmuring her incantation and paused like she was "listening" for the dark magic outside. "For now. He's withdrawn, and I can't find him."

"He's gone," Donnelly confirmed. "And we will figure out how to locate him. He and his witch will slip up. Power leaves a trail that's impossible to eradicate completely. Now that we know what to look for, we'll find traces of that trail and follow it to him." The set of his jaw told me that Donnelly now considered this to be personal. "When we do—we'll finish this."

A knock at the door drew our attention. I went to answer, as Sorren moved back to look out the window. With the wardings still intact, only a small number of people could get through to reach my front door. Mrs. Teller stood on the porch as I opened the door.

"Cassidy. I've narrowed it down. I think I know who the Weaver witch behind all this might be."

CHAPTER FOURTEEN

I WELCOMED MRS. TELLER AND STEPPED ASIDE TO USHER HER INTO THE living room. She smiled as she saw the group assembled there.

"Well, this saves time. I won't have to say things twice," she said. Donnelly stood to offer her his chair, and she sat, folding her hands in her lap.

"You have a lead on who the Weaver might be who's been causing trouble?" Teag asked.

Mrs. Teller frowned. "I've taken on a lot of students in my day. Been doing baskets and root work for a long time, and when you've been around awhile, folks start to come to you and ask you to teach them. Some you can, some you can't. And some you know you shouldn't."

I went to the kitchen and fetched a glass of sweet tea for her, which she accepted gratefully.

"I've had students who wouldn't apply themselves, and they never came into the power that they might have claimed," she went on. "I've sent some home because they didn't want to do the hard work," Mrs. Teller added, with a look of disapproval on her face.

"But only a few times have I refused to teach someone because I knew in my bones that they wanted to use their power to do harm.

They didn't like being turned away, but I had the power to make it stick, and they knew better than to come back at me," she said, her lips drawn in a firm line.

"And you think that the person who's been leaving the cursed fabric around the city and selling the spelled clothing is one of those people you turned down?" I asked.

"I do," Mrs. Teller replied. "I didn't make the connection, at first. Never saw the person at the Market who sold those awful pieces of clothing that did such harm. But something in the power I've sensed felt familiar; only it's taken me a while to place it." She gave a grim smile. "I have a lot of memories to sort through, after all my years."

"Did you narrow it down?" Teag asked.

"I might have," Mrs. Teller said. "I don't think any of the three people I'm going to give you have the power to do this on their own. But I think they might be crazy enough to use the magic they have to tap into things they shouldn't ought to be messing with to amplify what they do have. And a couple of them have what you might call 'anger management issues,' a big fat chip on their shoulders, which is why I sent them packing in the first place."

"They're Weavers?" I asked, opening an app on my phone so I could take down the names.

Mrs. Teller nodded. "Yes. Hannah McCloud, Kerrie Carson, and Carmen Vincente."

"Do you know where they are?" Sorren asked.

"I have addresses for them, but I haven't tried to contact them," Mrs. Teller replied. "I didn't want to spook them."

"Tomorrow, let's go see them," I suggested.

"I'll come with you," Teag volunteered.

"No, you won't." Sorren and Anthony spoke at the same time. I could see Teag bristle at being told what to do. Anthony turned to him and laid a hand on his arm.

"Holmgang alone is scary as fuck," he said. "And this other witch —we don't know anything about what she can do. Please, Teag. Stay where you're safe."

Secona turned toward him. It seemed so uncanny that the presence using Alicia's body could be so utterly different from Alicia herself. "You place yourself at risk for no purpose if you leave these wardings," she cautioned.

"There is a purpose," Teag argued. "I'd be protecting my friends."

"Who would be even more at risk because you were with them," Donnelly challenged. "If Holmgang is trying to abduct you, then we have to think that he believes imprisoning you will make him stronger or will remove you as a threat to his plans. Either way, you're not safe outside these wardings."

Anthony's hand tightened on Teag's arm, a wordless plea to stay. I watched the conflict in Teag's eyes, and I could imagine his struggle. Had our positions been reversed, I would have fought against being sidelined when there was work to do and friends in danger. Finally, I saw the surrender in Teag's face.

"All right," he said, with an edge in his voice that told me he was unhappy about the decision, but resigned. "I'll stay here. But I can research, and I can coordinate the information that everyone else finds. Even if I can't go out, it doesn't mean I have to be useless."

Relief brightened Anthony's expression. "Thank you," he murmured. "I'll stay with you, and do everything I can to help."

Teag looked to Sorren and Donnelly. "I'll stay in for now," he clarified. "But when the time comes to go up against Holmgang, I need to be part of the fight." He glanced at Secona. "Whatever it takes to stop this bastard."

"Agreed," Sorren replied, and Donnelly nodded, although Anthony looked unhappy. "I suspect that we'll need both of you," he added, indicating Secona, "to finish the job."

MRS. TELLER and I set out in search of the three Weaver witches the next morning. Maggie promised to handle the store, and I promised her a raise. Anthony arranged to work remotely, agreeing to stay with Teag. Secona, still possessing Alicia's body, also remained at the house, in part to protect Teag and Anthony, and also to avoid tipping our hand to Holmgang and his collaborator that Secona had returned. Sorren went to ground, promising to return at dark.

We had agreed that both Donnelly and Rowan were powerful enough that their presence might scare the Weaver witches. But we also knew that they were right insisting we take back-up. Since Sorren couldn't accompany us in daylight, I called Chuck Pettis.

Chuck was waiting for me on the sidewalk the next morning. I heard him ticking as I fell into step beside him. "Thanks for calling me in on this, Cassidy," he said. "You know I love playing bodyguard," he added with a grin.

I took in Chuck's appearance. Nothing about him suggested the arsenal of weapons I knew he would have secreted beneath his coat, including no small number of devices that could blow things up or melt them down. Chuck might not have magic, but he could make things go "poof" just fine. On the way over to pick up Mrs. Teller, I filled Chuck in.

"Damn, Cassidy. You can't do anything halfway, can you?"

I rolled my eyes. "It's not like I go looking for trouble. I was minding my own business…"

"Isn't that how it always starts?" he asked with a grin.

He was right, and we both knew it, so I gave him the stink eye.

"So can't your witchy friends put some kind of magic tracer on these Weavers?" Chuck asked.

"They might be able to, if we can get a personal item from each of the Weavers," I replied. Teag might be benched temporarily, but he intended to spend his time using his computer to investigate the three suspect witches. His own hacking skills were impressive, and with Secona's help there shouldn't have been a database—official or other-wise—they couldn't crack. Anthony was likely maintaining his plau-sible deniability by reading in the other room. Then again, when push came to shove, Anthony had been known to call in a few favors from law enforcement to track license plates or run a name through the system.

"I'm surprised Rowan or Donnelly couldn't snap their fingers and wiggle their noses for something like this."

"You've been watching the oldies TV channel again, haven't you?" I asked with a smirk. "Donnelly's magic only works to find someone if the Weaver witch is dead. Rowan needs something to focus on, like a personal item. So at the moment, we're stuck with good, old-fashioned legwork."

When we pulled up outside Mrs. Teller's home, I saw her in the doorway. Then she turned as Niella came up behind her. From the stiff way Mrs. T held her shoulders, I guessed they were arguing. Mrs. Teller emerged, her eyes narrowed, and her jaw set, and the door shut harder than necessary behind her as she went down the steps.

"Problems?" I asked as she slid into the back seat.

"Just drive," she growled. After we pulled out into traffic, I heard her sigh. "Niella wanted to come with us. I told her we would be fine, and that if she wanted to help, she could weave our strongest magic into cords and cloth. She didn't like it, but she'll do it."

I knew that wouldn't be the end of it. Niella might do as she was told, but she was a grown woman every bit as stubborn as her mama, and there would be words about this later. Lucky for me, I wouldn't be in the line of fire when that happened.

"Who's first?" Chuck asked.

"Hanna McCloud," I replied. I wove through back streets until I reached the last known address we could find for Mrs. Teller's old student. I parked in front of a small, shotgun-style house in a questionable neighborhood. Even without magic, I knew we were being watched, although I couldn't spot anyone in the windows.

Chuck came around and opened our doors, then walked beside us up to the entrance. A harried woman in her middle years answered my knock.

"Whatever you're selling, I don't want it," she said, "and I don't need a new church, either." She moved to shut the door, and I stiff-armed the knob.

"We're looking for Hanna McCloud," I said with my most winning smile. "We need to talk to her."

The woman eyed me suspiciously. Behind her, I could hear the shouts and squeals of young children tussling, and figured she either ran a babysitting service or had gotten stuck minding the grandchildren. "She in some kind of trouble?"

"We're not sure," I replied truthfully. "We need to ask her some questions. Please, it's important."

"You don't look like cops," the woman said, looking at me and then to Mrs. Teller. She frowned when she saw Chuck. Even though he smiled and had his hands where she could see them, everything about the way he carried himself screamed "military."

"We're not," I answered. "But we think she may have information that could help us stop someone from committing a crime. Finding her could save lives."

I tried to read something from my gift as we stood on the porch. The noise of the TV and the loud children made concentrating difficult, but I picked up a faint sense of restlessness, despair, and a slow, simmering anger that squared with what Mrs. Teller remembered about her former student. Still, I got that kind of vibe from a lot of perfectly harmless people who had been dealt a bad hand. So by itself, that didn't prove she was our rogue Weaver.

The worn-looking homeowner turned and yelled over her shoulder for the kids to quiet down. Then she turned her attention back to us. "She owned this house before I bought it at the sheriff's sale last year. Never met her, but the neighbors say she went to jail for dealing. Don't think she's coming back anytime soon."

Mrs. Teller and I exchanged a glance. I turned back to the woman in the doorway. "Do you know which jail?"

"No idea. Don't know, don't care." A crash sounded loud enough to make us all jump, followed by the piercing wail of a child. "Gotta go." The door shut in our faces.

"Well, we struck out on that one," I said as we headed back to the car.

"Not necessarily," Chuck replied, standing guard until we were inside with the doors locked. "If she's in jail, she wasn't running around hiding cursed pieces of cloth in the storm drains," he continued as he slid into the passenger seat. "And odds are good she wasn't weaving spelled fabric in her cell."

I texted what we'd learned to Teag, figuring that he could take it from there on Hanna McCloud. "If there's anything worth knowing, Teag will figure it out," I said. "Next up is Kerrie Carson."

Kerrie's house in a nice suburb outside the city limits didn't look like the home of a psychotic evil Weaver witch. The bungalow-style home sat behind a tidy white picket fence, with all the charming "curb appeal" of a house on the Home and Garden channel. It made me wonder whether we might have tracked down the wrong Kerrie Carson, then I remembered how often we'd found the horrors that could lurk behind an unremarkable facade.

This time a man came to the door. He might have been in his early thirties, but he looked worn and tired.

"We're looking for Kerrie Carson," I said, plastering on what I hoped looked like a friendly smile.

He flinched, and looked away. "She's not here," he replied. "Can I help you?"

"We'd like to talk with her. She might be able to help us find some people who are looking to cause problems," I answered. Before he could protest, I held up a hand. "She's not in any trouble," I assured him. "But we're trying to head off a situation, and we really could use her help."

He motioned for us to come inside. Chuck followed last, on alert for any danger, but all we found was an unremarkable living room in need of decluttering. I looked around, at what I could see of the messy house. The sense my gift picked up from the stacks and jumble around me spoke of the owners being overburdened, not untidy. A second glance at our host revealed the dark circles beneath his eyes and the too-thin hollow to his cheeks, like he hadn't slept or eaten well lately.

"I'm David Carson," he said, as we moved into the living room. "Kerrie's my wife. Please excuse the house. Kerrie was in a terrible car accident three weeks ago, and I haven't had my mind on housework, if you know what I mean."

We all murmured our condolences. "How is she doing?" I asked. "Were the injuries serious?"

David looked pained. "Kerrie went through the windshield. Her seat-belt broke, and the airbag didn't deploy. The car rolled down an embankment. Hit and run. She hasn't regained consciousness. The doctors say she might not. Ever." His strained voice convinced me of the truth of his story.

"No clues about who was driving the other car?" Chuck probed.

David shook his head. "No. They think another car might have forced her off the road, but they haven't found any evidence yet. At least, none they've told me about. Believe me, if someone did that to her and left her behind, I'd like to get my turn at them." Only then did a bit of fire come into his eyes.

"Did Kerrie have any enemies? Anyone who might have wanted to hurt her?" I asked. When David looked as if he might balk, I gave him a wan smile. "I know we're not the police, and we're not trying to be. But we think that a former classmate of hers might have been planning to do something that would have hurt a lot of people, and we want to stop it before anything happens."

His eyes narrowed. "Why not go to the police?"

"Because we don't have the kind of evidence they'll believe," Mrs. Teller spoke up. I saw her fingers moving back and forth over a woven strip the size of a bookmark that she held in her hand. It looked like fidgeting, but I suspected she drew on stored magic in the fabric to help her coax David into telling his story.

"Which classmate?" he asked.

"Did Kerrie ever talk about a woman named Carmen Vincente?"

He frowned, thinking. "The name's familiar. I never met her. I did overhear Kerrie on the phone a few days before the accident. She was arguing with someone, but I could only hear her side of the conversation, so I don't know what it was all about. She called the other person 'Carmen,' and she said, 'Count me out. I'm done with that kind of thing. You're on your own.' The caller gave her grief about it, and Kerrie hung up. When I asked what was going on, she told me that someone she knew wanted her to go in on a business deal, but she wasn't interested, and the other person got angry she didn't want to invest."

"I know this may sound strange, but you wouldn't happen to be able to find that call in her phone's history, would you?" Chuck asked.

David sighed. "Her phone got lost in the wreck. She always carried it, but they didn't find it in the car or on her, and they said it never went into the ambulance with her. I even went back to where the wreck happened and looked around, but no luck."

"And you haven't heard back from this argumentative friend since then?" Mrs. Teller probed.

David shook his head. "No. Although I can't help wondering whether whoever was on the phone might have had something to do with the wreck. The cops haven't been able to trace the other car." He looked from one of us to the next. "If you know anything, or if you find out anything, please call me. It's bad enough with things the way they are, but not knowing—that's even worse."

We repeated our condolences and headed back to the car. "Looks like Carmen is our witch," Chuck said.

"Carmen had a bad temper," Mrs. Teller said from the back seat. "She held grudges. But I don't understand how she got caught up in this. I was afraid that she might use her magic for petty grievances, like getting back at a neighbor who annoyed her, or a co-worker she was jealous of. Taking over the world seems like a stretch."

"If something happened that might have expanded her horizons, Teag will find it," I assured her. "But we need to have a plan. What happens if we get to her house and she's there?"

"I'd rather subdue her peacefully," Mrs. Teller replied. "But if she won't cooperate and she attacks, I should still be stronger than she is, magically."

"Worst comes to worst, a flash-bang does a nice job of taking the piss out of someone," Chuck said cheerily. Much as I love him as a friend and an ally, sometimes the man scares the crap out of me.

"Yeah. Let's try to avoid that if we can," I said. "Truly worst case scenario."

"Just sayin'," he replied.

"I'd be very surprised if she's at her house," Mrs. Teller said. "She may not know about Secona, but we've shut down her plans several times now. Carmen was brash and had a chip on her shoulder, but she wasn't stupid."

"All we need is something that belonged to her," I replied. "Even smart people get careless."

The address I had for Carmen led us to a well-maintained home in a nicer suburb. It looked like a family home, and I wondered if we would find a partner or roommate present even if Carmen had bolted. But as we pulled up to the curb, I noticed that the grass looked overgrown, and the drawn shades gave the impression that the building had been abandoned.

"I don't like this," Chuck muttered, eying the house. "Closed blinds are always a bad sign."

We got out of the car, and Chuck did a quick reconnaissance trip around back to get an idea of what we were dealing with. "There's no car in the driveway," he reported. "Trash cans are empty, and the backyard is weedy. Doesn't look like anyone's been here for at least a week, maybe more."

"If Carmen's involved with the problems downtown, she might have gone into hiding right around the time the 'grouch flu' started," Mrs. Teller said. "That would have been the smart thing to do because none of us had any reason to go looking for her at that point."

"I'll go in through the back," Chuck volunteered. He held up a hand to silence our objections. "I'll be careful, and I'll sweep for traps. But we can't break in through the front door in broad daylight."

"I'll go with you," Mrs. Teller replied, and her narrowed gaze challenged either of us to object. "I'm most familiar with Carmen's magic and the feel of Weaver energy. Chuck can check for physical traps; I'll look for magical ones."

"And what about me?" I argued.

Chuck grinned. "You get to be the lookout. And the getaway driver."

I dallied in the car for several minutes after the others headed around back, sizing up the neighborhood. At this time of day, most people would be at work, and from the lack of toys in the nearby yards, I didn't think there were a lot of parents home with young children.

Nosy retirees were another threat, but nowadays the odds of finding people with nothing better to do than rock on their porch and spy on the neighbors were slim when they could be out kayaking or doing Yoga.

I locked the car and walked up the sidewalk like I had a right to be there, then knocked on the door and waited, doing my best to look like a casual visitor. I heard the click of a lock and then the door opened. Chuck stood back from the entrance, in the shadows where someone on the street was unlikely to spot him.

"She's gone," Mrs. Teller said. "The place is stripped clean."

I looked around at bare walls and an empty living room. Maybe Carmen anticipated someone wanting to gain power over her through a left-behind possession, or perhaps she didn't intend to come back, but she'd moved out completely.

"I'm betting that she packed up in a hurry," I said. "She might have gotten sloppy. Let's see if we can find anything I can use to get a read on her."

We made sure both doors were locked, then split up and went to work. The one-story house wasn't huge, and the lack of either base-ment or attic meant we only had a few rooms to search. My check in the kitchen revealed rotting food in the refrigerator and some aban-doned boxes of cereal in the cupboards. While those might technically have been "owned" by Carmen, I'd learned that the kind of energy reading I'd pick up from them would be minimal or non-existent. People didn't tend to imbue their breakfast food with the resonance of deep emotions.

I checked the drawers and cupboards, but Carmen had taken every-thing except a few cans of soup. Even the plates and silverware were gone, and while I doubted they would have been much better than the cereal boxes for providing an insight, I wondered whether she had given thought to the possibility of other witches trying to track her.

Then again, while she had moved out suddenly, the lack of traps made me wonder. If Carmen had expected that opponents with magic might come looking for her, surely she was capable of leaving behind nasty surprises to slow them down, since her cursed fabrics had set all of Charleston on edge. Maybe that meant that she either didn't know we were on to her, or that she wasn't worried. I doubted we still had the element of surprise working for us, but it worried me if Carmen felt so sure of herself that she didn't fear anyone trying to stop her, and I wondered what she knew that we didn't.

"We found these," Mrs. Teller said when we reconvened in the living room. She held out her hand to reveal a button, a comb, and a single earring.

I smiled. "Those will do nicely." All of them were items that had a lot of body contact, which increased the resonance my gift could read of associated memories and energy. Chuck wrapped them in a bandana he pulled from his pocket and tucked them away for safekeeping.

"Let's get back to the house," I said, "and I'll see what the pieces you found have to tell me."

CHAPTER FIFTEEN

"She's a Nicholson." Teag announced his big news when we got back to the house. To my relief, we faced no hordes of zombies or demonic hounds, and if any attacks had been attempted, the wardings held fast. Baxter yipped and carried on when we returned, proving that no one was going to mount a sneak attack.

"What did you find?" I asked as we headed in to the living room. I kept on going to the kitchen since it was nearly lunch, and heated up the oven for a couple of frozen pizzas, since ordering take-out didn't seem like a smart idea right now. Then I came back and settled into an armchair, next to the end table where Chuck placed the bandana-wrapped pieces we found at Carmen's house.

Anthony had stepped into the hall to take a phone call, and I could hear his voice, but the words were too muffled to make out what he was saying. From the way she carried herself, I could tell that Secona still possessed Alicia. A silver chalice etched with runes sat in front of her, filled with a red liquid I hoped was wine.

"Carmen Nicholson ran away and married Diego Vincente," Teag replied. "You can guess that didn't go down well with Papa Nicholson, since Vincente had a criminal record."

"For what?" Chuck asked.

188

"Stupid teenage stuff," Teag replied. "Took a car for a joyride, stole money out of lockers at school, got nabbed for vandalism. Looks like Vincente straightened himself out, but he wasn't the kind of boy Carmen's dad envisioned as a son-in-law, and so she got an ultimatum to pick between her lover and her family, and Carmen picked Vincente."

"And?" Mrs. Teller prompted.

"Carmen's family cut her off, and there was bad blood for a long time," Teag continued. "Then Vincente got sick, and they needed money. Her father wouldn't help them, and Vincente died. That was six months ago."

I looked at Teag with a measure of awe and consternation. "How the hell did you find all that out?"

He smirked. "Anthony's mother. Apparently, she went to boarding school with Catherine Nicholson, Carmen's mother, and while they aren't close, they run in the same circles, so she knew all the gossip."

I shook my head. The blue blood network in Charleston could be confining and cliquish, but never let it be said that the inner circle of high society didn't keep tabs on its own. "Wow," I replied. "Did she wonder why he wanted to know?"

Teag grinned. "Actually, she figured Carmen had gotten herself in some kind of trouble, and she wanted to warn Anthony away from taking her case."

"So Carmen has a grudge against daddy-dearest, and it simmers for years, then really comes to a head when hard feelings cost her the man she loves," I mused. I glanced at Mrs. Teller. "You said she had a chip on her shoulder."

Mrs. Teller nodded. "I never pried into her personal business, but I could tell she was an angry young woman with a lot of unresolved issues. That kind of thing plays havoc with magic if you don't settle your old wounds before you try to control real power. Like I said, I was afraid she might use what she learned from me to harm someone, so I refused to teach her. She wasn't happy about it, but she knew to leave well enough alone and not try any of that crap on me."

I smothered a chuckle. Mrs. Teller didn't care for vulgarity, so her saying "crap" was the equivalent of a string of profanity from anyone else.

"So she's upset by her husband's death, pissed at her father, and still disowned by the family," I recapped, crossing my legs beneath me in the armchair. "She's got native magic, but she's half-trained, a real loose cannon. So how does she jump from there to summoning Holmgang and calling down the Wild Hunt?"

"The Nicholson family was a founding member of the Ashley River Rod and Gun Club," Teag replied. "As were the families of the men who fell out of the sky, and the zombies who crawled out of their graves at Magnolia Cemetery."

"And let me guess—both the families and the club had ties to Harrison Stables out in Aiken," I hazarded.

"Yep," Teag said. "It's all one big inbred tangle."

Since Anthony's family was every bit as blue-blooded as the Nicholson's clan, I knew Teag's comment focused more on the cliquishness of Charleston's upper echelon, but there was an element of truth to the harsh words. The city's old families tended to intermarry, and the bloodlines crisscrossed so often over the past few centuries with the same surnames popping up again and again that family trees tended to look more like snarled vines.

"Anthony gave you the tip about the Rod and Gun Club?" I asked.

"He confirmed it, but I asked Mrs. Morrissey about organizations that the key families had in common, and she rattled off a list. All the usual charity and non-profit boards, but those were too recent," Teag replied. "Lots of other groups, but the only one that went back far enough was the hunting club."

"Nice work," I told him. "But I still don't see how a bunch of fox hunters managed to call down the Wild Hunt."

"I've got a theory about that," Teag replied with a mysterious smile, "but I need Donnelly to confirm it for me, and he said he had an errand to run for Sorren, so he'll be back in a bit. Rowan went with them, too."

I chuckled, thinking of Sorren sending Archibald Donnelly on an "errand." The engraved chalice next to Secona drew my attention. "Is that the chalice Sorren mentioned?" I asked.

She nodded. "Yes. Its maker did well. I've been scrying on and off since you left. No insight into Carmen, but if you've brought one of her possessions, perhaps we can change that," Secona said with a nod toward the pieces wrapped in Chuck's bandana.

I'd been genuinely interested in what the others had done while we were gone, but to tell the truth, I'd also been stalling. Reading objects takes a toll on me, especially when the emotions associated with them are dark and upsetting. I settled into my chair, readying myself to touch the items from Carmen's house when Anthony ended his call and returned to sit on the couch next to Teag.

"I pulled in a favor from an old friend who knows people in Corrections," Anthony said. "Hanna McCloud is still in jail and has been for months. She's not likely to be the person you're looking for."

"And I confirmed that Kerrie Carson is in the hospital in critical condition," Teag added, omitting how he did the confirming. "Her accident happened at the very beginning of the 'weirdness.' So she may be a victim, rather than a perp."

"Maybe Carmen decided to get rid of the competition, and go after any other Weaver witches?" I wondered aloud. "Which would explain the attack on you," I added with a glance toward Teag.

He shrugged. "Could be. If she went after Kerrie first, maybe she already knew Hanna was out of the running. But that would leave me and Mrs. Teller—and Niella—as targets."

I excused myself to take out the pizza before it burned, keeping one ear on the conversation as I set out the pans.

"Carmen was always arrogant," Mrs. Teller said. "Thought a bit too highly of herself. If she got rid of Kerrie, I'd bet it was more of a personal grudge than the thought that anyone might out-magic her." Her eyes narrowed as she thought. "I think the attack on you had more to do with this Holmgang than with Carmen being afraid of rivals."

"I'm not sure whether that makes me feel better or worse," Teag replied.

I beckoned everyone into the kitchen to get some pizza, and we grew quiet as we ate. Once we finished, the conversation hit a lull, forcing me to confront the pieces we retrieved from Carmen's house. "All right," I said. "Let me take a look at the stuff we brought back. But I'd like to do it in the dining room, where I can sit at the table." I glanced at Teag. "Would you bring the bandana in, please?"

He nodded. "Sure. Do you want me to trance with you?"

I paused. "If we used a long spelled cord, could the others see what you see?"

"We can make sure they do," Mrs. Teller answered. "I'll boost the signal if I need to."

Usually Teag was the only one who glimpsed the impressions I received when I used my gift, and then only when we both held onto a piece of fabric with his magic woven into it. I'd never put on a show for a larger audience, and while that made me a little nervous, these were all trusted friends, and it would make the aftermath much easier if I didn't have to recap my vision.

I sat in the middle of one side on the big table I'd inherited from my grandmother. The scarred wooden dining table wasn't particularly valuable, but I remembered many family holiday meals, and that gave it a resonance of calmness and support that grounded me. Teag sat to my left, and Mrs. Teller sat on my right. The others found their seats, and Teag uncoiled a long braided cord, handing one end to me and then passing the rest of the rope down the line until Mrs. Teller grasped the opposite end.

"If this works right, you'll see what I see. Hang on. I never know what is going to happen," I warned. Teag used a pencil to nudge the button my way, steering it with the eraser to keep from touching it with his skin. I took a deep breath, reached for the button, and closed my eyes.

Buttons are some of my favorite things to read because they are worn close to the skin and soak up a lot of impressions. The button we found in Carmen's house had a mother of pearl sheen to it, high-end like it came off a dressy blouse. The smooth, cold disk warmed to my skin, and I felt my gift connect.

I saw the house through Carmen's eyes as it had been. The interior looked chic and color-coordinated, like something out of a magazine, and I wondered whether she had a good eye or she'd gone into debt to hire a decorator. Or maybe Carmen never lost the memory of Nicholson money, even as she followed her bad boy lover into family exile.

Anger permeated the sensations I read from the button, a low, persistent boil below the surface. Carmen had a mad on for the world, but underneath it all her father held a special place in her fury. I caught a glimpse of a photograph of Carmen with a handsome dark-haired man and figured that was Vincente. Grief lurked below the anger, dark as sin and deep enough to drown in. But one emotion burned brightly. Vengeance. Carmen had a plan, and the idea that those who had wronged her would get what was coming to them sustained her, helping her rise above the grief and filling her with purpose.

The image shifted, and I saw the house again, but everything was boxed, and the rooms were almost empty. I felt a tug of sadness as Carmen looked around the vacant rooms and remembered better times. Then a flare of anger drove away the regret, and I felt her resolve harden. She went back to the bedroom to retrieve a few containers to hand carry. The box on top held a small hand loom and several pieces of fabric that I recognized from the storm drain. When she looked at the cloth swatches, I could feel cold satisfaction and the anticipation that she would make people pay for their sins. She stretched down to pick up the boxes, and abruptly, the vision ended.

I came back to myself with a rush of breath and opened my eyes to find the others staring at me with various levels of astonishment.

"Nicely done," Mrs. Teller said, breaking the silence.

"An impressive gift," Secona murmured.

Anthony looked confounded. "I've seen you read objects before, and helped you through the aftermath, but somehow I never understood how real the visions are."

"That was pretty tame," I said, knowing that Anthony had been around to help gather my wits after a malicious object knocked me on my ass.

"So if I'm interpreting what you saw correctly, that nails Carmen as the person behind the woven fabric that caused havoc downtown," Teag said. Mrs. Teller and I nodded.

"She was running away," I mused. "So either she thought someone would come after her to stop her—maybe us—or she needed to go somewhere more private to finish the rest of her plan."

"I'll see what I can find in the registrar of deed's records when we're done," Teag volunteered.

"Ready for the comb?" I asked. The others nodded, and Teag pushed it toward me. Once again, I picked up the hard plastic and willed my gift to focus on whatever memories it retained.

There's a reason magic and ritual prefer basic materials like wood, metal, bone, and stone. The farther removed from nature an object is, the less well it conducts magic. Plastic can be tricky, and while I can get a reading from it, the images often aren't quite as clear.

Then again, from what I could see, maybe this time it worked out well that the reception was blurry.

Once more, I saw through Carmen's eyes, but this time, she stood in a large clearing. The image looked like a bad cable TV signal, fuzzy and breaking up a bit, but I could force my magic through the comb enough to hold the connection.

Carmen was in the middle of a circle made from braided rope. At her feet lay a shallow bowl filled with a dark liquid I bet was blood. Beyond the rope, I could see the discarded bodies of chickens and rabbits. Thick pillar candles burned at the four quarters of the warded circle. Carmen began to chant, and while I couldn't make out the words, the thrum of power, even at a distance, raised the hackles on the back of my neck.

The breeze stirred, fluttering her hair and her loose-fitting shirt. The candle flames flickered, and the tall grass bent in waves. I could feel Carmen's intense focus and an almost ecstatic urgency. The wind grew stronger, guttering the candles and whipping her hair wildly around her face. Fear and excitement warred inside as she called down old power and felt a response. And then, in the distance, I heard the howl of dogs and the pounding of hooves—

"Cassidy?" Anthony's worried voice cut through the mental fog as I struggled to come out of the vision.

"I'm okay," I assured him, but Teag pushed a glass of sweet tea at me anyhow, and I drank it greedily, needing the sugar. I pick up flashes of normal life from objects fairly often, and those little insights don't usually bother me. But when I focus my gift on an object full of dark resonance, the effort drains my psychic "batteries" pretty quickly. I could feel the beginnings of a headache in my temples, and I felt like I'd run a mile in the heat.

"We can do this later if you need a break," Anthony added. I waved him off.

"I'd rather get it over with. Then I can collapse on the couch and listen while the rest of you come up with a brilliant plan," I replied, only partly kidding.

Teag rolled the lone earring toward me. The single cultured pearl on a gold stud had been fairly expensive, the kind of loss someone would miss—if they weren't consumed by trying to summon the power of the ancient dead. The earring fit what we knew about Carmen, a woman who had left behind a privileged upbringing. I wondered if she even noticed it was missing.

I felt Mrs. Teller's gaze on me as I reached for the earring. She gave me an appraising look, not falling for my reassurances about being all right. Then again, all of us around the table except Anthony knew first-hand about the cost of magic, and what kind of price our gifts sometimes demanded.

My fingers folded around the earring, careful not to poke myself with the sharp post. I definitely didn't want to draw blood, not with an object like this. The strain from the readings made my hand shake, and I took a deep breath to steady myself. My magic latched onto the resonance of the earring with a sudden jolt, and I found myself in Carmen's dining room.

I realized that what I saw happened before she packed up and moved out because Carmen sat at a dining table spread with spell books and ritual objects. I saw the shallow bowl that I'd glimpsed in the previous vision and guessed it was a scrying tool. Two silvery objects caught my attention. One was a rune-inscribed brooch and the other a dagger with elaborate engraving. They looked familiar, and then I realized that I had seen both before. These were the stolen items from the Museum and the Archive. Up close, I could see the intricacy of the carvings, and feel the old power both resonated.

A small brazier the size of an incense burner sat on a protective pad, filled with glowing embers. Carmen reached into a velvet pouch and withdrew a handful of small seeds, then dropped them into the brazier. Smoke rose as they burned, and she leaned into the aromatic wisps, inhaling deeply.

I felt my head spin as the smoke filled my lungs, and my body felt strangely light. The room pulsed in time with my heartbeat, and the colors throbbed. Carmen's voice rose in a chant, rising and falling, her words slurred. The tethers that kept my soul in my body seemed loose as if I could float away. That idea felt both thrilling and terrifying.

Carmen's dining room dimmed, and I saw a cold, rocky shore on the verge of a dark sea. The shadowy forms of boats drifted in the moonlight. A bonfire near the cliff sent flames leaping into the sky, and when I looked up, the Northern Lights arced like a blazing ribbon of green fire.

Silhouetted by the bonfire stood a giant of a man. His dark cloak shimmered with iridescent colors like starling feathers, falling across broad shoulders and powerful arms. I could not see his face because a headdress in the shape of a bird's head obscured his features.

Giddy with the smoke, drunk on the borrowed power of Carmen's incantation, I watched the man turn. Across time and distance, I swore he knew we were watching him, and that shadowed face looked right at us. Although I couldn't see his eyes, I felt his attention on me, and my skin prickled as my gut clenched. And while I knew that the scene was of the memories imprinted on Carmen's lost earring, that the vision her smoke produced was in the past, still I also had the sense that the man, Holmgang, somehow knew that I was there, and his oppressive stare imparted a warning.

The scene vanished and I felt myself falling. Strong arms caught me, and I heard chanting again, but this time Alicia's voice led the litany. Gradually, my head cleared, and I realized that I lay stretched out on the couch, with the others crowding around worriedly.

"What happened?" I asked, still groggy.

Secona, still wearing Alicia's body, sat on the edge of the couch. She pressed a length of woven fabric into my hand, and almost immediately I felt the last of the fog lift from my mind. "The woman in the vision you saw burned henbane seeds. Very dangerous—and a way seers throughout the ages have gone walking without their bodies."

"A hallucinogen?" Anthony mused.

"Yes, but more than that," Mrs. Teller replied. "Not all hallucinations are false. In the hands of a skilled practitioner, henbane, peyote, wolfsbane, belladonna, and others can produce astral projection and clairvoyant visions…if they don't kill you."

Teag knelt next to me, bearing both another cold glass of sweet tea and several ibuprofen. "Did you see what I saw?" I managed, pleased that my words weren't as slurred as Carmen's.

"Yes, in all three cases," Anthony replied. "And I stand in awe of your courage, all of you. Five senses are overwhelming enough for me."

Teag steadied me as I sat up to drink, then fixed pillows so I didn't have to lie flat and could see everyone as they dragged chairs into my line of sight. "So what did everyone get out of all that?" I asked, grateful that Teag kept my glass refilled.

"We know what happened to the missing relics," Teag observed.

"And the visions linked Carmen to both Holmgang and the Wild Hunt," Secona replied. "But calling to something is very different from commanding it. I wonder if she realizes that."

"What now?" Mrs. Teller asked. "We don't know where Carmen is, or when she'll make her next move. And while Carmen might not be able to control the forces she's toying with, we aren't guaranteed to be able to stop them, either."

Baxter suddenly sat up from where he lay on the floor, ran to the foyer, and barked like he'd lost his mind. My head hurt too much for me to worry about the newcomer since I knew the warding would prevent a stranger from entering. But I was surprised to see Donnelly and Rowan enter. Rowan bent down and murmured a few words to Baxter, who immediately stopped yipping and ran in a happy circle around her feet before trotting off toward his food dish.

"Did you learn that from Sorren?" I asked. "That's cheating."

Rowan chuckled. "Sorren can glamour the dog. I just reminded him of his food."

"Sneaky," Teag replied.

I frowned, trying to make out what Rowan carried. Then I realized she had a wooden staff, about three feet long, darkened with age and inscribed with complicated markings. "Where did you get the staff?" I asked.

Teag gave me an apologetic look. "Forgot to mention that. While you and Mrs. Teller were out, Secona said that if the Nicholson family had a history of Weaver witches, there should be a staff, especially if their power dates back to the Norse times. I remembered that clothes press in one of the bedrooms at the mansion had a bunch of old walking sticks in the corner. Didn't think anything about them at the time, so it never occurred to me before now that there might be a *Seiðr's* staff in with the canes and hiking poles."

"Archibald and I offered to go look, and Teag pulled a few strings through your friend at the Archive to get permission," Rowan supplied.

"That's no ordinary walking stick," Mrs. Teller said, coming around the couch to get a closer look. Rowan held the staff in the light so we could all see.

"Those are Norse runes," Secona said, rising from her seat to examine the staff. "It is a *Seiðr's* tool, one of considerable power." She ran a hand above the surface of the wood without touching it. "It still holds echoes of its last user's magic, but they're very faint. No one's channeled energy through it in a long time. A pity, because it's badly starved."

"Starved?" Anthony echoed. "Are you saying that the staff is alive?"

Secona's expression grew pinched as she struggled to explain. "Not as you think of life. Not sentient, like a person or an animal. But... reactive, and instinctual. A staff becomes an extension of the witch who wields it. It resonates with energy and magic—and memory. It... responds...over time to the imprint of its master's power," she said.

"And when such a staff isn't used for a long time, the magic...dries out," Secona continued. "Almost as if the energy is a sap running through it and keeping the staff primed for use. Without magic, the staff grows brittle, physically and in its energy. This will need to be cleansed and charged before we can use it against Holmgang, but once restored, it will be a fine weapon indeed."

I thought about the walking stick that Sorren had given me, a gentleman's sword-cane that once belonged to his maker, Alard. While my wooden spoon athame drew on memories of my grandmother to let me summon a white-cold force, Alard's walking stick channeled my energy into a bolt of flame. I might not have the kind of power that either Secona or Holmgang possessed, but I understood what it felt like to have a bond with my athame. So I could only imagine what a seasoned, very old staff might be able to channel in the hands of an ancient and powerful sorceress.

Donnelly cleared his throat when we were all done ogling the *Seiðr* staff. "I think I have the last piece of the puzzle, the way to connect Carmen to the Wild Hunt," he announced. "I just need to summon a couple of ghosts, and make them spill a few old family secrets."

CHAPTER SIXTEEN

My curiosity over the chance to see Archibald Donnelly work his necromancy when I wasn't fighting for my life won out over the dregs of the headache from my vision. The daylight had faded to twilight as we trooped out into the walled garden that served as my backyard since Donnelly said he worked best when he could stand between earth and sky.

I knew he could marshal his considerable magic inside if need be, but I also understood that just because you *can* do magic under certain conditions doesn't mean that's the most effective way. And if he wanted to use my garden to stop an ancient horror and a mad Norse warlock, I wasn't going to say no.

Rowan and Secona helped Donnelly prepare. He walked in a circle around a small grassy area, going to the left and then to the right. He repeated the effort, creating a second, concentric circle. Donnelly withdrew a bone wand from inside his jacket, and I wondered if it was the relic entrusted to Sorren in Alard's will.

Sundown, that time when it's no longer day but not yet night, was a time of power, perfect for thinning the Veil to the other side. Donnelly looked normal, in a tweed jacket with a knit scarf over a button-down shirt and khaki pants. Only his wild white mane might suggest otherwise. But standing there in a blessed circle holding a relic of power in the half-light of dusk, Archibald Donnelly looked every bit the necromancer that he was, even without the trappings of a flowing robe or flapping cape.

When he spoke words of power, they had a guttural sound, harsh and clipped, like the grinding of rock against rock. Nothing at all like Secona's almost musical chant or Carmen's nasal, sing-song invocation. I felt Donnelly's power like a brooding storm, an electric crackle in the still air. The temperature dropped until our breath puffed in white clouds and I couldn't help shivering, both from cold and from the rising energy all around me.

Donnelly dropped several items onto the ground outside the warded circle—a man's ring, an old riding crop, and a silver medallion that might once have hung from a champion's ribbon.

"Oliver Nicholson, Maxwell Lawton, I command you to come forth!" Donnelly's voice brooked no disobedience, and he thrust forward with the bone wand. Its tip ripped into the still night air, opening a dark gash. In the next instant, the gray forms of two men stood inside the second circle.

The ghosts appeared nearly solid, but ashen in both skin and clothing, like a faded black and white photograph. They wore clothing from the late 1800s, and from the cut of their suits and the way they held themselves, I knew they had been men of means. Nicholson, no doubt, had once owned the plantation that bore his name. The Lawton name was equally renowned in Charleston society. Neither spirit looked pleased at the summons.

"What do you mean, sir, troubling us like this?" The man on the right demanded. He resembled one of the portraits at the plantation, so I felt sure he was Nicholson.

"This is an outrage," the shorter gentleman on the left agreed.

"Silence!" Donnelly thundered, and both ghosts obeyed. "I want to know what unholy bargain you struck to win that medal, and I will know if you tell me less than the full truth."

The two ghosts looked by turns furious, then worried and both spoke at once, arguing about Donnelly's right to call their spirits.

Finally, when Donnelly would brook none of their arguments, they fell silent, like men awaiting their sentence.

"Nicholson—this was your idea?"

The taller man gave a curt nod, with a miserable expression, as if he wished to be anywhere else. "We never thought it would go this far."

"You never thought at all, except about winning your damned blue ribbon," Donnelly snapped. "How did you work the spell?"

"I found a book," Lawton said, raising his head defiantly. "A fellow I went to university with knew Latin, and he had studied at seminary, so he had a flair for ritual."

"A half-trained priest and an old grimoire, and it never occurred to you that you might be selling your souls for a horse race?"

"It wasn't just any race," Lawton said, a spark of anger animating his ghostly features. "It was the Derby."

"Since I'm cleaning up your mess a century—and dozens of dead men—later, forgive me if I'm not impressed," Donnelly retorted. "Now, out with the rest of it. What happened?"

I marveled at the power it must have taken for Donnelly to require two unwilling ghosts to answer his summons, and then compel them to show themselves so clearly and speak aloud. Suddenly, my headache felt like the mark of a rank amateur.

"We'd only started the club," Nicholson replied, sounding petulant. "But we'd all been horsemen for years. Spent a bloody fortune on horses and jockeys, trainers—the whole lot. Wanted to see some payback for our investment."

Lawton turned on him. "Can't you admit that we wanted to show up those bastards from Newport who strutted around like they owned the place? The nerve, coming to Aiken, down here, after what their army did to our state—"

"Enough!" Donnelly rumbled. "You wanted to win, badly enough to do anything. Lawton found a book and a priest. And then what?"

Nicholson's jaw clenched with anger. "We'd get what we wanted. And show up those sons of bitches in the process."

"This deal you made. What did it involve?" Donnelly looked like judgment incarnate. The ghosts shrank back, and I thought about what it took to strike fear into the hearts of the dead.

"We would win the Derby that year," Nicholson replied. "But when he needed replacements for his Hunt, we would give him what he needed."

"I swear we thought he just wanted horses and dogs," the other ghost said. "Not us and our sons."

"More than your sons," Donnelly countered. "Your grandsons on down through the generations. Was the glory of a shiny cup and a bouquet of flowers worth it?" He did not give them time to reply. "Who holds your deal? A demon? A dark witch? Lucifer himself?"

"We never asked his name," Nicholson replied. "But he had a head like a horned goat."

Donnelly looked like he might burst a blood vessel at the sheer magnitude of the ghosts' stupidity and greed. "Well, that narrows it down—not by much. Just a slew of demons, Krampus, Perchta…"

"Perchta." Alicia's quiet voice silenced us all. "He is known to lead the Wild Hunt, depending on who is telling the tale. It would be like him to make such a bargain."

Donnelly turned back to the ghosts, glowering with anger. "What were the terms—exactly?"

Nicholson fidgeted. "I didn't handle the actual negotiation myself. Our friend the lawyer looked it over—"

"You outsourced reading the contract with a supernatural being?" Donnelly shouted.

Nicholson's ghost shied back. "We really didn't think it was binding, since there was a question about whether or not the jurisdiction was real—"

"Son of a bitch!" Donnelly rumbled. "So you signed and figured your lawyers would wiggle you loose later, is that it?"

Nicholson shrugged, and I suspected the approach had served him reasonably well in life.

"Could the contract be assumed by someone else?" Donnelly pressed.

"I don't know—it was a long time ago," Nicholson hedged. "But the terms were clear. It was only supposed to last seventy-five years."

"I'll take that as a yes," Donnelly said, a look of utter annoyance on his face. He looked back to the ghosts. "You belong to neither heaven nor hell, so there's nothing I can do for you. Go back to whence you came, and watch this sorry business play out." He waved a hand at them in dismissal, and both ghosts vanished.

Donnelly broke the wardings and opened the circle. He looked tired, but the working that fatigued him would have killed a less powerful witch. "Well, you heard it," he said, pulling out a kerchief to mop his brow. "All this, over a horse race."

We headed into the house, where both sweet tea and bourbon were in demand. "So Carmen might have been able to 'buy out' Perchta, or at least make a second deal?" Teag asked.

"If she planned to summon Holmgang, perhaps she promised Perchta additional resources for his help," I suggested. "Although I'd think the original deal would have given her what she wanted—but since the disappearances continued after when the first deal should have ended, someone must have re-upped."

"That would be the second time a Nicholson horse won the Derby and the Preakness," Teag supplied, looking up from his laptop. "Man, their negotiator sucked. Didn't even net them a Triple Crown."

"When would it have ended again?" I asked.

"If the terms of the second deal were the same as the original bargain, the term would have been up earlier this year," Teag answered.

"So maybe Carmen found out about the bargain and didn't want to let her family off the hook, not when the Hunt was going to claim its due from the current family members who caused her grief," Anthony mused.

"And this time she added in a couple extra favors to the deal. Maybe if she intends to partner up with Holmgang, she promised Perchta a steady supply of hunters, from more than the Rod and Gun Club families."

"Might be why he was culling his team," Teag said. "Those dead men who fell from the sky. Free agents, so to speak."

"And the zombies and angry ghosts were unintended consequences?" Mrs. Teller questioned.

"Or diversions," I speculated. "Pretty damn good ones, if you ask me. Kept us busy elsewhere while Carmen got everything set into motion."

"So we find Carmen and then what?" Mrs. Teller asked.

"Do I get a vote?" Donnelly asked. "Because I suggest turning both Carmen and Holmgang over to the Hunt, and then banishing their asses."

"Can you do that? Banish the Wild Hunt?" Anthony asked.

Secona's lips quirked in a half-smile. "Probably not. But we might be able to convince Perchta to take them as his tribute and consider this cycle complete."

I glanced at the scrying chalice. "Can you find her? Because I sense she's got something else planned."

Secona drew the goblet closer. I could see that red wine, and not blood, filled it almost to the lip. "I've searched before. Something— perhaps Holmgang—is blocking me. But I will search again."

I laid a hand on her arm. "How long can you remain present without hurting Alicia? Because while I'm glad for your help, Alicia's our friend, and we want her back."

Secona's expression changed and became completely Alicia. "I'm all right, Cassidy. Thanks for worrying, but Secona and I...have an understanding. I'm okay."

"Thank you," I murmured, as something undefinable shifted, and Alicia became Secona once more.

"I keep my word," Secona replied. Donnelly poured himself another bourbon as Secona readied for the scrying. The rest of us drew back to give her space while staying close enough to watch.

Her fingers traced runes in the air over the cup, and I could have sworn that the shapes burned like fire for an instant before vanishing. As Secona chanted, I thought of the vision I'd seen of Holmgang in his raven mask by the bonfire and realized that these two ancient sorcerers provided a glimpse of a world that had been gone for nearly a millennia.

The surface of the wine shimmered, but although I strained to look, I saw nothing but the red depths. Secona stared at the cup's contents, entranced by a vision the rest of us could not share.

"I see a large home, old and grand." Secona's voice was languid in her trance. "This woman, Carmen, has gone to the home. I see lights and people. A party? Then darkness. Dark magic. A skull and a post. Cursed." Her voice became more agitated as the vision went on. "Niding horse. Sacrifice. Kill them all. Kill them all. Kill them all—"

Teag and Mrs. Teller acted together, each clutching a swatch of spell-woven cloth, and reached out to grip Secona by her shoulders. Abruptly, the seer gasped and jerked awake. She pulled back, blinking rapidly, as she struggled to break free of the vision. I moved the chalice away to keep it from spilling and felt a frisson of lingering power through my skin.

"Tonight," Secona said when she had returned to herself enough to speak. "There's a big event at an old mansion, and Carmen means to summon the Hunt to take everyone there. It will seal her bargain with Perchta, their souls for whatever she and Holmgang wanted in return. Whatever their plan, it won't be good for the rest of us."

"What's a niding horse?" Anthony asked, sliding closer to Teag and slipping an arm around his waist, but whether he meant to give or receive support, I couldn't tell. Maybe a little of both.

"An old and powerful curse." We looked up to see Sorren in the doorway, and only then did I realize that night had fallen. "A horse head—or skull—on a rune-scribed post sets the curse, and it can only be lifted with a challenge. The curse is potent and dangerous."

"You've been through this before, after Alard passed," I said.

Sorren nodded and looked to Secona. "Where is the niding horse?"

"At the Nicholson mansion. The curse makes this all more difficult," she replied.

"What does the curse do?" Teag looked from Sorren to Secona for answers.

"It's a binding spell, and a summoning," Secona replied. "I suspect that Carmen—and Holmgang—couldn't use it against us here or at the store because of your wardings." She smiled at Sorren. "You've learned well."

He inclined his head in acknowledgment. "I try not to make the same mistake twice."

Obviously an entire silent history lay bound up in those few words, but it made sense now why Sorren had been adamant that we hole up at my house. Lucinda and Rowan were working on stronger wards for Teag and Anthony's house, but magic can't be rushed and wardings take time to sink in and permeate. So for now, we were safer here.

"What does it summon?" Anthony looked worried, and I couldn't blame him. Out of all of us, he was the one with no magic, the one who would be left behind to worry when we all went off to battle.

"Land sprites," Secona replied. Anthony looked like he might laugh, but something in Secona's expression sobered him. "They're nasty little things. Vicious, and fast. Normally sprites aren't harmful, but Holmgang catches them and...abuses and twists them. They're difficult to banish." She glanced over to Sorren and met his gaze. "I've learned a thing or two since the last time, also. But we'll need more people to do what needs to be done."

"I've already put out the call," Sorren replied.

Carmen and Holmgang, bitter and angry and scary powerful in their magic, backed up by the primal power of the Wild Hunt and eager for revenge, were going to make their big move tonight. No one would be safe, and both Teag and Mrs. Teller would be at the top of Carmen's list to win over or destroy. "Then we need a plan," I replied. "Because it's time we went hunting."

CHAPTER SEVENTEEN

THE NICHOLSON MANSION SAT DARK AND SILENT. TEAG CONFIRMED that the Rod and Gun Club did indeed have a gala that night at the old estate, but no lights blazed from the windows, and nothing but silence met our approach. It looked like the power was out. I glimpsed what might have been candlelight flickering at a few windows, and imagined a frightened group of partygoers huddled next to decorative lamps and lanterns pressed into emergency service.

Tumultuous energy roiled from the surrounding land, thick and filthy like a sewage spill. I closed my hand around my agate necklace to keep from being tainted, but it felt like walking through existential muck. If this was the psychic field that accompanied Holmgang, then he was loathsome as well as dangerous.

"Mrs. Morrissey confirmed the event attendance at twenty-five," Anthony's voice came over the earpiece. Kell had shown up along with Father Anne, Chuck Pettis, Lucinda, and Niella Teller, ready to do whatever he could to help. As the "civilians" in the group, Kell and Anthony stayed at my house—under protest—until Sorren pointed out that they could be used as hostages against Teag and me. That ended the argument, and they took over the command center. Several of us wore earpieces, and Kell gave me some remote sensors and small action cams that would help him monitor the situation via his laptop so he and Anthony could relay information and find any details we might require.

"So we've got twenty-five people trapped in the house, surrounded by land sprites," Chuck echoed. "Can the sprites get inside?"

"No idea," Sorren replied. "When we faced the sprites before, it was at our store in Antwerp. They couldn't get through the wardings."

"I think we'd hear a lot more screaming if they could get into the house," I said. "Maybe the whole point is to hold them hostage?" I frowned as I remembered how Carmen had drained the magical items at the Museum and the Archive and used the cursed cloth in the storm tunnels to create discord. "Or could Carmen use their fear to power her magic?"

"Maybe," Mrs. Teller replied, staring at the house as she thought. "If she got into the house ahead of time and left cloth inside that she'd spelled to tune in on emotions, she might have worked out a kind of relay."

"We can't get rid of the sprites until the challenge is fought, right?" Father Anne asked, hands on her hips as she surveyed the manor's grounds like a general. Our vantage point kept us well beyond where the sprites had gathered, but with a good view of the estate. "But nothing says we can't distract them."

Despite the clerical collar around her throat, she gave us a wicked grin. "If Chuck and I come up with a way to distract the sprites and get the guests out safely, then Carmen loses her 'battery back-up.'"

"Don't underestimate the sprites," Sorren warned. "They're not like in the children's stories."

Father Anne gave the mansion an appraising look. "There's a boxwood hedge all around the house except for the doorways, and an iron fence as well. The doors have iron hinges and decoration. That might be keeping the sprites out. Chuck and I can create a corridor to get the guests out to the cars, if we put some of the natural protections to good use."

She turned to Secona. "Any idea what the range is for that niding horse?"

Secona gave a wan smile. "I don't know that it's been measured, exactly. But old curses are particular. It affects what the skull of the horse points at, which is the house. No way to know if it includes the most recent Nicholson or the members of the club. They might not be able to leave, no matter what you do. But you might get other guests to safety."

Father Anne turned to assess the ornate grounds, and I had no doubt that she searched for anything usable as a weapon. She glanced at Rowan. "Could you strip that boxwood hedge behind us and drop the leaves on the driveway?"

Rowan grinned. "That's easy."

Chuck withdrew a grenade launcher from his pack. "You bring the leaves; I've got the iron filings."

Father Anne raised an eyebrow. "A grenade launcher?"

Chuck shrugged. "Got the idea from a friend in Pennsylvania. It'll work."

Father Anne nodded. "All right. We've got this."

Donnelly and Lucinda were our best bets against the Wild Hunt. That meant the rest of us—me, Teag, Sorren, Secona, Rowan, Mrs. Teller, and Niella—needed to keep Carmen and Holmgang busy and destroy them if we could.

I used night vision goggles to watch Chuck and Father Anne make their way down the slope toward the mansion, staying wide of the strange shadow that marked the territory claimed by the land sprites.

Rowan called to the wind, and it answered her magic, racing through the high boxwood hedge behind us, and sweeping over our heads, carrying with it a dark green tide. I saw Chuck take aim at the horse skull on its carved post, heard the ping of rock against bone, and saw the head turn so that its nose pointed toward a stacked stone shed in the opposite direction of the driveway.

The shadow that followed the sprites shifted, swarming over the shed. As soon as the darkness massed around the small structure, Chuck lobbed something, and an instant later the shed erupted in flames and a spray of dust.

Seconds later, we heard the blast of a grenade launcher. Chuck and

Father Anne ran toward the driveway, and in the distance, we heard them shouting to the hostages inside the mansion, then the roar of engines.

"There goes Step One," I said.

I turned away from the mansion and scanned the lawns for two figures, Donnelly and Lucinda. We didn't know where the Wild Hunt would manifest, but a necromancer and a Voudon mambo were our best chance of holding it at bay.

Now for Carmen.

Spoiling her surprise with the niding horse flushed her out from her bolt hole. Carmen rose from her hiding place amid the topiary, shrieking spells at the top of her lungs. I didn't need Weaver magic to know that the clothing she wore was redolent with power. My gift picked up a jumble of disquieting visions from the land beneath my feet: the discontent and acquisitiveness of the Nicholsons, the shadow of the long-ago bargain with Perchta, the jagged edge of Carmen's madness, and the fear that permeated and poisoned the land ever since the curse claimed the family bloodline.

Rowan struck first, raising her hands with fingers splayed wide. Sparks crackled around her, making her hair rise with static electricity, as lightning arced from her palms. Her power touched down all around Carmen, a warning for the other witch to stand down. Carmen laughed as the fiery blasts burned the grass and kicked up dirt, filling the air with the smell of ozone.

Mrs. Teller and Niella had already laid out long braids of spelled rope that bought us a temporary haven, but I knew it wouldn't last for long. Sorren slipped through the darkness, using his vampire speed and stealth to circle around, looking for a weak point. All of us wore extra charms and protective amulets drawn from a variety of traditions and beliefs. Secona/Teag, Rowan, Father Anne, and both of the Tellers had been up late into the night blessing the talismans we already owned and making some special protections of their own design. Considering the foe we battled, even Sorren consented to protections.

I let my athame fall into my right hand, and jangled Bo's collar on my left. His ghost appeared beside me, and he fixed immediately on

Carmen, giving a low growl. I had Alard's walking stick holstered in my belt, and I drew it, taking comfort from its heft and age, and the weight of the centuries of memories it held. My weapons felt woefully inadequate, but they would have to do.

The most significant change was that Alicia stayed back at my house to recover, with our assurances that she had gone above and beyond the call of duty. Now, Secona's spirit possessed Teag, simultaneously augmenting their combined power and frustrating Holmgang's desire for an easily snatched victim.

Secona held the *Galdrastafur*, the Viking wand Rowan had "borrowed" from the mansion. None of us knew for sure what power it held, but channeling Secona's substantial magic made it our most likely weapon of massive destruction.

Carmen reached out amid the lightning strikes and plucked the bolts of power from the air, hurling them back at us like the god of thunder. Mrs. Teller threw a weighted silver net into the air, and its glowing strands trapped the arcing power as if they were shining birds, bearing them harmlessly to the ground.

Carmen strode toward us, and her flowing garments shimmered with energy. Threads laced through the cloth, glowing like embers in sigil patterns and Norse runes. She threw back her head and laughed, drunk with magic, mad with vengeance, and sure of her victory.

Secona and Niella chanted, their voices rising above the din. They wove threads between their fingers, then as I watched, the fine webs glowed bright and turned to ash. Each time, Carmen stumbled as if invisible fetters tugged at her, hobbling her ankles or dragging her backward.

Carmen screamed in fury and jerked to break free from the magical bonds, but Secona and Niella kept up their attack, slowing her approach. Overhead, clouds parted across the moon, and on the hilltop by the stables, I saw a tree hung with the bodies of large, dark birds, a blood sacrifice like in Teag's visions.

I shook off my fear and closed my fingers around the ancient spindle whorl that grounded me with echoes of Secona's magic. Pulling on that power, I leveled my athame and sent a blast of cold white force at Carmen, driving her back and interrupting her chant. She turned her attention to me and made a weaving gesture with her fingers, cutting off my air as if she tightened a rope around my neck.

Bo's ghost bounded toward her, snapping and snarling, and he leaped for her throat, forcing her to refocus her attention and shift the target of her magic. Bo's teeth sank deep into one arm, and she shook free, tearing him loose at the cost of a bloody gash. Bo landed on all fours so hard his claws dug into the ground, and then he sprang at her again, diving onto her from behind and knocking Carmen off balance. The attack broke her concentration, and I could breathe again.

Gasping, I loosed a stream of fire from the silver tip of Alard's cane. Carmen threw her hands up, holding a swath of fabric that glowed with runes, deflecting the fire.

"This is none of your business!" Carmen screamed. "It's a family matter. You have no right to be here."

"It stopped being a family matter when you brought the rest of the city—and the old families—into your vendetta," Secona replied in Teag's voice. "Do you really think you can command the Wild Hunt? Whatever Holmgang promised you, know this. He lies."

Carmen's laughter sent a chill through me. "Holmgang's spirit came to me. He chose *me* to be the instrument of his vengeance. And he would be my champion."

That's it. Keep her monologuing.

"You think Holmgang cares for your family squabble?" Secona countered. "What does he need from you, once he has a vessel and commands the Wild Hunt? You think that Vincente's death means anything to him? He's using you."

Somewhere in the darkness, I knew Sorren closed in on Carmen, waiting for an opportunity. Niella and Mrs. Teller had stepped back into the shadows, forgotten by Carmen as she vented her fury on Secona.

"They cast me out. Turned *their* backs on us when we needed the most," Carmen raged. "Diego was a much better man than my father ever was, and they let him die."

"So you want to call down the Hunt and Holmgang on the whole world to avenge him?" Secona challenged. "Is that what a good man would want? What Diego would want?"

"Diego wanted to live!" Carmen roared. "They stole that from him. And I swore I'd make them pay."

Movement closer to the mansion caught my attention. I saw Father Anne battling the land sprites that had survived the blast and figured she was putting her blessed boline knife to good use. Chuck's shotgun unloaded blast after blast of shells filled with iron pellets, helping them drive the land sprites back to keep them pinned close to the mansion and away from us.

Mrs. Teller and Niella kept up the invisible Woven fetters, making Carmen fight to free her arms and legs. I sent a blast of cold force against her, and Carmen stumbled backward, nearly falling into Sorren's arms as he closed the distance and threw a spelled blanket over her, one that Mrs. Teller assured could nullify magic—at least for a little while.

Carmen went down in a heap with Sorren pinning her. Temporarily stripped of her magic by the Weaver's blanket, she was no match for his vampire strength. I grinned, happy that we'd battled two foes— Carmen and the land sprites—and kept them at bay. Then I felt the energy shift around me yet again and knew we weren't done yet.

"You should not have returned, Secona." A dark figure with a black cloak and a head like a raven appeared out of nowhere. He carried a long staff in one hand.

"I have a claim on this world," Secona replied, drawing Teag's body up in a regal posture, back straight, head high, and chin lifted. "You do not. I will give you one warning. Leave now."

Holmgang's cold laughter carried across the dark lawn. "This time, Secona, I will win. And you will be the one banished."

Those of us in Team Secona stood within a warded circle reinforced with spells, salt, and holy water. That barrier didn't prevent a physical attack, but it afforded some protection against low-level magical assault. Sorren and Carmen—who was now bound in iron chains and still covered with the spelled blanket—were outside the warding, but the woven fabric's null spell limited what Holmgang might send their way. Sorren had also used spelled fabric as gag and blindfold, effectively stopping Carmen from working even the mildest incantation. Sorren and Holmgang regarded each other with mutual loathing neither one tried to disguise.

"You wretched witch!" Holmgang thundered at Carmen. "You promised me a vessel, and you failed me!"

He turned, looking at Secona and the other Weaver witches, and beneath his raven headdress, his grin spread cold and wicked. "Join me. With the Hunt at our command, we can rule this sordid little world, have the power of the ages flowing through our blood."

"Go to the Devil," Secona spat.

Holmgang chuckled. "He is a myth. I am real—and I do not forgive." He thrust out his hand, sending a torrent of darkness toward our warded circle that grew and spread like a noxious cloud of smoke. Secona gestured, and a thin, iridescent scrim of power rose from within the spelled rope barrier, blocking his attack. I lent the glistening energy wall all the power I could send, drawing on my protective charms and the resonance of the potent objects I carried.

He shifted his stance, and his magic changed as well, this time a bright white fire that burned the grass around the perimeter of our circle but could not pass the shimmering curtain of magic that kept us safe. In the next breath, he leveled his staff and pointed it toward Carmen and Sorren. A fierce wind tore across the ground, straining our warding and ripping at Carmen and Sorren.

The gust forced Sorren to dig in his heels to keep from being tossed aside. He wrapped his arms around Carmen, securing the blanket that kept her powers at bay, holding on with all of his enhanced strength.

With one hand, Holmgang kept up the assault against our position, requiring us to sustain the barrier that protected us but also kept us from retaliating. With the other, he sent hurricane-force gales against Sorren, intending to rip him away from Carmen and strip away the blanket that neutralized her magic. The wind howled, coursing through the trees at the edge of the lawn with enough force to bend them like saplings. I heard the crack of a tree as it snapped, and felt the winds batter the pearlescent scrim of power that protected us from flames hot enough to reduce our bodies to ash.

With a final surge, the wind shrieked like a mad thing, and sent Sorren and Carmen sprawling, overwhelming even Sorren's exceptional strength.

Carmen screamed Holmgang's name and rose from the shadows, still bound by iron but freed of both Sorren and the null-cloth.

"Fill me, and finish them!" Carmen shouted. Holmgang gestured, and the chains fell away. She flung her arms out, threw back her head, and called out the words of power that would allow Holmgang to possess her body. Holmgang's look of triumph terrified me as he saw his victory in sight.

The ancient Norse sorcerer sent a final blast of energy toward us, and then he took up Carmen's chant. Their voices rose, at first clearly separate, but then in unison, as the soul-shift began. Holmgang's dark spirit-form wavered, blurring as the power of the spell caught his life force in its pull and sent what remained of his essence into his willing host.

At that instant, with Holmgang distracted, Secona pushed both her hands, palm out, toward the wall of energy. The shimmering curtain thickened, absorbing the fire and then folding in on itself to smother the flames.

As soon as the fiery onslaught stopped, we struck.

Secona held the *Galdrastafur* staff in one hand drew the bone wand with the other. Holmgang was as vulnerable as he would ever be, caught mid-shift as he began his possession of Carmen. Secona slammed the staff's end down into the ground, sending out a shockwave of power that rocked us, and struck against Holmgang's twisted magic. Bo's ghost sprang at Holmgang, only to be sent sprawling with a wave of the dark sorcerer's hand. Angry, I leveled Alard's cane and delivered a blast of fire that Holmgang barely managed to deflect.

Mrs. Teller and Niella focused on Carmen, working the air with their fingers as nimbly as they wove sweetgrass into their baskets, crafting a loose net of pure energy and flinging it at Carmen. Rowan alternated between firing off attacks, first at Carmen and then at Holmgang. But the energy of their soul-transfer seemed impervious to her assaults as if the transference spell carried its own protections.

From the shadows, I heard the savage barks and growls of something that sounded far too big to be a dog, and way too vicious to be natural. I suspected Holmgang had found a way to keep Sorren occupied with a *grim* to prevent him from rejoining the fight, at least for long enough so Holmgang could claim his borrowed body.

Magic might not be able to touch them as their souls fused, but iron might be another matter. Carmen's body was still human, at least until Holmgang fully possessed her, and so if we were going to strike, it had to be now.

I jumped the warding rope and ran at Carmen, drawing an iron blade from a sheath on my belt. Secona ran beside me, outpacing me, and swung the *Galdrastafur* two-handed, striking Carmen in the head with enough force that it should have split open her skull. She reeled but remained standing as Holmgang's dark essence poured into her. I launched myself at her, iron knife raised, and sank the blade deep into her chest. Secona's magic flung the bone wand like a dart, and its point caught Carmen in the throat. Her body jolted, and I knew that something had struck her from behind.

"Clear!" Secona yelled, charging forward with the *Galdrastafur* like it was a lance, and slammed into her abdomen, taking her to the ground like a jouster unhorsed. We had hit Carmen at all of the main chakra points, the places in the body where energy gathered. Striking with spelled weapons or iron disrupted those chakras.

A bloodied form broke from the shadows, and before I could even recognize Sorren, he dove for Carmen, covering her once again with the null-blanket, sprawling across her to keep her from rising, and assuring that Holmgang's weakened spirit remained trapped inside her failing body.

Secona walked toward us with Rowan beside her. I frowned, trying to make out the weapon in Secona's hand, then realized it was the dagger we had reclaimed from Carmen, the one she had stolen from the Museum.

The two witches stopped when they reached where Sorren pinned

Carmen to the ground. Secona gestured for him to move out of the way.

Rowan and Secona fell to their knees beside Carmen, and they folded their hands around the hilt of the Norse-runed dagger. They chanted under their breath as they brought the blade up, then fell together, driving the sharp point through the blanket and into the body beneath, right to the heart.

The form beneath the blanket bucked and trembled. Holmgang fought death, but we had caught him at his moment of true vulnerability—not in the shift between bodies, but when he had not yet fully occupied his willing host. Trapped by the blanket and the hurried magic of the chants Secona and the Tellers raised, drained by the blows from our spelled weapons, and unable to flee his vessel because of the null blanket, Holmgang had nowhere to run.

"We need to burn the body." Sorren stood, feet braced wide as if standing took all his remaining strength.

The moonlight made it difficult to fully assess Sorren's injuries, but his clothes were soaked in blood, and one sleeve hung in tatters over deep gashes. He moved as if everything hurt, and I knew that his immortality was not absolute. Sorren was hard to destroy, but severe enough damage could exceed even his ability to heal. I'd seen him at that threshold once and hoped never to see it again. From what I could make out, and the curt nod he gave as if he guessed my thoughts, Sorren judged himself still ready for duty.

"Then let's get to it," Secona replied, mouth in a grim line, voice cold. Hearing another person speak through Teag gave me chills, because I could tell it wasn't him. I missed the spark in the eyes that was truly Teag.

We stood around Carmen and Holmgang like a funeral escort and raised our magic. Secona held out *Galdrastafur*, willing the power through it, into a stream of fire that hit the body like a blowtorch. I lifted Alard's cane, and my fire joined theirs, a fitting tribute to Sorren's maker. Rowan's blue-white bolt added to the flames, as did the golden glow of the fiery net of woven energy Mrs. Teller and Niella formed over the corpse. Carmen and Holmgang burned on a pyre of magic flame, and as the body disintegrated, Holmgang's trapped spirit screamed impotent curses until the fire rose so hot we had to look away.

Dimly, I realized that Donnelly and Lucinda had begun to chant. I saw dark shapes coming toward us from the mansion and wondered if Chuck and Father Anne had lost their fight against the sprites. We'd come so far, but it wasn't over yet.

That's when we heard the baying of the hounds and the thunder of ghostly hooves. Holmgang was gone, but the Wild Hunt had answered his final summons.

Holy shit. Nothing prepares you to face off against creatures from ancient legend. The wind rattled through the trees like dried bones, sweeping across the lawn and bowing the branches. In the distance, I saw the Hunt against the clouds, a long black undulating cavalcade. The howls of phantom dogs and the rhythm of spectral hoof beats grew louder as the Wild Hunt approached, and the most primal wiring in my brain screamed for me to hide.

Another glance toward the house told me that Father Anne and Chuck still battled the sprites, but the rest of us stepped up to face this new foe, uncertain that anything we could do might avert a threat older than humankind. The Hunt gyred through the night sky like a drunken wagon train, and as it grew closer, I heard the snap of reins, the whinny of long-dead mounts, and the exultant shouts of hunters closing in on their prey.

Now the fearful revenants loomed close enough that I could make out their features in the moonlight. The riders had once been men, members of the Nicholson family or of the Rod and Gun Club that cared so much about winning that they would barter their eternal rest and immortal souls in exchange for fame and trophies.

I had seen old woodcuts and medieval paintings of the Wild Hunt and chalked them up to fanciful tales or an artist's dark dreams. But now that I stood before the legendary host, I knew that the pictures did not come close to conveying the true terror.

The riders wore the attire of the times in which they lived, but their fine riding jackets were faded and their breeches tattered like shrouds.

Time made them animated mummies; skin pulled tight over prominent bone, teeth bared in a rictus grin, eyes wild and mad. The horses, too, were skeletal, eyes red, hooves sharp, and stained with blood, teeth champing. Cadaverous dogs ran alongside, howling and baying at the moon.

The Hunt settled to the ground, horses pawing impatiently and dogs shuffling. One horseman edged to the front, a fearsome figure with a horned skull for a head and the emaciated body of a reaper. Perchta, the Master of the Hunt, looked down at us from his seat atop a giant steed more war horse than hunting mount. Six horns twisted from Perchta's skull, bending in all directions, and his hideous face was the stuff of nightmares. Glowing yellow eyes peered balefully from the dark sockets of the skull, taking our measure. In one hand he held the reins for his wraith mount, and in the other, a sharp-edged flail for a riding crop.

Seven of us stood against the power of the storm.

"Where is my tribute?" Perchta's voice sounded like boulders falling and wind howling, and I could not be certain whether I heard it aloud or in my mind.

"This is the final reaping." Archibald Donnelly stepped forward, and if he felt fear in the presence of Perchta and his horde, it did not show in his grim expression or confident stance. That's when I realized he had an army at his back, a ghostly phalanx of men, horses, and dogs. "Your agreement ends tonight, and it will not be renewed."

One of those spirits moved to the forefront, an old man whose straight spine and truculent expression suggested that he expected to get his way in the hereafter as much as he had commandeered what he desired in life. "We are your tribute," he said, "the men of the Nicholson family you have not claimed. We offer ourselves as payment for a debt that never should have been incurred. Take us, and spare the living from our greed and folly."

Lucinda remained in the background. I saw her in the moonlight, clad all in white, her hair tied up with bright cloth, drumming and chanting. Power coalesced around her, as heavy as the smoke from her candles and the incense she burned to woo the Loas, the Voudon gods whose favor she sought with the offerings that lay beside the makeshift altar. Lucinda moved fluidly to the beat of the drum, and I'd seen her trance enough times to know she called out to powers far beyond this world, more than the equal of Perchta and his hunters.

"Let the dead rest." A new and unexpected voice startled me. I turned to see Jonathan Nicholson, the latest scion of the plantation's owners, standing at the fore of a grim-looking posse. I bet that Carmen's curse made it impossible for them to leave when the other party guests fled to safety. Stripped of other options, I also wagered they decided to go down with a semblance of dignity rather than be dragged away screaming from their hiding place inside the mansion. "We will be the last tribute. But this bad bargain ends tonight."

Perchta's gaze came to rest on Teag and I wondered if he sensed Secona's presence. "I know you, though your form is not your own," he wheezed.

She inclined her head. "I'm honored that you remember. We have traveled some paths together, in the past."

"A past that few recall," the Master of the Hunt replied. Next, he regarded Sorren. "You, I also remember. I sought you, and with her help," he added with a nod toward Secona, "you eluded me."

"You came for someone else. I was unlucky enough to be in the way," Sorren replied, in a gravely respectful tone as if he addressed Death himself.

"Nobody goes anywhere if I refuse to dig their grave." We turned to see Lucinda swagger toward us, and I knew one of the Loa possessed her. How fitting that devotees referred to possession as being "ridden" and the willing spirit-host as a "horse." When I looked at Lucinda, my vision blurred, as if another face and figure overlaid her own. I saw Lucinda, but I also saw a tall man with a skull-white face. He wore a black tuxedo and a top hat, as well as dark glasses and he carried a cigar.

"Baron Samedi, I presume?" Perchta growled. "This is not your business."

Lucinda gestured toward our brave but woefully outgunned band of would-be heroes. "These are my people, and that makes this my business," she replied. Lucinda long-ago learned to soften her accent for her professional persona, but Baron Samedi's drawling cadence and thick accent spoke of bourbon and cane sugar. Behind him stood the translucent figure of a bent-legged old man puffing on a pipe with a rangy dog at his side, and I knew that Papa Legba had also answered Lucinda's call. The air smelled vaguely of cigar and pipe smoke, and a hint of dark rum.

I held my breath, in awe of the primal forces that surrounded us. Compared to them, my gift at its strongest was insignificant. Even Sorren's age and abilities meant nothing compared to beings that were truly immortal, and perhaps gods.

"We made a bargain," Nicholson spoke up, and I gave him credit for having brass balls. "You came for riders, fresh for the hunt. Our grandfathers signed with their blood, and we're willing to pay with ours, but it all ends. Now."

"It's a good bargain," Baron Samedi replied through Lucinda. "Might be wise to take it, and be on your way."

We did not need old gods getting into a pissing match. I shivered as Perchta turned to regard both the Baron and Papa Legba. His gaze raked over us, and we did our best not to flinch. Donnelly's army of Nicholson dead shifted to stand beside their living progeny, a show of solidarity in the face of a bad agreement, but commendable in its doomed honor.

"I have enjoyed our dealings," Perchta rumbled, turning back to Nicholson. "Surely you would like to keep your glory from fading away?"

Nicholson's jaw twitched. "I would not visit this curse on another generation, not for all the wreaths and trophies in the world." The men beside him looked pale and terrified, but to their credit, they held their ground.

"Then I accept your offer," Perchta said, with the sweep of his arm as if he were being magnanimous. "And with your addition to the Hunt, I will trouble your house no more."

Then he looked at us, and I saw a glimmer of greed in his yellow eyes. "I would take all of you."

"These belong to me." Lucinda's voice had ceased to be her own, and I heard the honeyed steel tones of the Baron speaking through her. "I will not dig their graves, so they cannot pass the Veil." She inclined her head toward where Papa Legba waited near the altar, content in the knowledge that all things alive and dead came to him in the end. "And Papa Legba will not open the threshold for them. You've gotten the best of the bargain. Do not force me to meddle further."

Perchta and Baron Samedi regarded each other in a silent dispute that held our lives and afterlife in the balance. Finally, Perchta looked away.

"I concede," he rumbled. "Your offer is acceptable."

Perchta gestured with his flail, swinging it toward Nicholson and his doomed cohort. "Ride with me," he intoned, and as he spoke the living men became gray spirits, and the ghosts grew more solid. Each man appeared astride a ghastly horse. "Mount up!"

Spectral hunting horns sounded a terrifying and mournful note, carrying across the night. Dogs bayed, and horses stamped their feet. The newly taken souls fell into place amidst the cavalcade, and then in the next instant, the whole dark horde rose skyward. For a moment, their silhouette stood out against the moon, and then with a final horn blast, they were gone.

Donnelly turned toward Lucinda. "Thank you," he said, making a deep bow to Baron Samedi and to Papa Legba. "We are in your debt."

A deep, masculine chuckle rolled from Lucinda's throat. "Don't you of all people know, it's a dangerous thing to owe someone like me, necromancer?"

Donnelly smiled a terrible smile, part challenge and part inside joke. I had the distinct feeling that he and the Baron were, if not old friends, at least well-acquainted. "And you remember that I always pay my debts," he replied. I knew that whatever lay behind their words was a mystery I would never solve.

The Baron turned to Secona. "My lady," he said, and Secona in Teag's body made a courtly bow. "We meet again. It is always an honor and a privilege."

At that, Lucinda walked back toward where the spirits of Papa

Legba and his dog waited. She turned once more, gave a wink that was pure Baron, and then raised her arms to the sky. When I blinked, Lucinda was herself again, and Papa Legba was gone, though the waft of pipe and cigar smoke assured me that I had not imagined their presence.

"Did we miss it? What happened?" We all turned as Father Anne and Chuck made their way toward us. "The sprites vanished. Is it over?"

Neither Father Anne nor Chuck were prepared when the rest of us broke out laughing. Maybe they could hear the edge of hysteria and relief that tinged our humor, or perhaps they just thought us mad.

"Let's go back to my house," I said. "It's been a long night. I promise, we'll tell you everything."

EPILOGUE

Secona continued to possess Teag as we returned to my house. Without Carmen's "grouch flu" and the threat of the Wild Hunt or Holmgang, the tension and dread that had hung so heavy over us were gone. I wondered if Secona was waiting to release Teag because he might collapse when her spirit left him.

Anthony and Kell rushed to greet us, hanging back long enough to assure that neither of us were badly hurt. We'd both taken some hits, but compared to some of the battles we fought, everyone came back in pretty good condition. Alicia looked up from where she sat bundled in blankets in an armchair, with Baxter on her lap. She looked tired, and I wondered how much of that was the strain of having channeled Secona's spirit.

Kell hugged me close and gave me a kiss. Anthony started toward Teag, then must have remembered that Secona still possessed him, because he stopped awkwardly in mid-motion.

"Is it over? Holmgang and Carmen, are they gone?" Anthony asked. He moved closer to Teag and tentatively slipped an arm around him, guiding him to the couch.

"They're gone," I confirmed. "It's over."

Rowan came up beside me. "Anthony, when Secona releases Teag, he's going to be fatigued. Could you please make him a cup of hot tea with a lot of sugar?"

Anthony nodded and then got up and headed to the kitchen. Lucinda sidetracked Kell with a question, while Rowan pulled me closer to Teag. I knelt in front of him, while Rowan sat on the couch beside him.

"Teag, you need to know that Carmen was dead seconds after Holmgang began possessing her," Rowan said quietly. "Secona can show you the truth of that, if you doubt me. The way Secona possessed Alicia and you was different. Secona didn't want to harm either of you. Holmgang enjoyed the power trip. So when we stabbed her—"

Teag looked up, and I knew Secona had pulled back her power so that we were seeing him and not her, though she still possessed him. "You're trying to convince me I didn't help murder someone in cold blood?" he asked quietly, guilt thick in his voice.

"Carmen was already dead," Rowan repeated. "All we did was extinguish Holmgang. No different from any other monster we've destroyed—Nephilim, shifters, vampires. He intended to destroy the city—or more. And if she'd have been alive, Carmen would have been right beside him all the way."

Teag clasped his hands in front of him. "I know. But this time, it felt different."

"Are you ready for Secona to let you go?" I asked gently. He nodded, but still didn't make eye contact.

"Thank you." This time, the voice was still Teag's, but the mannerisms were Secona's. "I know you did not want to be possessed, but I think we fought rather well together back there. You are clever and brave. I have been honored to share your vessel."

With that, I felt the energy shift, and Teag slumped just as Anthony returned with the cup of tea. I shook my head, letting Anthony know Teag was okay, and Rowan stood to give Anthony room beside Teag on the couch. Teag straightened as if he had woken from sleep, and looked at us, bleary-eyed.

"She's gone," he said quietly, sounding utterly worn out. Anthony handed over the tea, and Teag sipped it slowly. "That was…weird. But I guess it worked."

Anthony wrapped an arm around his shoulders, and Teag leaned into him. Despite the assurances from Secona and Rowan, I knew it would be a while before Teag could convince himself that he'd done the right thing about Carmen.

"There are going to be side effects," Mrs. Teller said, from where she and Niella stood, watching to make sure Secona departed as promised.

"What kind of side effects?" Anthony asked, worried.

"Won't know until he's up to doing some lessons, but I wager having a Weaver of Secona's strength and experience in his head taught him a few things," Mrs. Teller replied with a grin. "He saw how she did her magic, felt how it worked. That'll be like cramming in a lifetime of lessons, maybe, if he remembers. Won't be surprised if his magic is stronger, too."

"What happened?" Kell asked, sidling over to join me. "We heard some of it on the headsets, but that's no replacement for a visual."

Sorren recounted the events of the evening. Meanwhile, Father Anne got out the medical kit and took care of our injuries. I noticed that he didn't go into detail about Carmen's death, and saw the spark of gratitude in Teag's eyes.

"So it's really done?" Kell asked.

Sorren nodded.

"Holmgang is banished, and this time I think he'll be much harder for anyone to summon, if that could even work again," Sorren replied. "Holmgang killed Carmen, so that threat is resolved. Perchta removed the body, which means there won't be awkward questions from the police."

"Except for the missing Rod and Gun Club people," I said. Kell gave me a puzzled look. "Nicholson and his buddies offered themselves as payment to the Hunt, to end the curse. Perchta took them, so they'll be permanently 'missing.'"

Anthony winced. "I'm going to pretend I didn't hear that. Although

I guess there's no way to bring charges against the master of the Wild Hunt."

"If it makes you feel any better, you can blame Nicholson and his cronies for a century and a half of missing persons and chalk up their racing wins to fraud," Lucinda said tartly. "So not exactly innocent victims."

"What about Kerrie Carson, the Weaver who was in the car accident?" Teag asked. "Do you think being rid of Carmen will bring her out of her coma?"

"I'll stop by the hospital tomorrow and check on her," Rowan promised. "If there's magic that can help, Mrs. Teller and I can take care of it."

"I guess the missing horses and hunting dogs from Harrison Stables are gone for good," I said. Valerie's cousin would be saddened, but perhaps not surprised. I had the feeling he suspected that the chance of retrieving the missing animals had been slim, given the supernatural nature of the theft.

"What now?" Kell asked. Teag finished his tea and set the cup aside, then curled against Anthony, letting his partner wrap both arms around him. Kell slid an arm around my waist, drawing me to him, and I rested my head on his shoulder.

"I don't know about you, but I'm tired," I replied. "I want a hot shower and a good night's rest. We've earned it. There's no telling what crazy new threat might pop up tomorrow."

AFTERWORD

Charleston, South Carolina is a real place. Some of the landmarks and a few of the historical figures in this book do exist, and some (but not all) of the historical events were real. But the characters and their shops are all a work of fiction. So for example, if you go to Charleston (and I hope you do, because it's a lovely place to visit), you can see the real Charleston City Market and walk down King Street, but you won't find any of the businesses or restaurants I've mentioned by name. Any resemblance to real people or actual businesses is completely coincidental.

Many people in Charleston will tell you that the ghosts, however, are real. My ghosts are fictional, but that's because Charleston has enough of its own already. But don't take my word for it. See for yourself.

I hope you enjoyed the adventures with Cassidy, Teag, and Sorren. If you want more, check out more Deadly Curiosities Adventures collected in *Trifles and Folly*, *Trifles and Folly 2*, as well as the full-length novels, *Deadly Curiosities* and *Vendetta,* available in paperback and e-book. Cassidy has more short stories and novellas coming!

Visit the website: www.DeadlyCuriosities.com for the latest news.

Thank you for supporting independent authors!

This book was written and published by an independent author. Independent authors work outside the large, traditional publishing industry, which means we can be more responsive to our fans and readers, bringing you more of the kinds of stories you want to read.

When you support independent authors, you're helping them make a living, providing an income for their families, and helping to guarantee that they can continue writing the books you enjoy reading.

By helping spread the word about the books and authors you enjoy, either in reviews on sites like Amazon and Goodreads or by personal recommendation, you help others discover these books for themselves, and you help make it possible for the writers you enjoy to keep on writing. This is especially important for independent authors, because we don't have a big name publisher promoting our books or the benefit of being shelved in bookstores.

If you've enjoyed this book, or other books by independent authors, the biggest way to show your thanks is by reviewing online and spreading the word. And please, never download 'free' books off pirate sites. Doing so harms the author by robbing him or her of the sale, and makes it harder for authors to stay in business, writing the books you love.

Thank you for reading!

ABOUT THE AUTHOR

Gail Z. Martin is the author of *Vengeance*, the sequel to *Scourge* in her Darkhurst epic fantasy series, and *Assassin's Honor* in the new Assassins of Landria series. *Tangled Web* is the newest novel in the series that includes both *Deadly Curiosities* and *Vendetta* and two collections, *Trifles and Folly and Trifles and Folly 2*, the latest in her urban fantasy series set in Charleston, SC. *Shadow and Flame* is the fourth book in the Ascendant Kingdoms Saga and *The Shadowed Path* and *The Dark Road* are in the Jonmarc Vahanian Adventures series. Co-authored with Larry N. Martin are *Iron and Blood*, the first novel in the Jake Desmet Adventures series and the *Storm and Fury* collection; and the *Spells, Salt, & Steel: New Templars series (Mark Wojcik, monster hunter)*. Under her urban fantasy MM paranormal romance pen name of Morgan Brice, *Witchbane* and *Badlands* are the newest releases.

She is also the author of *Ice Forged, Reign of Ash*, and *War of Shadows* in The Ascendant Kingdoms Saga, The Chronicles of The Necromancer series (*The Summoner, The Blood King, Dark Haven, Dark Lady's Chosen*) and The Fallen Kings Cycle (*The Sworn, The Dread*).

Gail's work has appeared in over 35 US/UK anthologies. Newest anthologies include: *The Big Bad 2, Athena's Daughters, Heroes, Space, Contact Light, With Great Power, The Weird Wild West, The Side of Good/The Side of Evil, Alien Artifacts, Cinched: Imagination Unbound, Realms of Imagination, Clockwork Universe: Steampunk vs. Aliens, Gaslight and Grimm, Baker Street Irregulars, Journeys, Hath no Fury,* and *Afterpunk: Steampunk Tales of the Afterlife.*

Find out more at www.GailZMartin.com, at DisquietingVisions.com, on Goodreads https://www.goodreads.com/GailZMartin, and free excerpts on Wattpad http://wattpad.com/GailZMartin.

ALSO BY GAIL Z. MARTIN

Other books by Gail Z. Martin

Deadly Curiosities

Deadly Curiosities

Vendetta

Tangled Web

Trifles and Folly

Trifles and Folly 2

Darkhurst

Scourge

Vengeance

Ascendant Kingdoms

Ice Forged

Reign of Ash

War of Shadows

Shadow and Flame

Chronicles of the Necromancer / Fallen Kings Cycle

The Summoner

The Blood King

Dark Haven

Dark Lady's Chosen

The Sworn

The Dread

The Shadowed Path

The Dark Road

Other books by Gail Z. Martin and Larry N. Martin

Jake Desmet Adventures

Iron & Blood

Storm & Fury

Spells, Salt, & Steel: New Templars

Spells, Salt, & Steel

Open Season

Deep Trouble

11506110R00141

Printed in Great Britain
by Amazon